Alexander Solzhenitsyn
STORIES AND PROSE POEMS

Translated by Michael Glenny

RLI: VLM 7 (VLR 5–8) / IL 9–Adult

STORIES AND PROSE POEMS
*A Bantam Book / published by arrangement with
Farrar, Straus & Giroux, Inc.*

PRINTING HISTORY
Published in Germany under the title
Im Interesse der Sache, by Luchterhand Verlag
Farrar, Straus & Giroux edition published July 1971
2nd printing .. September 1971
3rd printing ..... October 1971
Book Find Club edition published June 1971
Serialized in MADEMOISELLE *Magazine in June 1971 and*
LITERARY CAVALCADE *Magazine in November 1971*
Bantam edition published September 1972
2nd printing .... January 1973
3rd printing
4th printing

*Bantam Books are published by Bantam Books, Inc. Its trade-
mark, consisting of the words "Bantam Books" and the por-
trayal of a bantam, is registered in the United States Patent
Office and in other countries. Marca Registrada. Bantam
Books, Inc., 666 Fifth Avenue, New York, New York 10019.*

PRINTED IN THE UNITED STATES OF AMERICA

Contents

Matryona's House

For at least six months after the incident took place every train used to slow down almost to a standstill at exactly a hundred and eighty-four kilometers from Moscow. The passengers would crowd to the windows and go out onto the open gangway at the end of the carriages to find out whether the track was under repair or if the train was ahead of schedule. But these were not the reasons for the delay. Once it had passed the level crossing, the train would pick up speed again and the passengers would go back to their seats. Only the drivers knew why they had to slow down.

And I knew too.

In the summer of 1953 I was returning from the hot, dusty wastelands, making my way aimlessly back to Russia. No one had sent for me and no one was waiting for me, because my return had been delayed by a little matter of ten years. I simply wanted to go somewhere in central Russia, somewhere where it was not too hot and where leaves rustled in the forest. I just wanted to creep away and vanish in the very heartland of Russia—if there were such a place.

A year earlier, the most that I could have got in the way of a job on the other side of the Urals was labouring work. I would not even have been taken on as an electrician on a decent-sized construction site. And my ambition was to be a teacher. People in the teaching world told me that I was wasting money on a ticket, as the journey would be fruitless.

But the atmosphere in the country had already started to change. As I climbed the stairs of the Regional Education Department and asked for the personnel branch, I was amazed to see that personnel was no longer situated behind a black leather door but simply on the other side of a glass partition as in a chemist's.

I approached the window timidly, bowed, and asked: "Excuse me, have you any vacancies for a mathematics teacher somewhere far away from civilisation? I want to settle there for good."

They scrutinised every detail of my documents, scuttled from room to room, and made telephone calls. I was a rare case for them; as a rule, everybody asked to be sent to a town and the bigger the better. Suddenly they presented me with a little place called High Field. The name of the place alone cheered me up.

It did not belie its name. Situated on a slope among hills, encircled by a wood, with a pond and a dyke, High Field was the very place where a man would be glad to live and die. I sat there on a tree stump in a copse for a long time, wishing that I could do without my daily meals and just stay here and listen to the branches rustling against the roofs at night, when there was no sound of a radio from any direction and everything in the world was at peace.

But it was no good. They did not bake their own bread there. They did not sell anything to eat. The whole village dragged its foodstuffs in sacks from the local town.

So back I went to the personnel branch and stood imploringly at their window. At first no one would see me. Then once again they scurried from room to room, made telephone calls, scratched their pens, and typed on my assignment form: "Peatproduce."

Peatproduce? If only Turgenev were alive today to see what violence is being done to the Russian language.

On Peatproduce Station, consisting of a grey temporary wooden hut, hung a warning sign: "Trains may only be boarded from the platform." Someone had scratched on the notice with a nail: "Even if you haven't got a ticket," and beside the ticket office the following grimly humorous message was carved permanently in the woodwork: "No tickets." I realised the full meaning of these comments only much later. It was easy to get to Peatproduce but not to get out of it.

2

Before the Revolution and for some time after it, the place had been covered with silent, impenetrable forest. Then the forest had been cut down by the peat diggers and the nearby collective farm, whose chairman, Shashkov, had razed a considerable area of the forest to the ground and had sold it at a profit in the province of Odessa.

A straggling village was scattered among the peat diggings, consisting of some monotonous huts dating from the thirties and a few cottages put up in the fifties with fretwork trimmings and glassed-in verandahs. But in none of these cottages were there any partitions built right up to the ceiling, so that I could not find a room that had four proper walls.

A factory chimney poured smoke over the whole village. A narrow-gauge railway line wound its way through the place, and little engines, also puffing out thick clouds of smoke and emitting piercing whistles, pulled trainloads of raw peat, peat slabs, and briquettes. I was right when I guessed that a radiogram would be blaring out music all evening through the doors of the club, that drunks would be lurching about in the street, and that now and again they would knife each other.

This was the place to which my dream of a quiet corner of Russia had brought me. At least in the place I had come from I had lived in a mud hut that looked out over the desert, a fresh, clean wind had blown at night, and only the starry arc of heaven was stretched over my head.

I found it impossible to sleep on the station bench and it was hardly light when I set off to explore the village. Then I saw that it had a tiny market. Because it was so early, only one woman was there, selling milk. I bought a bottle and drank it on the spot.

The way she spoke surprised me. She did not so much talk as sing in an oddly touching way and her words made me feel nostalgic for Asia.

"Drink, drink, your heart's athirst. Are you a stranger here?"

"Where are you from?" I asked, delighted.

I learned that the region was not all peat workings, that beyond the railway track there was a hill and over

3

the hill a village called Tal'novo, which had been there from time immemorial, since the days when a "gypsy" lady had lived there and a haunted wood had stood all around. And beyond it a whole string of villages with names like Chaslitsy, Ovintsy, Spudni, Shevertni, Shestimirovo—each one more remote than the next as they stretched farther and farther away from the railway and nearer to the lakes.

The names wafted over me like a soothing breeze. They held a promise of the true, legendary Russia. So I asked my new-found friend to take me to Tal'novo when the market was over and help me look for a cottage where I could find lodgings.

As a lodger I was a good prospect: in addition to my rent, the school also provided a lorryload of peat for the winter. The woman's expression now betrayed a kind of concern that was less touching. She herself had no room to spare (she and her husband looked after her aged mother), so she took me around to some of her relatives; but their houses were noisy and crowded and none of them had a separate room to rent either.

By then we had walked as far as a little dammed-up stream crossed by a bridge. There was no prettier spot in the whole village—two or three willows, a crooked little shack, ducks swimming on the pond, and geese waddling up the bank to shake themselves.

"Well, I suppose we'd better try Matryona," said my guide, already growing tired of me. "Only her place isn't that well kept, she's let it go on account of her being so sick."

Matryona's house was nearby. It had a row of four windows along the side on which the sun never shone, a steep shingled roof with an elaborately ornamental dormer window. But the shingles were rotting away, the logs of the cottage walls and the once-mighty gateposts had turned grey with age, and much of the caulking between the logs had fallen out. Although the gate was shut, my guide did not bother to knock but thrust her hand underneath and undid the bolt—a simple precaution against stray cattle. There were no sheds in the yard, but instead the cottage had several outbuildings clustered under the one roof. Just inside the entrance,

4

there were some steps leading up to a broad passage, open to the roof timbers. To the left, some more steps led up to the outhouse—a separate room but without a stove—and another flight of steps down to the storeroom. To the right were the living quarters with their attic and cellar.

It had been solidly built a long time ago, intended for a large family, but now a woman who was getting on towards sixty lived there alone.

The spacious room, and especially its brighter end by the windows, was set about with flower pots and tubs of fig plants on stools and benches. Silent yet alive, they filled the loneliness of Matryona's life, growing in wild profusion as they strained to catch the sparse northern light. As the light was fading and because she was hidden by the chimney, the owner's round face looked yellow and ill. Her bleary eyes showed how much her illness had exhausted her.

She talked to me lying prone on the stove, without a pillow, her head facing the door, while I stood over her. She showed no sign of pleasure at the prospect of acquiring a lodger but merely complained about the attack from which she was now recovering: the sickness did not come every month, but when it did strike, ". . . it stays for two or three days, so I wouldn't be able to get up or do anything for you. But the house isn't bad, you'd be all right here."

She listed other landladies whose cottages might be quieter and more comfortable and suggested that I should go and try them. But I could already tell that I was fated to settle in this dark cottage with its tarnished mirror, in which it was completely impossible to see yourself, and its two cheap, brightly coloured posters hung on the wall for decoration, one advertising the book trade and the other campaigning for the harvest.

Matryona made me try the village again, and when I arrived the second time she made countless excuses like "Don't expect any fancy cooking." But she was up and about and there was even a glint of something like pleasure in her eyes because I had come back.

We agreed about the rent and the peat that the school would supply.

5

I only found out later that Matryona Vasilievna had not earned a penny from anywhere for a long, long time, because she was not given a pension and her relatives hardly ever helped her out. She worked on the collective farm not for money but for ticks—the ticks entered in her well-thumbed workbook.

And so I settled in with Matryona Vasilievna. We did not divide up the room: her bed was in the corner by the door, near the stove; and I set up my camp bed by the window. I pushed Matryona's beloved fig plants aside to let in more light, and put a table by one of the windows. They had electricity in the village; it had been brought from Shatura as early as the twenties. In those days the newspapers used to publicise Lenin's electrification scheme with catchwords like "Ilyich lamps," while the peasants blinked and called it "magic fire."

Perhaps to someone from a better-off village Matryona's cottage would not have seemed an ideal place to live, but we were very comfortable there that autumn and winter. Despite its age, it kept the rain out, and the embers in the stove warded off the icy winds pretty well—except towards morning, and hardly at all when the wind was blowing from the cold quarter.

Besides Matryona and myself, the other occupants of the house were a cat, some mice, and the cockroaches.

The cat was rather old and lame. Matryona had adopted it out of pity and it had settled down with her. Although it walked on four legs, it limped heavily in order to spare its one bad leg. When it jumped from the stove onto the floor, the sound it made when it landed was not a typical soft catlike sound but a thump of three legs hitting the floor simultaneously—crash!—a noise so loud that at first, before I got used to it, it startled me. It would land on three feet at once so as to spare the fourth.

It was not lameness that prevented the cat from dealing with the mice in the cottage; it would corner them and pounce like a flash of lightning and carry them off in its teeth. The reason why it caught so few was that once, when times were better, someone had papered Matryona's room with some greenish ribbed

6

and checked wallpaper, and not just one layer but *five.* The coatings of wallpaper were stuck firmly to each other but in many places all five layers had ceased to adhere to the wall, thus giving the house a sort of inner skin. The mice had made paths for themselves between the planks and the wallpaper where they pattered impudently back and forth, even running about under the ceiling. The cat would glare angrily at their rustling but could never get at them.

Sometimes the cat would even eat cockroaches, but they made it feel sick. The only thing that the cockroaches respected was the line of the partition dividing the stove and the kitchen from the clean part of the house. They never penetrated into the living room. But they made up for it by swarming all over the kitchen at night, and if I went into the kitchen late in the evening and switched on the light, the entire floor, the large bench, and even the walls were almost a solid, heaving mass of reddish-brown. Once when I brought home some borax from the chemistry lab at school, we mixed it with dough and slaughtered the cockroaches. Their numbers diminished, but Matryona was afraid of poisoning the cat as well, so we stopped putting down poison and the cockroaches flourished once more.

At night, when Matryona was asleep and I was working at my table, the occasional sound of the mice darting about behind the wallpaper was smothered by the ceaseless, monotonous rustle behind the partition, like the distant roar of the ocean. But I grew accustomed to it, for there was nothing false or deceptive about it. It was their nature; they couldn't help it.

I even got used to the crudely drawn girl on the poster, eternally offering me copies of Belinsky, Panfyorov, and a pile of other books, but never speaking. I got used to everything in Matryona's house.

Matryona would get up at four or five o'clock in the morning. She had bought her old-fashioned kitchen clock at the village store twenty-seven years ago. It was always fast, but Matryona didn't mind; at least it wasn't slow, so she would not be late in the mornings.

She would switch on the light in the kitchen and quietly, considerately, trying not to make a noise, stoke up the stove. Then she would go and milk the goat (her entire livestock was one dirty white goat with a crooked horn), fetch water, put three saucepans on the stove to boil—one saucepan for me, one for herself, and one for the goat. From the store in the cellar she picked out the very smallest potatoes for the goat, small ones for herself, and a few for me the size of a hen's egg. Her kitchen garden was incapable of producing large potatoes; its sandy soil had not been manured since before the war and was never planted with anything but potatoes.

I hardly ever heard her doing her morning chores. I slept long, woke up late with the wintry sun and stretched, poking my head from underneath my blanket and sheepskin coat. With a quilted jacket from my prison-camp days which covered my feet, and a sack stuffed with straw as a mattress, I stayed warm all night, even when the north wind set our little windows rattling in their rotten frames. Hearing the muffled noises coming from behind the partition, I would solemnly say:

"Good morning, Matryona Vasilievna."

And always the same kindly response would be echoed from the other side. It began with a sort of low purring noise that grandmothers make in fairy tales: "Mm-m-m . . . and the same to you."

And a moment later: "Your breakfast's ready."

She never said what was for breakfast, but it was not hard to guess: an unpeeled potato, 'taty soup (as they called it in the village), or millet porridge. Any other kind of cereal was unobtainable in Peatproduce that year, and even millet was hard enough to get—as it was the cheapest sort, they bought it by the sackful for pig food. It was not always salted properly and it was often burnt; it left a film on your palate and gums, and it gave you heartburn. However, this was not Matryona's fault. There was no butter in Peatproduce either, margarine only now and then if you were lucky, and the only readily available fat was low-grade lard. What was more, the Russian stove, as I soon realised, was extremely awkward: the cook was unable to see the food cooking, and the heat reached the saucepan unevenly and sporadically. I suppose the reason why our forefathers have retained this kind of stove since the Stone Age is that once it is banked up before dawn, it keeps food and water for man and beast warm all day; and it's warm to sleep on.

I dutifully ate everything that was cooked for me, patiently removing any foreign bodies such as a hair, a lump of peat, or the leg of a cockroach. I did not have the heart to reproach Matryona. After all, she had warned me not to expect any fancy cooking.

"Thank you," I would say with absolute sincerity.

"What for? It's yours—you're paying for it." Having disarmed me with her dazzling smile, she would then look at me guilelessly with her pale blue eyes and ask: "Well, what shall I cook you for supper?"

I ate two meals a day, as we used to do on active service. What could I order for supper? It was always either potatoes or 'taty soup.

I reconciled myself to this, because experience had taught me not to regard eating as the main object of life. I set greater store by the smile on her round face, which, when I eventually took up photography, I tried in vain to capture on film. Whenever Matryona saw the cold eye of a lens staring at her, she would put on a look that was either strained or exaggeratedly stern. Only once did I manage to catch her smiling at something out of the window.

Matryona had a lot of trouble that autumn. Her neighbours had persuaded her to apply for a pension. She was all alone in the world, and since she had started being seriously ill, she had been dismissed from the collective farm. Altogether, Matryona was treated most unjustly: she was sick, but she was not certified as disabled; she had worked on the collective farm for a quarter of a century, yet because she had not been directly engaged on production she was not entitled to a personal pension but only to one on her husband's behalf—that is, on the grounds of loss of the breadwinner. But her husband had been dead for twelve years—since the beginning of the war, in fact—and it was not easy to get the necessary documents certifying how long he had worked and how much he had been paid. It had been trouble enough collecting all these certificates

9

—getting someone to write down that he had earned three hundred roubles a month, then getting another to certify that she lived alone and was not supported by anyone, and for how long—then taking it all to the social-security office, then doing it all over again because something had been entered wrong. Even at the end she was still not sure whether she would get a pension at all.

All this effort was made still more difficult by the fact that the social-security office which dealt with Tal'novo was twenty kilometres to the east, the district soviet was ten kilometres to the west, and the village soviet was an hour's walk to the north. They chased her from office to office for two whole months—sometimes because of a missing period, sometimes because of a misplaced comma. Every journey meant a whole day. She would go to the district soviet, and the secretary would be out that day: he was just absent, for no particular reason, as happens in the country. Come again the day after tomorrow. And four days later she would have to go again; out of sheer carelessness (all Matryona's documents were pinned together in one sheaf), someone had signed the wrong piece of paper.

"They're wearing me out, Ignatich," she complained to me after several of these fruitless journeys. "I get so worried."

But her brow did not stay furrowed for long. I noticed that she had an infallible means of restoring her good spirits: work. She would immediately pick up her spade and dig potatoes, or go off with a sack under her arm to fetch some peat, or wander far into the woods with a wicker basket to pick berries. Instead of bowing to office desks, she would lean over the bushes in the forest. Then, her back bending under the weight of her burden, Matryona would come beaming back to her cottage, thoroughly delighted.

"Now, I really know where to get the good stuff, Ignatich," she would say about the peat she had dug. "You should see the place; it's a treat."

"Isn't my peat enough, Matryona Vasilievna? There's a whole lorryload of it, after all."

"Pooh, your peat! If you got twice as much, or more,

10

it might just do. When the wind really starts blowing in the winter, you need all the peat you can get simply to keep warm. You should have seen how much we pinched last summer. I'd pinch three lorryloads if I could. But they catch you. They took one of our women to court."

She was right. The terrifying breath of winter was already starting to blow. We were surrounded by woods, but there was nowhere to gather fuel. Although excavators were digging peat out of the bogs all around us, none of it was sold to the local inhabitants; but if you were one of the bosses or ranked among the boss class—teachers, doctors, factory workers—then you got a lorryload. The local people in Tal'novo were not supposed to be given fuel, and it was no use asking for it. The chairman of the collective farm walked around the village looking at people earnestly or innocently and talking about everything under the sun except fuel. After all, he had his own supply. Winter didn't worry him.

Just as people had once stolen wood from the landlord, now they scrounged peat from the Trust. The peasant women banded together by fives and tens, because they felt bolder in a gang, and went in daytime. In summer the peat was stacked up all over the place to dry out. The great thing about peat is that when it is dug it cannot be removed right away: it has to dry out until the autumn, or until the snow if the roads are impassable from the autumn rains. It was then that the women stole it. You could get six slabs of peat into a sack if it was damp, or ten slabs if it was dry. A sackful, carried three or four kilometres (it weighed sixty pounds), was enough to fire the stove for one day. Winter lasts two hundred days, and you have to stoke two stoves every day—the Russian stove in the daytime, the tiled stove at night.

"There's no two ways about it," Matryona said, losing her temper with some invisible "them." "Since there's been no more horses, if you want stuff in the house you've got to fetch it yourself. My back never stops aching. If I'm not pulling a sledge in winter, I'm humping baskets in summer. It's true, you know."

11

The peasant women went more than once a day to scrounge peat. On a good day Matryona might bring home as many as half a dozen sackfuls. She made no secret about my peat, but hid her own under the passage, covering the hiding place every evening with a loose floorboard.

"Bet they can't guess where it is, the nosey-parkers." She grinned as she wiped the sweat from her forehead. "And if they can't, they'll never find it in a lifetime."

What could the Peat Trust do? They weren't allowed enough staff to post watchmen all over the bogs. They probably coped with the problem by exaggerating their production figures and then writing off a certain percentage to loss from the effects of rain and crumbling. Now and again, at random intervals, they would send out a patrol and catch the women as they returned to the village. The women would drop their sacks and scatter. Sometimes too, when an informer gave them a tip-off, they would make a house-to-house search, compile lists of people caught hoarding illegal peat, and threaten them with prosecution. The women would stop pilfering peat for a while, but winter was coming on and drove them to it again—at night this time, and with sledges.

Observing Matryona, I noticed that every day was taken up with some major task, in addition to cooking and housework. She somehow kept a record in her head of the proper routine of these jobs, and whenever she woke up in the morning, she always knew what she was going to be doing that day. Apart from collecting peat and scrounging old tree stumps rooted up by the tractors in the peat bogs, gathering bilberries, which she bottled for the winter ("Give yourself a treat, Ignatich," she would say as she offered me some), digging potatoes, and tramping the countryside seeing about her pension, she also had to find time to gather hay for her one and only nanny goat.

"Why don't you keep a cow, Matryona Vasilievna?"

"Well," Matryona explained as she stood in the kitchen doorway in her dirty apron and turned towards my table, "the goat gives enough milk for me. If I had a cow, she'd eat me out of house and home. No good cutting hay beside the railway track—that belongs to other people; the Forestry owns the hay in the woods, and they won't let me cut hay on the collective farm because I'm not a member any longer. The people on the farm won't give you the skin off their teeth. Ever tried looking for grass under the snow? There was a time when you could get all the hay you wanted on the verges, at hay harvest. Lovely hay, that was . . ."

Collecting hay for one milch goat was very hard work for Matryona. She would set off in the morning with a sack and a sickle and go to the places where she remembered that grass grew along the boundaries between fields, by the roadside, on tussocks among the peat bogs. Her sack stuffed with heavy, freshly cut grass, she would drag it home and spread it out to dry in her yard. A sackful of grass produced the equivalent of one pitchforkful of hay.

The first thing that the new town-bred chairman of the collective farm did was to reduce the size of the kitchen gardens allotted to disabled ex-members, so Matryona was left with fifteen square yards of sandy soil while the ten square yards docked from her old allotment simply lay fallow and went to waste on the other side of the fence. And when the farm was shorthanded and the women flatly refused to work overtime, the chairman's wife visited Matryona. She was a townswoman too, a determined creature in a short grey half-length coat, with a brisk, military air.

She went into the house and stared fiercely at Matryona without bothering to greet her. Matryona looked embarrassed.

"Right," the chairman's wife said crisply. "Comrade Grigorieva, you must come and lend a hand on the collective farm. We need some help to shift manure tomorrow."

Matryona's face creased into an apologetic smile, as though she was ashamed to tell the woman that the farm was not entitled to pay her for any work she did.

"Well," she said hesitantly, "I'm sick, you see, and I don't belong to the farm any longer." Then she hurriedly changed her mind. "What time shall I come?"

"Bring your own pitchfork," ordered the chairman's wife as she marched out with a swish of her stiff skirt.

"Huh!" Matryona fumed, "Bring your own pitchfork!' The farm never has any pitchforks, or spades either. Here am I, without a man to stick up for me . . ."

She talked to me about it all that evening.

"What else can I do, Ignatich? Of course I'm bound to help them—what sort of a harvest will they have if the muck doesn't get spread? Only, the way that place is run, it's a wonder they ever get any work done; the women stand around leaning on their shovels just waiting till the factory whistle blows at twelve. And they waste time arguing about the hours they've worked, who's on and who's off. Now to *my* way of thinking, when you work, you work—no gossiping, but get on with the job, and before you know where you are, it's suppertime."

Next morning, off she went with her pitchfork.

Not only the collective farm but any distant relative or simply a neighbour might accost Matryona one evening and say: "Come and help me tomorrow, Matryona. I need the rest of my potatoes dug." And Matryona could never refuse. She would abandon her private affairs, go and help her neighbour, and then when she returned say without a trace of envy: "Oh, she's got such huge potatoes, Ignatich. It was a pleasure to dig them up. I didn't want to stop, honest."

Matryona was equally indispensable when it came to ploughing up the kitchen gardens. The Tal'novo women had very sensibly worked out that it was much slower and harder work for one person to dig her garden singlehanded than for them to borrow a plough, harness six of them to it, and plough up six kitchen gardens in one go. Here again, Matryona was always called in to help.

"Do they pay her for it?" I once asked.

"She won't take any money. You'd have to force it on her."

Another of Matryona's great problems came when it was her turn to feed the village goatherds. One was a big, strapping creature who was a deaf-mute, and the other a boy with a soggy cheroot permanently stuck between his teeth. The job only came round once every six weeks, but it cost Matryona a lot of money. She would go to the village store to buy tins of fish and even things which she herself never ate, such as sugar and butter. Apparently the housewives all competed with each other to see who could feed the goatherds best.

"You should beware of tailors and shepherds," she explained to me. "They go round every house in turn, and if things aren't just right for them, they'll say terrible things about you to all your neighbours."

As if she did not have cares enough in her busy life, Matryona was regularly laid low by her ferocious illness. She would collapse and lie prone for a day or two at a time. She never complained or groaned; in fact, she hardly moved at all. When this happened, Masha, her lifelong friend, would come and tend the goat and stoke the fire. Matryona herself never ate or drank when she was ill and never asked for anything. No one in Tal'novo ever thought of sending for the doctor from the village clinic to call on them at home; it was regarded as vaguely insulting to one's neighbours, who might think one was putting on airs. Once, when the doctor was sent for, it turned out to be a disagreeable woman who simply told Matryona to lie down until the pain went and then come to the clinic herself. Matryona went very unwillingly. They did some tests on her and sent her to the district hospital, where the illness just subsided. Matryona, of course, was blamed for wasting their time.

Her everyday chores were what summoned her back to life. Soon Matryona would start getting up, moving slowly at first, then more briskly.

"You never saw me in the old days, Ignatich," she explained. "I used to be the one who carried all the sacks—a hundred pounds was nothing. My father-in-law used to shout at me: 'You'll break your back, Matryona!' I never needed any help harnessing the horse into the shafts, either. Ours was an army horse, a tough brute called Wolfcub . . ."

"Why an army horse?"

"They took ours for the war and gave us a wounded

army horse in exchange. He was a bit crazy. Once he shied at something and galloped off with the sledge, heading straight for the lake. The men all jumped out of his way, but I grabbed him by the bridle and stopped him—I did, you know! Liked his oats, did that horse. Our men always fed them on oats and then they could pull anything."

However, Matryona was by no means a fearless woman. She was afraid of fires and of lightning, and most of all she was terrified of trains.

"Once when I wanted to go to Cherusti the train came from Nechayevka, flashing its great eyes, the rails humming; it brought me out in a sweat, I can tell you, and my knees started shaking." Matryona was amazed at herself and shrugged her shoulders.

"Perhaps you were nervous about not having a ticket, because they don't sell them at the local station."

"You mean at the ticket office? They do—but only 'soft' class. Anyway, when the train came in, it was one big scramble. We rushed up and down trying to find somewhere to get on. The men either hung on to the steps or climbed up on the roof. We found a door that wasn't locked and pushed straight in without tickets. And all the coaches were 'hard' class, best you could hope for was to lie down on a luggage rack. Don't know why they wouldn't give us any tickets, the brutes . . ."

That winter Matryona's life took a turn for the better. At long last she started to get her pension of eighty roubles a month, in addition to slightly over a hundred roubles paid by the school and by me for bed and board.

"Matryona doesn't need to die now!" Some of her neighbours were already starting to envy her. "The old woman's got more money than she knows what to do with."

Matryona ordered a new pair of felt boots, bought a quilted jacket, and had an overcoat made out of a second-hand railwayman's greatcoat which she had been given by an engine driver from Cherusti, the husband of her adopted daughter Kira. The hunch-backed village tailor lined the material with cotton-

16

wool padding and made an overcoat more splendid
than any she had made herself in all her sixty years.

In the middle of winter Matryona sewed two hundred roubles into the lining of that coat. The money
was for her funeral and it gave her great satisfaction.

December and January passed, two whole months in
which she was spared an attack of her illness. Matryona
took to visiting her friend Masha more often in the
evenings, when they would sit talking and cracking
sunflower seeds. She never invited anyone to her home
in the evening, out of consideration for my need to
work. Only once when I came home from school did I
find the cottage full of people dancing. It was a chris-
tening party and I was introduced to her three sisters.
Since Matryona was considerably older than they were,
they treated her more like an aunt or a nanny. Until
then, we had seen or heard practically nothing of Matryona's sisters, probably because they were afraid Matryona needed help and would become a burden to
them.

For Matryona this celebration was saddened by only
one thing. She had walked three miles to church for the
blessing of the water and had put her bowl among the
others, but when the ceremony was over and the wom-
en jostled forward to collect their bowls, Matryona was
at the back of the crowd; when she finally got there, her
bowl was missing, gone as though the devil had spirited
it away.

Matryona went around asking all the women in the
congregation: "Did anybody take a bowl of someone
else's holy water by mistake?"

As no one owned up, it was probably stolen by one
of the little boys who had been brought to church.
Matryona came sadly home.

However, this did not mean that Matryona was really a fervent believer. If anything, she was a pagan and,
above all, superstitious: if you went into the garden on
St. John's day, that meant there would be a bad harvest
next year; if a storm was whirling the snowflakes round
and round, it meant that someone had hanged himself;
if you caught your foot in the door, it meant a visitor.

For as long as I lodged with her, I never once saw her say her prayers or cross herself. Yet she always asked for God's blessing before doing anything and she invariably said "God bless you" to me whenever I set off for school in the morning. Perhaps she did say her prayers, but not ostentatiously, being embarrassed by my presence or afraid of disturbing me. There were ikons in the cottage. On ordinary days they were unlit, but on the eve of feast days and on the feast days themselves Matryona would light the ikon lamp.

Yet she had even fewer sins to atone for than her lame cat. The cat, after all, did kill mice . . .

Having been slightly shaken out of the rut of her rather dull life, Matryona also started to listen more attentively to my radio (I had taken care to put up a good "area," as Matryona called it).

When she heard on the radio that some new machine had been invented, she grumbled from the kitchen: "Nothing but newfangled things these days. People won't want to go on working with the old machines, so where'll they put them all?"

During a broadcast describing how rain was induced by "seeding" clouds from an aeroplane, Matryona shook her head as she bent over the stove. "If they tamper with things much more, we won't know whether it's winter or summer."

Once they played a record of Chaliapin singing Russian folk songs. Matryona stood and listened for a long time, then said firmly: "He sings beautifully, but he doesn't sing our way."

"Oh, really, Matryona Vasilievna—just listen to him!"

She listened a bit longer, then pressed her lips together disapprovingly. "No. He hasn't got it right. That's not the way we sing. And he plays tricks with his voice."

Another time, Matryona made up for it. There was a recital of some of Glinka's songs, and suddenly, after half a dozen of his concert arias, Matryona appeared excitedly from the kitchen, clutching her apron, with a film of tears misting her eyes.

"Now that's . . . our sort of singing," she whispered.

18

2

And so Matryona and I grew used to each other and got along excellently together. She never pestered me with questions. Either because she was devoid of the usual female curiosity or because she was so tactful, she never once asked me whether I were married or not. All the women in Tal'novo would badger her to find out everything about me, but all she would say to them was: "If you want to find out, ask him yourself. All I know is, he's from far away."

When after quite a while I told her that I had spent a long time in prison, she merely nodded in silence, as though she had already suspected it.

For my part, I only saw Matryona as she was then, a lonely old woman, and I too refrained from prying into her past; indeed, I never suspected that there was anything of interest in it. I knew that she had married before the Revolution and had immediately moved into the cottage in which we were now living and straight to this same stove. Neither her mother-in-law nor any elder sisters-in-law were still alive then, so from the very first day after her wedding Matryona had taken over all the housework. I knew that she had had six children and they had all died very young, one after the other, so that no two of them had been alive at one time. Then there was Kira, who was her adopted daughter.

Matryona's husband did not return from the last war, and not even a funeral service was held for him. Men from his village who had served in the same company said that he had either been taken prisoner or was missing without trace. By the time the war had been over for eight years, Matryona herself had come to the conclusion that he was dead. And it was just as well that she did. If he had survived, he would probably be married and living somewhere in Brazil or Australia, and both the Russian language and the village of Tal'novo would have long since faded from his memory.

One day I came home from school to find a visitor in the cottage. A tall, dark, elderly man, his cap resting on his knee, was sitting on a chair which Matryona had put out for him in the middle of the room, near the Dutch stove. His whole face was framed in thick black hair that was scarcely touched with grey. His dense black beard merged with a thick black moustache that made his mouth almost invisible, while a pair of black side whiskers, almost hiding his ears, ran up in an unbroken line to join the black hair at his temples. To crown it all, his eyebrows met in an unbroken black line across the bridge of his nose, while his forehead rose like a gleaming dome towards the crown of his bald head. It seemed to me that the old man's whole appearance radiated wisdom and dignity. He was sitting there calmly with his arms folded on his walking stick, which was resting weightily on the floor, sitting in an attitude of patient expectation without making much attempt to talk to Matryona, who was busy behind the partition.

As I came in, he turned his magnificent head towards me in a dignified movement and suddenly spoke to me: "Good evening to you! I don't see very well, but you must be my son's teacher; his name's Antoshka Grigoriev . . ."

That was all he needed to say. For all my impulse to be helpful to this worthy old man, I knew exactly what he was going to say and I discounted it in advance as pointless. Antoshka Grigoriev was a chubby, red-cheeked lad in class 8-G who looked like a cat that has just eaten a bowl of cream. He treated school as a place to come for a good rest, where he could just sit at his desk, grinning idly. Needless to say, he never did his homework. But unfortunately, as part of our efforts to keep up the high success rate for which the schools of our region and the surrounding provinces were famous, he was regularly moved up by a class a year, and he had clearly grasped that, however much the teachers might threaten him, they would move him up at the end of the year just the same, and there was no need for him to do any work. He simply laughed at us. Although he was in class 8, he could not do fractions and he was unable to tell one sort of triangle from another. He had been a permanent candidate for bottom place in the class for my first two terms, and he would be in the same position next term too.

But how was I to tell this elderly, half-blind man, more of an age to be Antoshka's grandfather than his father, who had had the courtesy to call on me, that the school had been deceiving him regularly year after year? I could not keep up the deception, because if I too turned into a yes-man I would harm the children in my class, and that would be a betrayal of all my work and the ethics of my profession.

So I patiently explained to him that his son was a spoilt child, that he told lies both at school and at home, that we ought to check his attendance book more often, and that both parent and teacher should be much stricter with him.

"But I can't be much stricter with him," the visitor assured me. "I beat him at least once a week as it is. And I've got a heavy hand, believe me."

While we were talking, I remembered that Matryona herself had for some reason once put in a word on Antoshka Grigoriev's behalf, but I had not asked how he was related to her, and on that occasion too I had refused to intervene. Now Matryona appeared in the kitchen doorway, a wordless supplicant. After Ilya Mironich, the boy's father, had gone out saying that he would come to the school and find out for himself, I asked her: "What has that boy Antoshka got to do with you, Matryona Vasilievna?"

"He's the son of my brother-in-law," Matryona replied curtly, and went out to milk the goat.

I finally worked out that this persistent old man was the brother of her husband, the one who had been posted missing without trace.

For the rest of the long evening Matryona did not refer to the subject again. Only much later that night, when I had forgotten about the old man and was working in a silence disturbed only by the rustle of cockroaches and the tick of the kitchen clock, Matryona suddenly said from her dark corner: "I almost married him once, Ignatich."

I had forgotten about Matryona. She said it with as much emotion as if the old man were still courting her. It was obvious that she had been thinking about nothing else all evening.

She rose from her ragged bedclothes and slowly came over to me as though following her own words. I looked up in surprise, and for the first time I saw a new, unsuspected Matryona.

There was no overhead light in our big room, where the fig plants clustered like trees in a forest. The only illumination was from the table lamp shining downwards onto my exercise books, and if you looked up, the rest of the room seemed to be in half darkness tinged with pink. Matryona now emerged from this gloom and for a moment her cheeks did not look their usual yellow but were flushed.

"He courted me first, before Efim ... He was the elder brother ... I was nineteen; Ilya was twenty-three ... They lived in this very house. Their father built it."

I gave an involuntary glance around. Suddenly, instead of this grey, decaying old house with mice running wild behind its pale green skin of wallpaper, I saw it just built, with its fresh, newly planed logs, and smelling deliciously of pitch.

"What happened?"

"That summer ... he and I used to go and sit in the woods," she whispered. "Where the stables are now, there used to be a wood, but it was cut down ... I all but married him, Ignatich. Then the German war started, and Ilya was taken off to fight."

As she said this, I had a momentary image of that blue, white, and golden July of 1914: the sky of a world still at peace, floating clouds, and the peasants busily gathering the ripe harvest. I imagined the pair of them side by side: the giant with his pitch-dark beard and a scythe over his shoulder; Matryona, rosy-cheeked, clasping a sheaf of wheat. And the singing in the open air, a singing such as we have forgotten in this machine age.

"He went to the war, and he was posted missing . . . I waited for three years—not a sound, not a word . . ."

Wrapped in her faded, old-woman's kerchief, Matryona's round face gazed at me, lit by the soft indirect light of the lamp, and I saw it as though all its wrinkles had been smoothed out and the shabby, workaday clothes were gone. I saw the face of a bewildered girl faced with a terrible choice. I could see it happening . . . the leaves withering and blowing away, the snow falling and melting again. Another season's ploughing, another sowing, another harvest. Again autumn, again the snowfall; first one revolution, then another, and the whole world turned upside down.

"Their mother died, and Efim began courting me. 'You wanted to come and live in our house,' he said, 'so you might as well come—as *my* wife.' Efim was a year younger than me. Well, marry in haste, repent at leisure, they say. On Trinity Sunday I married Efim, and at Michaelmas . . . his brother Ilya came back from Hungary, where he'd been a prisoner of war."

Matryona closed her eyes.

I said nothing.

She turned towards the doorway as if someone were standing there.

"There he stood on the doorstep. I cried out and fell down on my knees to him. But it was no good. 'If he wasn't my own brother,' he said, 'I'd murder the pair of you.'"

I shuddered. Her anguish and fear had summoned up a vivid image of Ilya, black and angry, standing in the doorway and brandishing his axe at Matryona.

She calmed down, leaned on the chair back in front of her, and went on in her lilting voice: "Oh, the poor man! There were any number of nice girls in the village, but he wouldn't marry any of them. He said he'd only marry someone with the same name as mine. And he did, too. Brought a girl called Matryona from Lipki and built himself his own house. They still live there—you pass it every day on your way to school."

So that was it! I now realised that I had seen the other Matryona several times. I did not care for her: she was always coming to my Matryona to complain that

23

her husband was beating her, that he was a skinflint and worked her to death. She would come and weep for hours and her voice always seemed to be on the edge of tears. Matryona, it seemed, had missed nothing by not marrying him; Ilya had beaten his Matryona throughout their married life and had terrorised the household right up to the present day.

"He never beat me once," Matryona said of her husband, Efim. "He'd punch another man in the street, but he never touched me ... Well, there was one time—I'd quarrelled with his sister, and he hit me over the head with a ladle. I jumped up from the table and screamed at him: 'I hope you choke, you brute!' And I ran off into the woods. He never touched me after that."

Ilya apparently had no grounds for complaint either, because the other Matryona bore him six children (including my Antoshka, the youngest and the runt of the litter), and all of them survived, while none of the children of Matryona and Efim lived longer than three months, although they never actually fell ill.

"One of my daughters, Elena, died as soon as they'd washed her right after she was born. Just as I got married on St. Peter's day, so my sixth child, Alexander, was buried on St. Peter's day."

The village had decided that there was a curse on Matryona.

"Yes, there was a curse on me," Matryona said, obviously convinced of it herself. "They took me to a nun to be cured. She gave me something to make me cough, then waited for the curse to jump out of me like a frog. Well, it didn't ..."

The years passed like running water ... In '41 Ilya was not conscripted because of his poor eyesight, but Efim was called up, and just as the elder brother had vanished in the First World War, so the younger brother was lost without trace in the second—and he never returned. Empty, the cottage which had once been so lively and noisy grew decrepit and rotten and Matryona aged too as she lived on in it all alone.

She begged the other Matryona to let her have one of her offspring, her youngest daughter, Kira—perhaps because it was a child of Ilya's. For ten years she brought her up in her home as if she were her own daughter, one of those she had lost. Not long before my arrival, she had married her off to a young engine driver in Cherusti. This was now her only source of help and comfort; occasionally they would send her some sugar, or some lard when they killed a pig.

Frequently ill and sensing that she had not long to live, Matryona expressed the wish that after her death the separate outhouse on the other side of the passage in her house was to be given to Kira. She said nothing about the cottage itself; each of her three sisters was aiming to get it.

That evening Matryona told me everything about herself. And, as often happens, no sooner had I learned the secrets of her life than they began to appear in the flesh. Kira came over from Cherusti and old Ilya began to get very worried. Apparently, in order to validate their tenure of a plot of land in Cherusti they had to build on it, and Matryona's outhouse was ideal for the purpose: there was no hope of getting the timber anywhere else. The person who was keenest on getting the plot of land in Cherusti was neither Kira nor her husband but old Ilya on their behalf.

So he started calling on us; he came once and then again, talking persuasively to Matryona, urging her to give up the outhouse now, while she was still alive. During these visits he struck me as quite unlike the decrepit old man who had leaned on his stick and seemed liable to collapse at a push or a rough word. Although slightly hunched with lumbago, for a man over sixty he was still a handsome figure with his vigorous, youthful black hair, and he pressed his case with ardour.

Matryona could not sleep for two nights. It was a hard decision for her to make. She did not mind about the outhouse, which was empty anyway, just as she never grudged her own labour or property; it was, after all, already bequeathed to Kira. But she was upset by the thought of dismantling the roof which had sheltered her for forty years. Even I, a mere lodger, objected to them tearing down the planks and wrenching out the

25

logs from her cottage. For Matryona, it meant the end of her life.

But her insistent relatives knew that they would succeed in breaking up her house while she was still alive.

Ilya and his sons and sons-in-law arrived one February morning, and soon there came the knocking sound of five axes, the squealing and creaking of planks being wrenched apart. There was a purposeful gleam in Ilya's eye. Although he could no longer properly straighten his back, he was nimble enough at clambering about under the rafters and shinning down to shout instructions to his assistants. Long ago, as a young boy, he had helped his own father build this cottage, and the extra room that they were now demolishing had been designed as the place where he, the eldest son, should bring home his bride. Now that the house belonged to someone else, he relished the idea of pulling it apart and carting it away.

Having numbered the joists and the planks of the ceiling, they dismantled the room and the cellar and made a temporary wooden wall for the rest of the cottage and its shortened passage. Carelessly they knocked holes in the wall; it was all too obvious that these wreckers were no builders and were acting on the assumption that Matryona was not going to live here much longer.

While the men hacked away, the women distilled moonshine vodka in preparation for the day when the timber would be loaded up; proper vodka would have been far too expensive. Kira brought thirty pounds of sugar from somewhere in the Moscow region, and under cover of night Matryona Vasilievna carried the sugar and the bottles to the still.

When all the timber had been dismantled and piled up in front of the gate, the engine driver son-in-law went off to Cherusti to fetch the tractor. But that day it began to snow. The blizzard swirled and howled for two days and obliterated the roads with vast snowdrifts. No sooner had the way been cleared, and one or two lorries had got through, than there was a sudden thaw in the space of a single day, a damp fog came down, the snow dissolved into gurgling rivulets and your boots sank up to the calves in mud.

It was two weeks before the tractor was able to come and fetch the dismantled outhouse, and throughout that time Matryona went around like a lost soul. She was particularly depressed by a visit from her three sisters, who cheerfully swore at her and called her a fool for having let the outhouse go. They departed, announcing that they were fed up with her. Soon afterwards her lame cat strayed out of the yard and was killed. These two incidents in quick succession greatly upset her.

At last a frost came and the thawing roads hardened again. The sun came out, which cheered everyone up, and Matryona had a pleasant dream before waking up. That morning she found out that I wanted to photograph someone working at an old hand loom (there were still two of them in working order in the village, used for weaving crude rugs). She smiled shyly.

"Wait a couple of days until we get rid of this timber, Ignatich, and I'll set up my loom—I've got one too, you know. Then you can take a picture of me."

She obviously liked the idea of being photographed working at the old craft. A faint pink light from the wintry sun filtered in through the frosted window of her truncated porch, and the glow lit up her face. People who are at ease with their consciences always look happy.

As I was returning from school before dusk, I noticed movement outside our house. A big new tractor-drawn sledge was already fully loaded with timber, but there was still plenty more. The whole of Ilya's family, and their friends who had been invited to help, were just completing a second, home-made sledge. They were all working like madmen, in the frenzied state that seizes people when there is big money or free drink in the offing, all shouting at each other and arguing.

The argument was about how to move the sledges—separately or together. One of Ilya's sons (the lame one) and his son-in-law (the engine driver) were saying that the tractor could not pull both sledges at once. The tractor driver, on the other hand, a burly, self-confident tough, insisted hoarsely that he knew what he was

27

talking about, that *he* was in charge of the tractor and he was going to tow both sledges together. His motives were obvious: he was being paid a lump sum to transport a certain quantity of timber, rather than so much per trip. If he had to do it in two trips—it was thirty-five kilometres each way—he would never complete the job in one night, and at all costs he had to return the machine to its garage by the next morning, because he was "borrowing" it illegally.

Old Ilya was impatient to have the outhouse timber removed that same day, so he persuaded his family to agree to move the load in one trip. Hastily cobbled together, the second sledge was coupled behind the stronger one.

Matryona ran busily around among the menfolk, helping to pile the logs onto the sledge. It was then that I noticed that she was wearing my quilted jacket and had dirtied it when she rubbed against the frozen mud sticking to the timber. Annoyed, I pointed this out to her. I was fond of that jacket; it had seen me through some hard times.

For the first time I lost my temper with Matryona Vasilievna.

"Oh dear, oh dear, I am stupid," she said apologetically. "I just grabbed it without thinking, I forgot it was yours. Sorry, Ignatich." She took it off and hung it up to dry.

When the loading was finished, everyone who had helped, about ten men in all, clumped noisily through the living room past my table and ducked under the curtain that screened off the kitchen. There followed a muffled clinking of glasses, the occasional thump as a bottle was knocked over; the voices grew louder and the mutual congratulations more extravagant. The tractor driver was particularly boastful. The powerful reek of moonshine soon drifted through to me, but they did not drink for long because they had to hurry to start before darkness set in. Conceited and aggressive, the tractor driver came staggering out. Ilya's son-in-law, the lame son, and another nephew climbed on the sledge to go with it as far as Cherusti. The others went home. Waving his stick, Ilya ran after one of the men and hurriedly made some last-minute adjustment. The lame son stopped at my table to light a cigarette and quite unexpectedly began telling me how fond he was of Aunt Matryona, that he had recently got married and that a son had been born not long ago. Then someone shouted to him to hurry. Outside, the tractor's engine started with a roar.

The last person to emerge from the kitchen was Matryona. She shook her head anxiously as the men prepared to leave, then put on her quilted jacket and a head-scarf. In the doorway she said to me: "Why didn't they get two tractors? If one broke down, the other could have pulled. As it is, God knows what'll happen if something goes wrong . . ." And she ran out after the others.

After the drinking bout, the arguments, and the tramping feet, the quiet in the empty cottage was particularly marked; the cottage had also been made extremely cold thanks to the constant opening of doors. Outside, it was now quite dark. I too put on my quilted jacket and sat down to correct exercise books. The sound of the tractor faded in the distance.

An hour passed, then another and a third. Matryona had not come back, but I was not surprised. Having seen the sledges on their way, she had probably gone to see her friend Masha.

Two more hours went by. The village was not only in darkness, but a profound silence seemed to have settled on it. At the time I couldn't understand it; later I realised that not a single train had passed all evening along the railway line that ran a quarter of a mile away from us. My radio was silent and I noticed that the mice were unusually active, scurrying about behind the wallpaper, squeaking and scratching more noisily and impudently than ever.

I looked up, startled. It was one o'clock in the morning and Matryona had still not returned.

Suddenly I heard several loud voices out in the village street. They were still far away, but something told me they were coming to our cottage, and sure enough, before long there came a sharp knock on the gate. A brisk, unknown voice shouted to be let in. I went out into the dense blackness with a pocket torch. The whole village was asleep, none of the windows was lit, and the rapidly thawing snow gave off no reflection. I slid aside the lower bolt and let them in. Four men in service greatcoats marched into the house. It is extremely unpleasant to be visited at night by loud-voiced men in uniform.

In the light I noticed, however, that two of the men were in railway uniform. The senior, a stout man with the same sort of face as the tractor driver, asked me: "Where's the owner?"

"I don't know."

"Did some people drive a tractor away from here, pulling a sledge?"

"Yes, they did."

"Were they drinking before they left?"

All four men screwed up their eyes as they peered into the semi-darkness around the table lamp. It was obvious that they had made an arrest or were intending to arrest someone.

"What happened?"

"Answer when you're asked a question."

"But . . ."

"Were they drunk when they left?"

Had someone been killed? Had they run into trouble? They gave me quite a grilling, but I said nothing because I knew that Matryona could get a heavy sentence for dispensing illicitly distilled vodka. I placed myself across the doorway into the kitchen to keep them out.

"Not that I could see." (It was true: I hadn't seen them, only heard them.)

With an artless gesture I waved my hand around the room to emphasise the innocence of it all—the peaceful lamplight on my papers and books, the row of fig plants, Matryona's neat, spartan bed. There was not a trace of an orgy to be seen.

Agreeing reluctantly that no drinking bout could have taken place here, they turned to go. On the way out I heard them say that even if there had been no drinking here, they were still convinced that drink was involved somewhere. I saw them out and asked what had happened.

Only when they reached the gate did one of them bark at me: "The whole lot caught it. Hardly even any bits to pick up."

Another added: "That was nothing. The nine o'clock express was damn nearly derailed, that was the worst of it."

And they hurried away.

Appalled, I went indoors. What did he mean by "the whole lot"? How had they "caught it"? Where was Matryona?

I pushed the curtain aside and went into the kitchen. The reek of moonshine hit me like a punch in the face. It was a squalid sight—overturned stools and benches, empty bottles lying on their sides, an upright one with some moonshine still in it, glasses, half-chewed bits of salted herring, onion, a smear of dripping mixed with bread crumbs.

Everything was deathly still except for the cockroaches cheerfully swarming over the battlefield.

They had said something about the nine o'clock express. Why? What did that mean? I began to wonder whether I shouldn't have shown them the scene in the kitchen after all, but then I angrily remembered their highhanded manner and their refusal to give me any proper information.

Suddenly the gate creaked, and I hurried out into the passage. "Is that you, Matryona Vasilievna?"

The front door opened and Matryona's friend Masha tottered unsteadily in, wringing her hands. "Matryona . . . Our Matryona, Ignatich . . ."

I sat her down and she told me the story, between sobs.

There is a steep hill leading down to the level crossing, which is ungated. The tractor had almost managed to pull the first sledge across when the rope snapped. The second, makeshift sledge struck an obstacle on the tracks and began to fall apart, because the wood which Ilya had given them to make it with was mostly rotten. They pulled the first sledge clear, then the tractor driver, Ilya's lame son, and, for some reason, Matryona,

31

came back to mend the rope and tow the second sledge away. What use could Matryona have been? She always had interfered in men's work; a horse had once bolted and nearly dragged her into the frozen lake. Why, oh why did she have to go back to that cursed level crossing? She'd given up her outhouse to them, done her duty by them and more . . . The tractor driver kept looking round to make sure there was no train coming from Cherusti, he would have been able to see its lights from miles away; but two engines coupled together, travelling backwards and without lights, came down the track from the other direction—from our station. Why they had no lights nobody knows, and when an engine travels in reverse, the driver is blinded by coal dust from the tender and can't see properly. The engines rammed the sledge at full tilt, and the three people standing between it and the tractor were smashed to mincemeat. The tractor was battered to pieces, the sledge reduced to splinters, the rails were ripped up, and both engines derailed and flung onto their sides.

"But why didn't they hear the engines coming?"

"Because of the noise from the tractor engine."

"What about the bodies?"

"They won't let anyone near them. It's been cordoned off."

"Didn't I hear something about the express? Was there an express?"

"The nine o'clock left our station on time and it was picking up speed towards the level crossing. But when the two engines crashed, the engine drivers managed to get out alive, they ran down the track waving their arms and managed to stop the train . . . Ilya's nephew, too, was crippled by a falling log. Right now he's hiding with friends so the police won't find out he was at the crossing. They're pulling witnesses in as hard as they can—better keep your mouth shut if you want to stay out of trouble. And as for Kira's husband—not a scratch. He tried to hang himself and they had to pull his neck out of the noose. My brother and my aunt were killed because of me, he says. Then he went and gave himself up to the police, but he's being sent to

32

the madhouse instead of prison. Oh, Matryona, Matryona . . ."

Matryona was no more. A beloved person was gone forever. And on her last day on earth I had scolded her for wearing my jacket.

The woman on the book poster, printed in bright yellows and reds, smiled joyfully.

Masha sat and wept a little longer. Then as she was getting up to go she suddenly asked: "Do you remember, Ignatich? Matryona had a grey shawl. She promised that after her death it should go to my little Tanya, didn't she?"

She looked hopefully at me in the semi-darkness, wondering whether I had forgotten.

But I remembered. "Yes, that's right, she promised it to her."

"Listen, then. Would you let me take it now? Tomorrow morning the whole clan will descend on this place and I might not get it."

She gave me a hopeful, imploring look. She had been Matryona's friend for fifty years and was the only person in the village who had been genuinely fond of her. It was surely right that she should have it.

"Of course, take it," I agreed.

She opened a chest, found the shawl, stuffed it under her skirts, and went.

The mice seemed to have been gripped by a kind of madness; they were racing furiously up and down the walls and the green wallpaper was heaving in almost visible waves.

Tomorrow I had to go and teach in school. It was three o'clock in the morning. The only refuge was to lock myself in and go to sleep. I could lock the door now, because Matryona would not be coming back.

I lay down, leaving the light on. The mice were squeaking so hard it was almost as if they were groaning. They raced tirelessly up and down. My exhausted, confused mind could not throw off an involuntary sense of horror. I had a feeling that Matryona was moving about, bidding farewell to her home. Suddenly, in the hallway by the front door I had a vision of Ilya, young,

33

black-bearded, with axe raised: "If he wasn't my own brother, I'd murder you both."

Forty years that threat had laid in the corner, like an old abandoned blade—and it had finally struck.

3

At dawn the women brought home all that remained of Matryona, drawn on a sledge and covered with a dirty piece of sacking. They removed the sack to wash the corpse. It was hideously mangled—no legs, half the torso missing, and no left arm. One of the women said: "The Lord left her right arm so she can pray to Him in heaven."

All the fig plants were removed, the plants which Matryona had loved so much that once, when she had woken up with the cottage full of smoke, instead of trying to save the building she had thrown the fig plants to the floor so they would not suffocate. The floors were scrubbed clean. Matryona's dim mirror was draped with a large old towel of homespun cloth. The gay posters were taken down from the walls. My table was moved aside, and the roughly carpentered coffin was placed on stools near the window, under the ikon.

And there in the coffin lay Matryona. Her severed, disfigured body was covered with a clean sheet and her head was bound with a white cloth. Her face, calm and looking more alive than dead, had remained whole.

The villagers came to stand and look. Mothers brought young children to see the dead woman. And if anyone began to weep, all the women, even those who had come out of mere curiosity, inevitably started weeping in sympathy as they stood round the walls and in the doorway, like a choir accompanying a solo singer. The men stood stiffly to attention, silent and bareheaded.

It was the role of the female relatives to lead the mourning. I detected in their mourning an element of cold calculation, of an ancient, established procedure. The more distant relatives stepped up to the coffin for a short while and muttered as they bent over it. Those who regarded themselves as more closely related to the deceased began their keening at the very doorway and when they reached the coffin leaned over to say their piece right into the dead woman's face. Each mourner struck her own note and gave vent to her own particular thoughts and emotions.

I also observed that the keening was not merely an expression of grief but contained an element of "politics." Matryona's three sisters descended, took possession of the cottage, the goat, and the stove, locked her chest, ripped out of the lining of her coat the two hundred roubles she had put aside for her funeral, and explained to everyone present that they, her sisters, were Matryona's only close relatives. And this was what they said as they mourned over her coffin:

"Oh, our dearest, dearest only sister, you lived such a quiet, simple life, and we always loved you and cared for you. And your house was the death of you. The outhouse drove you to the grave. Why did you let them tear it down? Why didn't you listen to us?"

Thus the sisters' wailing was directed at her husband's clan—accusing them of having forced Matryona to surrender the timber from her house. And the further implication was: "You may have taken the outhouse but we won't let you have the rest of the cottage."

The husband's clan—Matryona's sisters-in-law, Efim's and Ilya's sisters, and various nieces—came and mourned in these terms:

"Oh, dearest Aunt Matryona, you never spared yourself or took care of yourself, and now *they* say we were to blame. We loved you, but it was all your fault. The outhouse had nothing to do with it. Why did you go to the place where death was lying in wait for you? Nobody asked you to! Why didn't you stop and think?— then you mightn't have died! And why didn't you listen to us?"

These lamentations implied: "We weren't to blame

35

for her death, and as for the cottage—we'll see about that!"

Then came the "other" Matryona, a coarse, ugly woman. But the substitute Matryona, who had once taken Ilya simply because her name was the same, broke the rules by wailing in unaffected sincerity over the coffin:

"Dearest, dearest sister of mine, promise me you weren't offended at me! Oh, what times we once had, you and I, and how we talked! Forgive me, poor Matryona! Oh, you've gone to join your mother now and you'll be telling tales about me! Oh, please don't, please . . ."

At this final "please" she seemed to sob out her very soul, and she beat her breast again and again against the side of the coffin. When her keening went too far beyond the ritual limits, the women, as though acknowledging that she had well and truly made her point, said kindly: "That's enough, dear. You'd better go now."

Matryona went, but she came back again and sobbed even more violently. Then a very old woman stepped forward from a corner, laid a hand on her shoulder, and said sternly: "There are two great riddles in this world: How was I born? I don't remember. How shall I die? I don't know."

At once Matryona was quiet, and everyone in the room fell completely silent.

But a little while later that same old woman, who was much older than all the others and who, I thought, had hardly even known Matryona during her lifetime, began to wail in her turn: "Poor, unhappy Matryona! Why was it you who died and I was spared?"

The one person whose mourning was completely unceremonious was Matryona's wretched adopted daughter, Kira from Cherusti, for whose sake the outhouse had been dismantled and removed. She could only weep the natural, commonplace tears of our time, an age that has been no stranger to suffering and bereavement. Her waved hair was pathetically disordered, her eyes bloodshot. Despite the cold, she was unaware that her headscarf had slipped off, and when she put on her overcoat, her arm could not find the sleeve. She walked numbly away from the coffin of her foster-mother in one cottage to her brother's coffin in another; they now feared for her reason, as her husband was certain to be sent for trial.

Her husband, it seemed, was doubly guilty: not only had he been responsible for moving the timber, but being an engine driver by profession and therefore thoroughly versed in the regulations for ungated level crossings, he should have first gone to Tal'novo Station to warn them about the tractor. That night the lives of a thousand people on board the Urals Express, sleeping peacefully in their berths by the light of shaded lamps, had been nearly destroyed. And all because of a few people's greed—the urge to grab a plot of land, the refusal to make two journeys by tractor; because of the outhouse, on which a curse had lain since Ilya had stretched out his covetous hands to seize it.

The tractor driver had already passed beyond the reach of earthly justice. But the railway management was also guilty for leaving a busy level crossing unguarded and for allowing two coupled engines to travel without lights. This was why they had at first made such strenuous efforts to prove that the party had been drinking, and were now doing their best to mislead the court.

The track and the rail bed were so badly damaged that no trains ran for the three days that the coffins lay in the village; traffic was diverted onto a loop line. Throughout Friday, Saturday, and Sunday—from the end of the police investigation until the funeral—the track was under repair day and night. To keep out the freezing cold and to provide light in the dark, the repair gangs lit bonfires with the free fuel provided by the planks and logs from the second sledge which were scattered all over the level crossing. The first sledge, still fully loaded, was left standing nearby on the roadside.

It was this—the tantalising fact that one sledge was there, ready to be towed away, and that the contents of the second sledge might have been saved from burning —that really tortured the black-bearded Ilya all Friday and Saturday. Yet his daughter was on the verge of insanity, his son-in-law was to be prosecuted, in his own house lay the body of his son, and across the street lay the woman he had once loved—both of whom he had killed. Ilya stood tugging at his beard and did not stay for long when he came to pay his last respects to the departed. To judge by his furrowed brow, he was obviously deep in thought; but what he was thinking about was how to save the rest of the timber from the bonfire and from the grasping claws of Matryona's sisters.

Later, when I came to know Tal'novo better, I realised that there were plenty of other people like him in the village. It is both revealing and bitterly ironic that our language itself equates "good" with "goods" and that to lose property is universally regarded as shameful and ridiculous.

Ilya set off on an unceasing round of visits, to the village soviet, to the station, from one department to another. His back bent, supported on his stick, he stood in each office in turn, begging the authorities to have pity on his old age and to give him permission to recover his timber.

Somewhere, someone gave him permission, and Ilya gathered his remaining sons, sons-in-law, and nephews, and borrowed some horses from the kolkhoz. Then, by a roundabout route through three villages, he reached the far side of the damaged level crossing and carted the remains of the outhouse away to his own yard. He completed the work during the night between Saturday and Sunday.

On Sunday the funeral was held. The two coffins met in the middle of the village and the relatives quarrelled over which should go first. Then they placed them side by side on one sledge, aunt and nephew, and hauled them through the damp chill of an overcast February day to the cemetery that lay two villages distant. The weather was blustery and unpleasant; the priest and the deacon waited at the church, refusing to come out to meet the procession on the way.

Singing in chorus, the people slowly followed the

procession as far as the village boundary. There they stopped and went home.

Even on Sunday morning the women were still busy at their rituals: one old woman sat mumbling psalms by the coffin; Matryona's sisters fussed around the stove, stoking up the heat with the slabs of peat that Matryona had brought in a sack from distant peat bogs. They baked some unappetising little pies out of cheap, nasty flour.

On Sunday evening, after the funeral, we assembled for the wake. Several tables, joined together to form a single long one, now occupied the space where the coffin had stood that morning. They began by all standing around the table while an old man, the husband of one of Ilya's sisters, recited the Lord's Prayer. Then a small quantity of melted honey was served to each person in a bowl, which we ate with spoons in memory of the departed. After that we ate something else, drank some vodka, and the talk grew more lively. Before eating the final dish of *kisel'*, we stood up and sang "In Eternal Memory." They explained to me that traditionally this had to be sung before the *kisel'*. Then more vodka, after which the talk became louder still and no longer concerned with Matryona.

Ilya's brother-in-law said boastfully: "Did you notice at the church how they said *all* the prayers, without leaving any out? That's because Father Michael noticed I was there. He knows I know the service by heart. Otherwise he'd have just grabbed off half of it, tipped 'em in, and goodbye."

At last the meal was over. Once again we stood up, and sang "She is Worthy," then repeated "In Eternal Memory" three times. By now the voices were hoarse and out of tune, the faces were drunken, and no one any longer put the slightest feeling into their "Eternal Memory."

Then most of the guests departed, leaving only the close relatives; cigarettes were produced and lit, there were jokes and laughter. The talk turned to Matryona's husband, Efim, who had been reported missing without trace. Thumping his chest, Ilya's brother-in-law explained about Efim to me and to a shoemaker who was married to one of Matryona's sisters: "Yes, he died all right, did Efim. Otherwise, why didn't he come back? Even if I knew I'd be hung if I came home, I'd still come back."

The shoemaker nodded in agreement. He had been a deserter and had spent the whole war at home, hiding in his mother's cellar.

The stern, silent old woman, the one who was much older than the others, had decided to stay in the cottage for the night and was already installed on top of the stove. She gazed down in silent disapproval on the indecently loud behaviour of all these youngsters of fifty and sixty.

Only the unhappy adopted daughter, who had grown up in this house, went behind the kitchen partition and wept.

Ilya did not come to Matryona's wake, because he was taking part in the memorial ceremony for his son, but during the next few days he came over to the cottage a couple of times for some ill-tempered discussions with Matryona's sisters and the shoemaker.

The argument was about who was to have the cottage—one of Matryona's sisters or the adopted daughter. It looked as if they might go to court over it, but they were fairly soon reconciled and reached a settlement, agreeing that the court would probably allot the house to neither party but would hand it over to the village soviet. So a deal was made. The goat went to one sister; the shoemaker and his wife got the cottage; and because he had "built the place with loving care," Ilya was allotted the outhouse timber plus the shed in which the goat had lived and the internal fence that divided the back yard from the kitchen garden.

Once more, overcoming his sickness and rheumatism, the insatiable old man began to perk up and look younger. Once more he summoned his remaining sons and sons-in-law. They demolished the shed and the fence and he personally removed the timber on a little sledge, helped by his young son Antoshka from class 8-G, who for once worked with a will.

Matryona's cottage was handed over before winter

was out, so I moved over to one of her sisters-in-law who lived nearby. On various occasions she recalled things about Matryona and thus I learned to see the deceased in a new light.

"Efim didn't love her. He used to say that he liked to dress smartly, but she just wore any old thing, like a typical peasant woman. So once he realised he needn't spend any money on her, he blew all his spare cash on drink. And once, when he and I went to town to do a job and earn some money in the winter, he found himself a fancy woman and didn't want to go back to Matryona."

Everything she said about Matryona was disapproving: she was dirty, she was a bad housekeeper, she wasn't thrifty. She wouldn't even keep a pig, because she didn't like the idea of fattening up a beast to kill it. And she was stupid enough to work for other people without pay—though the very reason the sister-in-law had remembered Matryona was that she had been complaining that there was no longer anyone to help plough up the kitchen garden. Even though she acknowledged Matryona's kindness and simplicity, she did so in a tone of scornful pity.

Only then, listening to the disapproving comments of her sister-in-law, did I see an image of Matryona which I had never perceived before, even while living under her roof.

It was true: every other cottage had its pig, yet she had had none. What could be easier than to fatten up a greedy pig whose sole object in life was food? Boil it a bucketful of swill three times a day, make it the centre of one's existence, then slaughter it for lard and bacon. Yet Matryona never wanted one . . .

She was a poor housekeeper. In other words, she refused to strain herself to buy gadgets and possessions and then to guard them and care for them more than for her own life.

She never cared for smart clothes, the garments that embellish the ugly and disguise the wicked.

Misunderstood and rejected by her husband, a stranger to her own family despite her happy, amiable temperament, comical, so foolish that she worked for others for no reward, this woman, who had buried all her six children, had stored up no earthly goods. Nothing but a dirty white goat, a lame cat, and a row of fig plants.

None of us who lived close to her perceived that she was that one righteous person without whom, as the saying goes, no city can stand.

Neither can the whole world.

For the Good of the Cause

"Faina, who's got the electricians' timetable?"

"What do you want it for? You're in radio."

"Faina, turn it down by twenty decibels ... This is our new colleague—he wants to know."

"I'm sorry. What are you going to teach here?"

"Generators. And theory of electrical transmission."

"There's such a noise I can't hear a thing. Call themselves teachers! The timetable's over there in the corner, have a look."

"Susanna Samoilovna! How are you?"

"Lydia Georgievna? Lydia, my dear, you're looking marvellous. Where did you spend the summer?"

"Where d'you think? On the building site for the whole of July!"

"On the building site? Did you have a holiday or not?"

"Not really. Three weeks instead of eight. Still, it wasn't too awful. But you're looking rather pale."

"Grigory Lavrentich, what have you fixed up for the electricians' department? Just two days?"

"The other departments have only arranged classes until September 2. It's a provisional timetable. Comrades, who's that going out? Comrades! Attention, please! I repeat: Fyodor Mikheyich has asked that no one should leave."

"But where is he?"

"In the new building. He'll be back soon and we'll discuss the business of the move."

"We must make up our minds pretty soon. Students from other towns are arriving already. Should we send them out to lodgings? Or will there be a hostel?"

"God knows, it's been put off for so long. But why can't we ever do anything on time?"

"Maria Diomidovna, I've been given two rooms in the new building, which should be enough. Theory of electro-technology in one room, and electrical measurement in the other."

"I'm in the same position: electronic and ionic appliances are separate from insulating materials, which have been left with lighting engineering."

"I'm glad for your sake. Up until now you haven't even had a laboratory—just a heap of old glass!"

"All the stuff's still in crates—in the passage, down in the cellar—it's ghastly! But now we've sent the shelves over there, there'll be a place for everything: ignitron, thyratron, generating lamps . . ."

"Do stop smoking, Vitaly. When you want a cigarette, ask the ladies first."

"Let me introduce our new teacher, Anatoly Germanovich, an engineer. This is Susanna Samoilovna—she has the chair of mathematics."

"He's pulling your leg. What chair of mathematics?"

"Well, chairman of the faculty board. Isn't it the same thing? Except that you don't get paid for it . . . And now let me introduce you to Lydia Georgievna, a typical staff member."

"Don't you believe him. Actually, I'm the most untypical. You'll be more typical than me from the moment you start."

"Are you judging by my appearance? Because of my glasses, I suppose."

"It's because you've an engineering degree and, of course, you're a specialist. But I can easily be replaced. I'm just, well, sort of superfluous here."

"What do you teach?"

"Russian. And literature."

"You can tell from Lydia Georgievna's smile that she doesn't think she's superfluous. To begin with, she's the leader of our youth group."

"Is she now? Did the youth group choose you?"

"No, the Party bureau appointed me. They attached me to the Komsomol committee."

"Come now, Lydia dear, don't be so modest. The Komsomol members specifically asked for you. And for the fourth year running."

"Personally, I also think Lydia Georgievna was largely responsible for putting up the new building."

"Now you're pulling *my* leg."

"I don't understand—who did put up your new building? Was it the trust? Or was it you?"

"Both the trust and us, that's the trouble."

"Tell us about it, Lydia Georgievna. We've got to wait anyway."

"They put it to us like this: the trust hadn't got enough money for all its projects this year, and our building would take it another two years. We said couldn't we help? 'Of course you can! You can have the building by the first of September.' We jumped at the chance. We called a general meeting of the Komsomol . . ."

"But where can you hold meetings here?"

"Of course, there's no one hall big enough, but we can use the corridor and the staircase, and there are loudspeakers in the lecture halls . . . Anyway, we held the meeting. Should we take it on? Yes, we should. We split up into teams. To begin with, we put a teacher in charge of each team, but the kids made a fuss and said they didn't want one, they wanted to do it on their own. To be honest, we were very frightened about the young ones who were just out of school. After all, they're only about fourteen or fifteen—should they collapse or fall under a crane. In the end, the grownups did keep an eye on them, but the older ones wouldn't let us."

"And wasn't there complete chaos?"

"We tried to avoid it. The foreman told us in the Party bureau how many and what kinds of workers he would need each week. We set up a sort of headquarters where we decided how we would split up into teams. We even went to work on workdays, some of us before school hours and some after. In fact, we had a two-shift system. And we worked right through several Sundays. Our plans for the summer were that everyone should work two weeks of his holidays. Of course, for students from other towns we tried to make these two weeks at either end of the holidays, but anyone who happened to be picked for the middle of the holidays came then."

"That's really amazing."

"And that's not all. The really amazing thing was that no one had to be coerced. If anyone dropped out, the other kids somehow filled in for them. And the building workers were even more amazed than we were. They admitted to me quite honestly that the kids were better at the job than they were."

"Astounding."

"Don't you believe me? Ask anyone you like."

"N . . . ooo—it's not that I doubt it . . . I'm sure enthusiasm is a natural human quality and quite admirable. It's just that in our country the word has become sort of . . . hackneyed and debased. People use it completely indiscriminately, even on the radio. At the factory I keep on hearing: What's in it for me? What's the rate of pay for the job? Fill in an overtime claim! Not that it's surprising—material incentives are completely normal."

"What else did we do? Oh, yes—we copied the plans and made a model of the new building and carried it through the town in front of May Day processions as our symbol."

"Lydia Georgievna has started by telling the story from the emotional angle, but to understand it properly you need to see it from an economic standpoint. Our technical school has been going for seven years now, and since they gave us this building by the railway line and then another one beyond the town boundaries, we somehow just stayed here. Then they added on a single-story wing for the workshops, and gave us another small building half a kilometre from here. But it was still inconvenient all the same. Then Fyodor Mikheyich managed to lay his hands on a plot of building land right in the town. There were some little houses which had to be pulled down . . ."

"I suppose that took them about five minutes?"

"They cleared the site with mechanical shovels and laid two foundations straightaway—one for the technical school and one for the hostel, side by side. They even began to build the first floor, then everything

46

stopped dead. For three whole years after that, they insisted over and over again that there were no more funds. First they didn't include us on some allocation list, then the ministries were being split up, then they were being merged again and we were transferred from one to the other. Meanwhile, on the site it snowed, the snow melted, the rains came, and nothing had gone a step further. Then suddenly not long ago these Councils of National Economy were set up. They put us under one of them; it gave us money from the first of July of last year, and so . . ."

"Hey, Dusya, open the window, will you, dear? The men have filled the place with cigarette smoke—it's really disgraceful."

"Surely we don't have to go outside every time we want a cigarette?"

"Well, that isn't what the staff room's for!"

"And what sort of work was there for you to do?"

"Quite a lot. We dug the trenches leading from the boiler room . . ."

"Yes, we seemed to spend most of our time digging ditches. For the electricity mains, for . . . And we filled them all in ourselves, too."

"We unloaded bricks from the lorries and stacked them in the hoist, shifted the earth out from the foundations."

"And we carted the rubbish out from every floor, lugged radiators round to all the rooms . . . the pipes . . . the parquet flooring. And we washed and scrubbed."

"So the builders only had to employ specialists and no general labourers?"

"We even trained up some specialists too. We formed two teams of our own: apprentice plasterers and apprentice painters. And they really got to grips with the job—it was a great sight."

"Excuse me, is that noise coming from the street?"

"Forward Electronics, your victory's achieved!
In all communications, progress is our creed!
Ignorance is darkness, technology is light!
Radio, our watchword; radio, our might!"

"Are those your students? What are they singing?"

"Without even bothering to look, I can tell they're third-year vacuum physics."

"They sound terrific anyway. May I have a look at them? Can we see them from the window?"

"Let's get a bit closer . . . Marianna Kazimirovna, could you move your chair a little?"

"Oh, really! It's the barrel look—all the fashion now. It's got a narrow waist, then it widens out below and hangs in little pleats, then it gets very narrow again and finishes at mid-calf length . . ."

"Out past the canal there's a little lake I know—oh, the carp I've caught there! . . ."

"Lydia dear, why are you pushing your way out when everybody's sitting down?"

"Over here, Anatoly Germanovich. Squeeze your way through them. Look, there they are—that bunch of boys and girls over there."

> *"From the house to the shop floor,*
> *from the sky to outer space,*
> *Electronics researchers advance the human race!*
> *We strive for perfection,*
> *to give them what they need.*
> *Radio, our watchword; radio, our creed!"*

"Yes, what enthusiasm! They really sound as if they mean it."

"Well, they're proud of it because they made it up themselves and that's why they call it *The Electronics Song*. It's just because they're so enthusiastic that they won second prize at the town pageant. Do you notice, by the way—only the girls are singing, the boys are silent at the moment? At the pageant they were there just for appearances, but to make up for it they roar out in the chorus: 'Radio, our watchword; radio, our creed.'"

"For some reason the sight of them frightens me slightly. I'm used to teaching grownups. Once I went to the school where my young son's a pupil, to give a lecture on 'The Achievements of Science and Technology.' With my son there, I felt so ashamed—they weren't listening to me and they just did whatever they felt like. The headmaster banged on the table, but they didn't listen to him either. Afterwards my son explained to me: they'd locked the cloakroom and wouldn't let anybody go home. It's often like this, he said, when some delegation comes or there's some new rule to be announced. The children talk on purpose to be annoying."

"But you can't compare a technical school with an ordinary school; there's a different atmosphere here. There aren't any idlers just sitting out their time. And the principal here has greater powers—grants, the hostel . . . Though, in fact, we haven't had a hostel all these seven years; they've been living out in private digs."

"Does the college pay?"

"The school pays each student thirty roubles. This is the standard rate and it's supposed to be enough. But a bed costs a hundred roubles a month—a better one, a hundred and fifty—so sometimes two people share one bed. It can go on like that for years. And they get fed up. You seem to be doubtful about our enthusiasm, but there's one thing there's no doubt about: we're fed up with living badly, we want decent living conditions. Wasn't that why they started the scheme for doing voluntary work at weekends—to improve the standard of living?"

"It was."

"Well, that's how it was with us. Go on, lean out the window."

"Radio, our watchword; radio, our might!"

"How far is it to the level crossing?"

"Six hundred metres."

"But we have to cross that distance on foot. And lots of them have to do it twice a day, there and back. It's summer now and there hasn't been any rain for three days—but we still have to jump over puddles. You can never wear any decent clothes here, we have to wear boots all year round. In town it's been dry for ages, but we can't help looking dirty whenever we go there."

". . . watchword!"

"So we got together and we said: how much longer do we have to put up with it all? Our lecture halls are no bigger than cupboards. You couldn't arrange anything in the evening unless you hired the club hall. It was the evenings that made the kids more fed up than anything."

". . . might!"

"Lydia Georgievna! Lydia Georgievna!"

"Yes?"

"Some of the kids are asking for you. Can you manage to get out?"

"Okay, I'm coming. Excuse me!"

"It was a great goal. From the edge of the penalty area, he kicked it backwards over his head and right under the crossbar."

"Is this your cap? You're not still wearing that old thing? They only wear those upturned flowerpots nowadays!"

"Marianna Kazimirovna, may I trouble you . . ."

"I'm planning to take over part of the cellar as a shooting range. I've already promised the students."

"I'm not going away, Grigory Lavrentich, I'll be on the stairs . . ."

2

"Hello, kids. Who wanted me? Welcome back to anyone I haven't seen yet."

"Congratulations, Lydia Georgievna—we made it!"

"Lydia Georgievna."

". . . Georgievna."

"Well done, boys, and you too, girls—all of you!" Lydia Georgievna waved her hand high above her head so that everybody could see it. "You worked magnificently. Here's to the new term in the new place!"

"Hurrah!"

"But who's that trying to hide from me? Lena? And you've cut off that wonderful plait of yours!"

"But no one wears them nowadays, Lydia Georgievna."

"Aaah, what we girls have to do to keep up with fashion!"

Lydia Georgievna was wearing a blue-green suit with the black collar of her blouse outside—smart and very neat in appearance, and her expression was open and candid. As she stood on the top landing of the staircase by the staff-room door, she looked around at the young people crowding in on her from three sides—from the narrow corridors to her right and left, and from the narrow staircase below. Usually there wasn't much light here, but today it was sunny and there was enough to distinguish every colour; the headscarves, neckerchiefs, blouses, dresses, and flannel shirts here seemed to contain all shades—whites, yellows, pinks, reds, blues, greens, and browns—in spots, patterns, stripes, checks, and borders.

The girls were trying not to stand close to the boys, but girls in one group and boys in another were packed tightly together, chins resting on the shoulder of the person standing in front of them, and craning so they could see better—noisy and radiantly happy, poised in expectation of something from Lydia Georgievna.

She gazed around and could see distinctly how the girls' new hair styles had flourished over the summer; admittedly, here and there she still caught sight of some short, girlish plaits with coloured ribbons, and coy little partings, and the less coy kiss-curls and side curls. But how many there already were of those casual-looking styles, unkempt and half dishevelled but in reality elaborately contrived—flaxen, oaten, wheaten, and pitch. As for the boys, the long-legged and the short ones, the lean ones and the stockier ones, all of them were dressed in those gaily-coloured shirts and every single one had his collar unbuttoned—both the ones who had already smoothed out their boyish curls, and those whose hair was combed carefully back or bristled in a crew cut.

None of the very young ones, who were still almost children, was here; but even these senior students crowding around were still at that unprejudiced, pliant age when they can so easily be directed towards what is good, and they were glowing with enthusiasm.

She had hardly come out of the staff room when she took all of this in at a glance, engulfed by so many smiles and trusting eyes. Lydia Georgievna felt excited by what is a teacher's highest reward—the feeling that comes when your pupils cluster round and hang on your words. They could not have put a name to what it was they saw in her: it was just that, like young people, they loved everything which was sincere. Anyone could see from her face that she was saying exactly what she was thinking. And they had come to know her and love her especially as a result of the months spent on the building site. Instead of her smart clothes, she had worn an overall and headscarf. She had felt awkward at simply ordering them around: she would never tell anyone to do something she was not ready to do herself. She swept, scrubbed, and carried things along with the girls.

And so, even though she was nearly thirty, was married and had a two-year-old daughter, all the students called her Lidochka, though not to her face. The boys were proud to rush off on errands for her which she assigned with a slight but authoritative wave of her hand, and sometimes as a sign of special trust or confidence she would give one of them a gentle tap on the shoulder.

"Well, Lydia Georgievna, when are we moving?"

"Yes—when?"

"Look, we've waited for so long already, we can wait another twenty minutes. Fyodor Mikheyich will be back soon."

"But why haven't we moved yet?"

"There's still some more work to be done . . ."

"There's always more to be done!"

"We'll finish it off ourselves, go on, let's!"

The slim boy from the Komsomol committee in a reddish-brown shirt, who had called Lydia Georgievna from the staff room, asked: "Lydia Georgievna, we must arrange about the move. Who's to do what?"

"Look, kids, I've got an idea . . ."

"Shut up and listen."

"This is it: there'll be two or three lorries, of course, to move the machine tools and the really heavy things. But I suggest that we carry across all the other stuff ourselves, like ants."

"How many of us are there? How far is it?"

"A kilometre and a half."

"Fourteen hundred metres, I've measured it."

"How did you measure it?"

"I used a bicycle speedometer."

"Surely we're not going to wait a week for the lorries. Couldn't nine hundred of us carry it all over in a day?"

"Yes, let's carry it!"

"Let's ca . . . arry it!"

"Let's start now and we'll fix up a hostel here!"

"Let's get going before the wet weather starts!"

"Here's what we'll do, Igor," said Lydia Georgievna, prodding the chest of the young man in the reddish-brown shirt with an authoritative gesture like a general pulling a medal out of his pocket to pin it confidently to a soldier's chest. "Which of you belongs to the committee?"

"Almost everyone. There are a few more out in the street."

"Right. Then collect them together now. Write down a list of teams, but make it legible. Opposite each one, say how many people there are in it and which one will transport which laboratory or which office, and where the work is heavy and where it's lighter. If you can, assign a teacher to each team. Make sure that students get jobs appropriate to their age. And then we'll go straight to Fyodor Mikheyich with this plan, get it approved, and then each team will be put in charge of a teacher."

"O.K." Igor drew himself up. "Our last meeting was in the corridor, but over there we'll have a room. Hey, committee! Genka! Rita! Where shall we meet?"

"I suggest going down to the street," Lydia Georgievna called out loudly. "We're more likely to see Fyodor Mikheyich from there."

They poured down noisily out into the street, leaving the staircase free.

Outside on the waste ground in front of the school, which was dotted with a few stunted trees, there were two hundred more students. The third-year vacuum-physics class were standing in a tightly packed group. The girls, arms linked, were looking each other in the eyes and repeating:

"Radio, our watchword; radio, our creed!"

The younger ones were playing pig-in-the-middle and tag. Whenever the one who was "he" caught a victim, he would fetch him a satisfying wallop between the shoulder blades.

"Why are you thumping him on the back?" a tubby little girl asked indignantly.

"Not his back, his spine!" A youth in a flattened cap with a deflated volleyball tucked into his belt corrected her pompously. But noticing Lydia Georgievna wagging her finger at him, he jumped up and ran off.

Those who were even younger—the new boys who had just come from secondary school—were standing around in small groups, cleanly dressed, timid, looking attentively at everything that was going on.

A few boys came up with bicycles and took some of the girls for a ride on the crossbar.

Fluffy white clouds, like flecks of lather, were floating across the sky. At times they hid the sun.

"Oh, I hope it doesn't rain," the girls sighed.

Three fourth-year students from the radio department were standing on their own and chatting—two girls in blouses and a young man in a shirt, all worn hanging out. The girls' blouses were plain-striped; the boy's shirt was a gaudy yellow and splashed all over with fantastic pictures of palm trees, ships, and catamarans. Lydia Georgievna noticed this contrast and a thought which had long been a source of surprise to her ran through her mind: in her elder brothers' day and then among her contemporaries, boys used to dress

54

very simply, in dull colours; it was the girls who wore all the bright colours, the fancy things and new gimmicks, and rightly so. Then suddenly some time ago an unnatural competition had started up; the boys began to dress with great care and even more gaily and colourfully than the girls, and to wear crazy-coloured socks, as if it was not they who had to chase after girls but the other way round; and more and more often it was not they who took girls by the arm but the girls who took theirs. This unnatural behaviour vaguely disturbed Lydia Georgievna; she was afraid that the boys were losing something psychologically important to them.

"Well, Valerik," she asked the young man in the yellow shirt with the catamarans, "what d'you think—have you grown wiser over the summer?"

Valerik smiled condescendingly. "What—me, Lydia Georgievna? No, I've got stupider, of course."

"Doesn't that worry you? The girls won't respect you."

"Oh, yes, they will!"

Judging by the faces of both girls, it was obvious that his confidence was well-founded.

"But what have you read this summer?"

"Practically nothing, Lydia Georgievna," Valerik replied, still in the same condescending tone. He did not seem to be very keen on carrying on this conversation.

"But why?" Lydia Georgievna was put out. "What have I been teaching you for?"

"Presumably because it's in the syllabus," Valerik reasoned.

"But if you read books, then you can't go to the cinema or watch TV. When would there be time to do that?" the two girls chipped in. "The TV's on all day and every day."

Other fourth-year students joined them.

Lydia Georgievna frowned. With her thick fair hair brushed back, her forehead was completely bare and her disappointment and embarrassment were plain to see.

"I know you're here to learn all about TV sets, so it's hardly up to me to preach at you against watching it.

Watch it by all means, but give it a break now and then. And . . . don't compare it with books. A TV programme is like a butterfly, it only lives for one day . . ."

"That's why it's interesting—because it's alive," the young people insisted. "There's dancing!"

"And ski-jumping!"

"And motorcycle racing!"

"But a book lasts forever!" cried Lydia Georgievna, grim, though smiling.

"A book? A book only lasts for a day as well!" exclaimed one very serious-looking boy, who was so round-shouldered he was almost a hunchback.

"Where did you pick up that idea?" Lydia Georgievna said indignantly.

"Well, just go into a bookshop," said the round-shouldered boy. "There are so many of those novels turning yellow in the windows, and all the shelves are packed with them. You go in a year later and they're all still there. Where I live, we share a yard with a bookshop, so I know. Afterwards they pile them up and take them back. The driver says they're going to be turned back into pulp and then into paper again. So what do they print them for in the first place?"

Two years ago these same young people had been in her class, but they had never said anything like this. In those days they had always given the approved answers and earned top marks.

The conversation that had started was really one which should not have been held here—standing by the entrance and in the general din. But she found it impossible to give up.

"Then you must have another look and see which books they're taking away."

"I did have a look, so I can tell you." The round-shouldered boy stood his ground, and a slanting crease of intelligence ran across his forehead. "Some of them were ones which were highly praised in the papers . . ."

Others were airing their views and shouting him down. Anikin, an excellent all-round student, a healthy-looking youth with a camera slung over his shoulder (they always listened to him), pushed his way forward and said: "Look, Lydia Georgievna, let's be honest. When we left, you gave us a great long list of books to read. But every single one of them's at least five hundred pages long. How long is it going to take to read it? Two months? Or else it's some great epic, or a trilogy, and there's a sequel. Who do they print them for?"

"For the critics!" was the resounding answer.

"To make money!"

"That must be it," Anikin agreed, "because technological man—and that means most of us—also needs some time to read his technical literature and his specialist journals. Otherwise he'll just be an ignoramus, he'll get the sack and serve him right."

"Yes, serve him right!" the young people cried. "But when can they read the sports magazines?"

"And *Soviet Cinema*?"

"Lydia Georgievna"—Anikin let himself go—"I think it's unforgivable in this day and age for writers to churn out long books. When we do a circuit diagram, we have to find the most economical design. When we were examined on our diploma projects—I had to do it last year—they kept interrupting: 'Can't you make it shorter? simpler? cheaper?' But what do they write in the *Literary Gazette*? Okay, the images are conventional, the composition lacks form, but, on the other hand, what lofty ideas! It's just the same as if we were told: 'The current won't flow, the mechanism won't work, but how beautifully you've chosen the condensers!' So why don't they say: 'This novel ought to be ten times shorter'? Then people wouldn't get bogged down trying to read it."

"I agree, I'm all for brevity," Lydia Georgievna said decisively, thrusting her arm out in front of her. The group around her, which had been growing bigger all the time, howled with approval. This was why the students were so fond of her: she never told lies. If she said she agreed, she meant it.

"But don't you see, a book is a record of our time, of ourselves, and our great achievements . . ."

"But all these memoirs!" the boy in glasses with the funny short crew cut gabbled eagerly from the third row. "Nowadays, anyone who's survived for fifty years has to write his memoirs: how he was born, how he got married—any old fool can do that."

"It depends what he writes about," the teacher shouted. "Whether it's about himself and our time."

"And look what they reminisce about!" the boy in spectacles said in exasperation. " 'I got a fit of the shivers in the back garden.' . . . 'I arrived in town but there was no room in the hotel.' "

They pushed him aside and shouted him down.

"I'd like to say something about brevity, Lydia Georgievna."

"And I want to say something about classics," said another boy, raising his arm.

Seeing their excited faces, Lydia Georgievna smiled happily. Let them get worked up, let them go for her—you can always persuade people who argue. What she feared most of all in young people was indifference.

"All right, then!" She gave permission to the student who had asked to talk about brevity.

This was Chursanov, dishevelled, the collar of whose grey shirt was not only turned but patched. His father had died and his mother, who worked as a caretaker, had other, smaller children to look after as well. So after the seventh grade he had had to go to the technical college. Although he always got poor marks in literature and Russian, even as a little boy he had collected radio sets and was considered a brilliant radio technician in the school: he knew how to find a fault without referring to a circuit diagram, as though he could sense where it was.

"Listen," declared Chursanov abruptly. "Anikin was right when he said that time is short and so we must economise on it. So what do I do? I never read fiction at all!"

Everyone roared with laughter.

"You wanted to talk about brevity."

"That's just what I am talking about!" said Chursanov in surprise. "I turn on the radio, listen to the news, a commentary or whatever—and all the time I'm getting dressed, or having dinner, or doing something useful round the house: that's how I save time."

58

Everyone laughed again.

"What are you laughing at?" Chursanov was amazed.

"It's not funny at all." Marta Pochtennykh backed him up—a big, ugly girl with a broad face and thick black plaits growing loose at the ends.

"Lydia Georgievna, don't you agree? When's a book worth reading? When you can't find out what's in it anywhere else, isn't that right? But if you read the same things in a book as you hear on the radio or read in the paper, then what's the point of the book? In the newspaper it's shorter and clearer . . ."

"And more likely to be right. Newspapers don't make mistakes," someone shouted.

"But what about style?" a pink-faced girl with fair curls down to her shoulders asked shyly.

"What do you mean by style? Is newspaper style bad?"

"Lit-er-ar-y style!" said the pink-faced girl, shaking her little head at every syllable.

"What good is style?" Chursanov was puzzled. "If someone loves someone else, who cares about style?"

"Yes, my friends. Of course we need style." Lydia Georgievna was heated by now and clenched her hand over her heart as if it were her dearest conviction. "A book should give us psychological depth, explain to us the subtle . . ."

But they had already crowded in on her from all sides, although not all of them were listening to her—some were talking and jostling each other.

Lydia Georgievna's face became flushed.

"No, wait." She tried to calm them down. "I won't leave the argument like this. Now we're going to have a big assembly hall. In September we'll arrange a debate." She placed her hands heavily on the shoulders of Anikin and Pochtennykh. "All of you who've spoken now will be dragged out onto a platform so you can . . ."

"He's coming! He's coming! He's coming!" the juniors began calling out, followed by the older ones. The younger ones started running towards him; the older ones let them pass and turned to look. Teachers and students stuck their heads out of the first-floor windows.

The battered college jeep was approaching from the level crossing, jolting over the bumps and occasionally splashing through puddles. The principal and the driver could be seen through the cab window, swaying from side to side. The pupils who had rushed on ahead, shrieking, to meet the principal were the first to notice that Fyodor Mikheyich's face for some reason did not look at all happy.

Silence fell.

They ran alongside the jeep until it stopped. Fyodor Mikheyich, stocky, his hair greying, dressed in a plain, slightly worn suit, got out of the cab and looked around. His way in was blocked, as the young people were standing around him packed close together in the shape of a horseshoe, watching and waiting. The most impatient ones were the first to venture to say quietly:

"Well, what's happening, Fyodor Mikheyich?"

"When?"

Then, louder, from the back rows:

"Are we moving?"

"When are we moving?"

He again looked round at the dozens of waiting, questioning eyes. He realised that he would not be able to save his answer until he got to the second floor; he would have to give it here. "When?" "When are we moving?" The students had been asking these questions all spring and all summer, but the principal and the class leaders had just grinned and said: "It all depends on you. On how you work." Now, though, all Fyodor Mikheyich could do was to sigh and, without hiding his disappointment, say: "We've got to wait a while, comrades. The builders aren't ready."

His voice always sounded hoarse, as if he had a perpetual cold.

The crowd of students heaved a sigh.

"More waiting!"

"Still not ready!"

"But the day after tomorrow is September 1!"

"What happens now? Will we have to go back to our digs again?"

The student in the bright yellow shirt with the catamarans smirked and said to his girl admirers: "What did I tell you? It always happens. And that's not all, just wait and see!"

They began calling out: "Can't we finish it off ourselves, Fyodor Mikheyich?"

The principal smiled. "What—did you actually enjoy it? No, it can't be done."

Some girls in the front row started trying to persuade him with great earnestness: "Fyodor Mikheyich! Let's move anyway. What's there left to do over there?"

The principal, heavily built, with a broad forehead, looked at them with embarrassment.

"Look, girls, do I have to explain everything? Here and there the floors haven't dried out yet . . ."

"But we won't walk on them."

"Let's put boards across the wet parts."

"There aren't enough window latches."

"Well, so what? It's summer now."

"The heating system has to be tested a bit longer."

"Pooh—we won't be needing it until winter anyway."

"Yes, but there are other little jobs to be done . . ."

Fyodor Mikheyich gestured impatiently. A lot of lines had formed across his forehead. He couldn't tell the students that before he could take over the building he had to have an official deed of transfer; that the builder and the receiver had to sign this deed; the builder would probably sign it because he wanted to turn in the job as quickly as possible, and time was now so precious to Fyodor Mikheyich too that he would have signed if the school itself were the receiver. But the school could not be the receiver because it had no staff competent to check and approve the construction. Instead, this was the responsibility of the construction office at the local electrical-equipment factory, and this factory had absolutely no reason to hurry or change the building schedule. The director of the factory, Khabalygin, who had been promising Fyodor Mikheyich all summer that he would take over the building in August without fail, had said recently: "Not yet, comrades. We won't sign the deed until they've tightened the last nut." The fact was, he was right.

The girls were whining: "Oh! We want to move so much, Fyodor Mikheyich. We'd set our hearts on it."

"What had you set your hearts on?" Chursanov, standing above the others on a mound, called sharply to the girls. "We still have to go to the collective farm for a month. Does it matter which building we leave from—this one or the other?"

"Ye . . . es! The collective farm!" The others remembered too. Because they had been building all summer, they had forgotten about it.

"We won't be going this year," Lydia Georgievna said firmly from behind.

This was the first time that Fyodor Mikheyich had noticed her.

"Why can't we go, Lydia Georgievna? Why?" they began asking her.

"You should read the local paper, my friends. There was an article about it."

"An ar . . . ticle?"

"We'll go anyway . . ."

Fyodor Mikheyich pushed the students aside and went towards the doors. Lydia Georgievna caught up with him on the stairs. The staircase was the sort on which only two people can walk side by side.

"But, Fyodor Mikheyich, will they hand it over in September?"

"Yes," he answered distractedly.

"We've got a good plan—to take all the stuff across between Saturday lunchtime and Monday morning. Then we won't miss a working day. We'll split up into teams by laboratories. The committee's seeing to it now."

"Very good." The principal nodded, deep in his own thoughts. All the same, it was bothering him that the unfinished jobs left to do really were trivial; the client should have foreseen this two or three weeks ago; and it was perfectly possible to hurry things up and take over the building. But from the way some of the minor problems were being dealt with, it looked as if the client was being purposely obstructive.

"Now, Fyodor Mikheyich . . . We on the committee discussed Engalichev and he gave us his word. We will vouch for him. Will you give him back a grant as from the first of September?" She looked at him, pleading, yet confident.

"So you're his advocate," said the principal, shaking his head and looking at her with his bluish eyes. "But suppose he does it again?"

"Oh no, he won't," she assured him as she reached the top of the stairs, watched by the other teachers and the secretary.

"Well, we'll look into it."

He went into his tiny office, having meanwhile sent for the Director of Studies and the heads of departments. He wanted to make sure that, come what might, they were ready to start the new year and had already done everything necessary without being told to.

During the long years he had spent in this school, Fyodor Mikheyich's overall policy had been to run it so that as far as possible it functioned by itself with a minimum of intervention by him. He had graduated from the Institute of Communications before the war and could neither grasp all these new subjects which the fast-changing technical school specialised in nor keep up with his staff. A moderate, unambitious person, he held the view that a leader should be not a man who arbitrarily imported his own ideas but the essential focal point for a group of people who trusted one another and worked for a common aim.

The secretary, Faina, a highly independent, middle-aged spinster, with a colourful scarf tied under her chin so that when she walked fast the loose end fluttered like a triangular pennant behind her, brought in a completed diploma and put it down in front of the principal, then opened a bottle of Indian ink.

"What's this?" Fyodor Mikheyich did not understand.

"It's Terentieva's diploma. Because of illness, she took her oral examination late . . ."

"I see."

He tested his pen, dipped it into the ink again, gripped his right hand by holding the fingers of his left hand tightly round it like a bracelet, and only then signed his name.

When he had been wounded for the second time in Transylvania, not only had the tips of his fingers been cut off and grown back unevenly, but he had also suffered from severe concussion. His hearing had begun to fail and his hands still trembled, so that he could not sign anything with his right hand alone.

3

An hour and a half later, most of the teachers had gone. Only those who had practicals to prepare had stayed behind with their lab assistants. Students were crowding round in the accounts department, trying to register for lodgings. Lydia Georgievna was with the committee, drawing up her plans for the move, to which she then had to get agreement from the principal and the heads of departments.

Fyodor Mikheyich was still sitting with the Director of Studies when Faina, her pennant fluttering, rushed into his study and announced the sensational news that two Volga cars were approaching from the level crossing. The principal looked out the window and saw that two Volgas, one sea-green, the other grey, were in fact jolting over the uneven ground towards the school.

It could only be the authorities, and he ought to go down to meet them. But he was not expecting any official visit and just stood there by the open first-floor window.

Large smoky-white clouds were floating across the sky.

The cars cruised up to the main entrance and five men wearing hats climbed out of them: two of them were in stiff green trilbies as worn by the local governing body; the others wore light-coloured hats. Fyodor Mikheyich recognised the man in front: it was Vsevolod Borisovich Khabalygin, director of the electrical-appliances works, who "held the deed" to the new building. He was a very influential figure, but although he operated on a much higher level than Fyodor Mikheyich, he always treated him in a friendly manner. Fyodor Mikheyich had already rung him twice that day to try to persuade him to permit his committee to accept the building on behalf of the technical school after all, having listed the jobs still to be done. But both times they had told him that Vsevolod Borisovich was out.

Now a thought flashed through Fyodor Mikheyich's mind and he said to his deputy, who was as tall and thin as a post: "I say, Grisha, perhaps this delegation has come to speed things up!" And he hurried to meet the visitors. The stern, businesslike deputy, who was the terror of the students, followed him.

Fyodor Mikheyich had only managed to go down one step when he met all five of them climbing up to the landing, one behind the other. In front was Khabalygin, a short man who, although he was not yet sixty, had grown very stout, had long passed eighteen stone, and suffered from his overweight. The hair on his temples had turned silver.

"A ... ah." He stretched his hand approvingly towards the principal. Stepping up onto the landing, he turned round. "This," he said, "is a comrade from our Ministry."

The comrade from the Ministry was much younger, but also decently plump. He let Fyodor Mikheyich hold the tips of three of his soft white fingers for a brief moment, then went on up the stairs.

In fact, "our" Ministry had paid no attention to the school for the past two years, since it had come under the Council of National Economy.

"You know, I phoned you twice today." Fyodor Mikheyich smiled delightedly at Khabalygin and touched him on the sleeve. "I very much wanted to ask you ..."

"This," said Khabalygin, "is a comrade from the Committee for ..." He said what sort of a committee it was, but Fyodor Mikheyich was confused and failed to hear the end of it.

The comrade from the committee was a very young

65

man, slim, good-looking, and fashionably dressed, down to the smallest detail.

"And this," said Khabalygin, "is the inspector of electronics from . . ." He named the place, but as he said it he was already moving on up the stairs and Fyodor Mikheyich again missed the end of his sentence.

The inspector of electronics was a squat, swarthy, polite man with a small black moustache just under his nose.

And last came the inspector from the Department of Industry of the regional Party committee, who was a good friend of Fyodor Mikheyich. They shook hands.

None of them was carrying anything.

On the top landing, by the handrail round the stair well, the severe-looking deputy principal was standing to attention like a soldier. Some of them acknowledged him with a nod of the head; the others ignored him.

Khabalygin heaved his corpulent figure up the stairs. It was well-nigh impossible to walk alongside him or pass him on the narrow school staircase. When he reached the top, he was panting. Were it not for his constantly lively, energetic look, one would have sympathised with his difficulty in moving about. Every action was a struggle with his vast form, whose unsightly bulk was concealed by his skilful tailors.

"Shall we go to my office?" Fyodor Mikheyich said as they reached the top.

"Oh, no. What's the point in sitting down?" exclaimed Khabalygin. "Lead on, Principal, and just show us how you live. Eh, comrades?"

The comrade from the committee, moving back the sleeve of his smart, imported topcoat, looked at his watch and said: "Of course."

"How I live?" sighed Fyodor Mikheyich. And corrected himself to the plural form: "We don't live, we suffer! We have to work in two shifts. There isn't enough room in the lab for everyone to work there. There are several different practical experiments being done in one room; every now and then we have to clear the apparatus from the tables and set up a new lot."

He sounded as if he were justifying and excusing himself as he looked from one to the other.

"Well, you're certainly making it sound bad enough," Khabalygin spluttered with a sound that was something between a cough and a laugh. The pendulous folds of flesh on his neck quivered like the dewlap of an ox. "It's amazing that you've managed to put up with it here for seven years."

Fyodor Mikheyich raised the fair bushy eyebrows above his bright eyes.

"But, Vsevolod Borisovich, there weren't as many departments before, and fewer students."

"Well, lead on, we'll see for ourselves."

The principal nodded to the deputy to see that all the rooms were open, and led them off on a tour of the building. The visitors followed, without taking off their hats and coats.

They entered a spacious room with equipment-laden shelves jutting out round the walls. The teacher, a lab assistant in a blue overall, and one of the senior students—Chursanov, with the patched collar—were preparing a practical. The room faced south and was filled with sunlight.

"Well," said Khabalygin cheerfully, "what's wrong with this? It's a beautiful room."

"But you must realise," said Fyodor Mikheyich, offended, "that there are in fact three laboratories here, one on top of the other: radio engineering and aerials, radio-transmitting and radio-receiving equipment."

"What does that prove?" The comrade from the Ministry, also offended, turned his large, striking head. "Do you imagine that there has been any more room to spare since our Ministry was reorganised? It's even more cramped than before."

"And what's more, the labs are used for related subjects." Khabalygin, very pleased with himself, clapped his hand on the principal's shoulder. "Don't pretend to be worse off than you are, comrade!"

Fyodor Mikheyich looked at him in amazement.

Every now and then, Khabalygin moved his lips and sagging cheeks as if he had just finished a good meal and bits of food were stuck in his teeth.

"But what are these for?" The comrade from the committee was standing in front of some strange, enormous, in fact almost giant-size gum boots with rolled-down tops, and touched them lightly with the pointed toe of his fashionable shoe.

"High-voltage overshoes," the teacher explained quietly.

"Overshoes?"

"High-voltage ones," Chursanov called out loudly, with the impudence of someone who has nothing to lose.

"A ... ah, yes, of course," said the comrade from the committee, and followed the others.

The instructor from the regional Party committee, who was bringing up the rear, asked Chursanov: "But what are they for?"

"For when you're repairing a transmitter," Chursanov replied.

Fyodor Mikheyich had intended to show them every room, but the visitors bypassed several and went into the lecture hall. Lists of English tenses and pretty pictures were hanging on the walls. The shelves of the cupboards were filled with stereometric models.

The inspector of electronics counted the tables (there turned out to be thirteen of them) and, smoothing down his prickly moustache with two fingers, asked: "How many people do you have in each group? Thirty?"

"Yes, generally . . ."

"That means there's less than three to a table."

They went on.

In the small television lab, ten sets, some brand-new and some half dismantled, were standing on tables.

"Do all of them work?" said the comrade from the committee, nodding towards them.

"Only the ones that are supposed to," the smart young lab assistant replied quietly. He was wearing a sandy-coloured suit with some kind of technical badge in his lapel and a bright tie.

A batch of instructional pamphlets was lying there; the inspector turned one over and read under his breath: *"How to Calibrate a TV Set, How to Use a TV Set as an Amplifier, The Structure of Visual Signals."*

"There aren't any shelves here, but you can make do," Khabalygin remarked.

Fyodor Mikheyich understood less and less of what was going on; what did this delegation want? "Well, you see, everything's kept next door in the preparation room. Show us, Volodya."

"You mean to say there's a preparation room as well? You seem to be very well off."

The door into the preparation room was smaller than normal size, like a storeroom door. The slim, elegant lab assistant went in with ease; the comrade from the Ministry was barely managing to squeeze after him but then decided not to go in. The others just poked their heads in, one after the other.

The preparation room turned out to be a narrow crack between two rows of shelves which reached up to the ceiling. The lab assistant indicated them from top to bottom, gesturing like a tourist guide: "This is the equipment for the TV lab. This is for the power-supply lab. This is for radio instrumentation."

All the shelves were packed with instrument dials.

"What's this for?" said the comrade from the Ministry, pointing. He had been watching the lab assistant the whole time and had noticed that he was concealing a space on the wall not covered by appliances, where there was nailed a colourful, bosomy pin-up, carefully cut out round the curves of her body. Without the caption, it was impossible to make out whether this creature had been cut out of a Soviet magazine or a foreign one—she was just a beautiful woman with dark-brown hair, in a blouse with a red frill that emphasised her figure. Her chin was resting on her folded arms, which were bare to the elbows; she was holding her head slightly to one side and giving the young lab assistant and the experienced comrade from the Ministry a distinctly unofficial look.

"You say you haven't any space here," he growled, finding it hard to turn round to get out, "but look what you hang on your walls, for God's sake!"

And with another quick glance at the pin up, he went out.

The news of the sinister delegation had already

69

travelled round the school, and here and there faces peeped out of doors or flashed past along the corridor.

Lydia Georgievna ran straight into the delegation. She moved to one side, almost gluing her back and palms to the wall, and surveyed them anxiously. Although she could not hear what they were saying, she could tell from the principal's face that something was wrong.

Fyodor Mikheyich took the inspector from the regional Party committee by the arm and, moving aside with him, asked quietly: "Listen, who sent this delegation? Why isn't there anyone from the Council of National Economy?"

"Victor Vavilich told me to come along. I don't even know myself."

When they had all reached the top landing of the staircase, Khabalygin cleared his throat, the yellow creases of excess fat on his neck quivering more than ever, and lit a cigarette.

"Well then, shall we carry on?"

The comrade from the committee looked at his wristwatch. "I think it's all pretty clear."

The inspector of electronics stroked his moustache with two fingers and said nothing.

The comrade from the Ministry asked: "Not counting this one, how many more buildings are there?"

"Two more, but . . ."

"Two . . . oo more!"

"But—you don't know what they're like. Only single-story. Very inconvenient. And miles apart. Come and have a look at them."

"Are there workshops there?"

"But don't you realise the sort of conditions we live in?" Fyodor Mikheyich blurted out, throwing off the constraints of politeness and the spell cast by such high-ranking visitors. "We haven't even got a hostel. This building should be a hostel. The young people are living out in lodgings all over town, and they're often highly unsuitable. All our work educating them goes to hell; anyway, where can we teach them—on this staircase?"

70

"Come now! Oh, really!" the protesting voices of the delegation echoed around him.

"Education is your job," said the young man from the committee sternly.

"You can't blame anyone for that," the instructor from the regional Party committee added.

"You've no cause to say that . . ." Khabalygin gestured with his chubby hands.

Fyodor Mikheyich involuntarily turned his head, and his shoulders twitched, seemingly in an attempt to ward them all off or to jerk himself out of the vulnerable position of defendant. If he didn't ask the questions himself, they would obviously never understand the situation. His fair bushy eyebrows bunched into a frown. "Forgive me. All the same, I would like to know who authorised you to come here? And what for?"

The comrade from the Ministry raised his hat and wiped his forehead with a handkerchief. Without his hat he looked even more impressive. The hair around the crown of his head was already rather sparse, yet very distinguished-looking.

"You mean you don't know yet?" he said with calm surprise. "Our Ministry and this"—he indicated them with a nod—"committee has decided that an important high-level scientific research institute planned for this town will be located in the buildings originally assigned to your technical school. Isn't that so, Vsevolod Borisovich?"

"Yes, that's right," Khabalygin confirmed, nodding his head in the hard green hat.

"Yes, that's right." He gave the principal a sympathetic look and a friendly pat on the shoulder. "You'll just have to stick it out for another couple of years, then after that they'll put you up a new building, an even better one. That's how it must be, my dear fellow, don't be disappointed. It can't be helped; it's for the good of the cause."

Normally squat, Fyodor Mikheyich now seemed to sag even lower and looked around strangely, as if he had been given a crack over the head with a stick.

"But . . ." he found himself saying irrelevantly, "we haven't painted here, we haven't done any repairs . . ."

71

Whenever Fyodor Mikheyich felt upset, his usual hoarse voice dwindled to a croak.

"Well, never mind," Khabalygin reassured him. "You must have painted last year."

The comrade from the committee took a step down the stairs.

There was so much to tell them and right now that the principal could not think how to begin.

"But what connection do I have with your Ministry?" he protested hoarsely, barring his visitors' path. "We come under the local Council of National Economy. You need a government decision for a transfer like this."

"That's quite correct." The delegation gently pushed him aside, already on their way downstairs. "Our job is to prepare the material for this decision, which will be passed in two days' time."

And all five of them went down, while the principal stood there, clutching the handrail at the top and staring blankly into the stair well.

"Fyodor Mikheyich!" Lydia Georgievna appeared from the corridor. For some reason she was clutching her throat, which was tanned from the summer spent on the building site and was revealed by her turned-down collar. "What did they say, Fyodor Mikheyich?"

"They're taking our building away," said the principal expressionlessly in a faint, sinking voice, without looking at her.

And he went into his office.

"What! Wha . . . aat!" she screamed, after a moment of disbelief. "The new one! Taking it away!" And she ran after him, her high heels clicking. In the doorway of the office she collided with the accountant, pushed her aside, and ran in after the principal.

He walked slowly towards his desk.

"Listen!" Lydia Georgievna screamed at his back in an unfamiliar singsong voice. "How can they be so unfair?" She was shouting louder and louder—as he should have shouted at them, but he was a principal and not a woman. Tears streamed down her face.

"What can we tell the students? We've ... cheated them."

He had never seen her crying before.

The principal sat down in his armchair and stared blindly at the table in front of him. His whole forehead was creased into tiny horizontal lines.

The accountant, a desiccated old woman with a bun of greasy hair on the back of her neck, was standing there with a cheque book in her hand.

She had heard and understood everything. She would have left at once and not bothered him, but she had only just rung the bank and they had told her she could come and collect the money. The cheque was already written out, the amount and date filled in. So she went in, put the long, blue-striped cheque book in front of the principal, and steadied it with her hand.

Fyodor Mikheyich dipped his pen, gripped his right hand with his left like a bracelet, and even lifted it, poised to sign. But although his fingers were clenched, they still fumbled.

He tried out his signature on some scrap paper. The pen began to write something strange; then it stabbed at the paper and splashed ink over it.

Fyodor Mikheyich raised his eyes to the accountant and smiled. The accountant bit her lip, picked up the cheque book, and hurriedly walked out.

4

His world had collapsed so suddenly, the delegation had won such a quick victory, that he had been unable to find the necessary words to fight back, and afterwards he could not imagine what his course of action should have been.

He rang the Education Department at the Council of National Economy. They listened to what he had to say, were indignant about it, and promised to clear it up.

This might have raised his spirits, but there was something behind the delegation's visit . . .

Fyodor Mikheyich now felt too ashamed to face the students, the teachers, and all the people he had called in to help put up the building, having confidently promised them that they would move to new premises; and all the plans for the building that he had discussed with his assistants for months and even years were so completely shattered that he would gladly, or so he thought, have given up his own flat for a worse one if only they would give the school back its new building.

Suddenly his mind became blank and, without saying a word or even putting on a hat, he went outside to clear his head.

He set off towards the level crossing without realising where he was going; he went over and over in his mind all the dozens of essential items which the school had forfeited together with the new building. The barrier went down in front of him; although Fyodor Mikheyich could have ducked under it, he stopped dead. A long goods train appeared in the distance. It rolled towards him, then roared away downhill. Fyodor Mikheyich did not consciously notice any of this. The barrier lifted and he walked on.

He suddenly realised he was standing in the yard of the new building. He had not gone there of his own accord. The main entrance, newly finished and glazed, was locked up. Fyodor Mikheyich started to walk out of the yard, which had been planned, cleared, and laid out by the students; it was big and they had intended to make a fine sports ground out of it.

The builders' lorry was standing there and workmen were noisily loading it with coping stone, pipes, and other things, but at that moment Fyodor Mikheyich did not realise the significance of what he saw. He went into the building and listened with pleasure as his footsteps echoed on the stone slabs of the spacious entrance hall with its two cloakrooms on either side, designed for a thousand people. All the revolving aluminum hat-and-coat hooks were polished till they shone, and they suddenly made him reflect on a fact which had not occurred to him until then, because he had been preoccupied with the school and not with the new owner: what could the institute want with a building like this? For instance, they would have to pull down these cloakrooms, because there would not be even as many as a hundred people in the institute. And what about the gymnasium with its huge wall bars, its fitted rings, horizontal bar, grilles and nettings on the windows? Would it all have to be stripped down and dismantled now? And the workshops with their concrete foundations especially laid for the machine tools needed for training? The whole system of electrical wiring? The layout of the building into lecture rooms? The blackboards? The great circular lecture hall? The assembly hall? The . . . ?

As these thoughts ran through his mind, some painters and a couple of carpenters carrying their tools passed him on their way out.

"Hey, listen!" The principal came to his senses. "Comrades!"

They were about to step out.

"Hey!"

They turned.

"Where are you going? It's not time to knock off yet!"

"We're packing it in," the younger of the carpenters said cheerfully. The older one went gloomily on his way. "Give us a cigarette. We're leaving."

"But where are you going?"

"They're laying us off. The boss said so."

"What do you mean, they're laying you off?"

"Didn't you know? We're going to another site. We've got to start a new job there today." The carpenter had noticed before that the grey-haired principal was not high and mighty, so he turned and tapped him on the arm. "Go on, give us a cigarette."

Fyodor Mikheyich held out a crumpled packet of cigarettes. "Where's the site foreman?"

"He's gone already. He was the first to leave."

"But what did he say?"

"He said turn it in, it's not our job any more. Some other lot's taking over."

"But who's going to finish?" Fyodor Mikheyich got

worked up. "What are you grinning for? How much was there left to do?" When he furrowed his brow, his face looked angry.

"Who cares?" the carpenter called out, as he went off after his mates, his cigarette already alight. "Don't you know how it's done? You're sacked and transferred to another job—that's how it goes, mate!"

Fyodor Mikheyich watched as the cheerful carpenter in his dirty overalls walked away. Was the Council of National Economy, which had taken over this ill-fated building when it had been bogged down at the foundation stage for three years and had raised it, finished it, and glazed it, now just backing out?

The Council of National Economy was running away, but the thought of the countless, utterly ridiculous alterations needed in this building gave the principal the strength to resist. He realised that justice was on his side. He too almost ran towards the exit, his footsteps echoing hollowly over the floor of the entrance hall.

The room where the functioning telephone was kept turned out to be locked. Fyodor Mikheyich hurried outside. The rising wind was starting to swirl and blow sand around. The builders' lorry was already driving out of the gates. The night watchman was on the other side of the gates, but the principal could not stop to go back. He fumbled in his pocket for some change and made for a telephone kiosk.

He rung up Grachikov, the secretary of the town Party committee. His secretary answered and said that Grachikov was at a meeting. He gave his name and asked her to find out if Grachikov could see him and, if so, when. She fixed an appointment for an hour later.

Fyodor Mikheyich set off, again on foot. As he walked along, and then as he sat waiting to go into Grachikov's office, he went over in his mind all the floors and all the lecture halls in the new building, and it seemed to him that there was not a single place where the institute would not have to knock down a wall or put up a new one. He began to add up in his notebook what it would all cost.

To Fyodor Mikheyich, Grachikov was not so much

the secretary of the town Party committee as an old wartime friend. They had served in the same regiment together, though not for long. Fyodor Mikheyich had been the regimental signals officer; somewhat later, Grachikov had arrived from hospital and replaced the battalion commander, who had been killed. They had found out that they both came from the same town, so they had got acquainted and sometimes during a night-time lull they would ring each other up and chat about home. Then a company commander in Grachikov's battalion had been killed. As always in a front-line regiment, the gaps were filled by staff officers, and Fyodor Mikheyich was sent to command the company temporarily. "Temporarily" turned out to be for two days and two nights: he was wounded forty-eight hours later, and when he came out of hospital, he landed up in a different division.

As he sat there waiting, he remembered that for some reason unpleasant things always happened to him at the end of August: when he had been wounded in '41 in Grachikov's battalion, it had been on August 29; in other words, yesterday. And in '44 he had been wounded on August 30. And now this.

People started coming out of the office and Fyodor Mikheyich was called for.

"It's a disaster, Ivan Kapitonovich!" the principal warned him in a hoarse, muffled voice, as soon as he entered the room. "A disaster!"

He sat down on a chair (all those armchairs which engulf people so that they can hardly raise their chins to the level of the desk top had been removed from the office on Grachikov's orders) and began to tell him everything that had happened. Grachikov rested his head on one hand, palm against cheek, and listened.

Nature had endowed Ivan Kapitonovich with coarse features: thick lips, a wide nose, and large ears. But although his hair was black and his forelock jutted out at an angle, making him look rather terrifying, his face as a whole was so expressively Russian that even if he had been dressed in a foreign suit or uniform, one would have instantly recognised him as a Russian.

"Be honest, Ivan Kapitonovich," said the principal,

his temper rising. "Isn't it plain? Forget the technical school, but just from the state's point of view?"

"Yes, very stupid." Grachikov gave his opinion confidently, without moving.

"Look what these alterations will cost—I've added it up on a scrap of paper. The whole building costs four million, right? Well, the alterations will cost two million, or at least one and a half. Have a look . . ."

And he read out from his notebook a list of the jobs to be done and how much they would cost. He felt more and more strongly that justice was indisputably on his side.

Grachikov listened and pondered carefully, without moving a muscle. He had once said to Fyodor Mikheyich that probably his greatest relief when the war ended was that he no longer had to take instant, personal decisions which were likely to be a matter of life or death. Grachikov liked to take his time forming conclusions, he liked to reason them out; he would think the issue over himself and then he would listen to other people's opinions. It was against his nature to end conversations and meetings by giving orders; he tried to convince his opponents to the bitter end, so they would admit "Yes, you're right," or would convince him that he was wrong. However stubbornly they objected to what he said, he would always keep the conversation on a friendly, informal note. All this, of course, took time. Knorozov, first secretary of the regional Party committee, soon noticed this weakness of his and hurled at him in his irrefutably laconic manner: "You're too soft. You don't act the Soviet way." But Grachikov stood his ground: "Why do you say that? Quite the contrary. I work in a Soviet way—I consult the people."

Grachikov had been made secretary of the town Party committee at the last regional conference, as a result of several conspicuous successes achieved by the factory at which he had been Party secretary.

"Have you heard anything about this scientific research institute, Ivan Kapitonovich? Where has it sprung from?"

"Yes, I have." Grachikov was still leaning his head

on his hand. "They were talking about it as early as the spring. Then it was put off."

"Yes," the principal complained. "If Khabalygin had accepted the building then, we would have moved in on August 20 and they wouldn't be pinching it from us now."

There was a moment's silence.

During the silence Fyodor Mikheyich felt as if the firmness which he had maintained so far was slipping away from under him. His calculation of a million and a half in alterations had not produced any noticeable effect; Grachikov was not grabbing the two telephone receivers, or jumping up, or rushing off anywhere.

"What is this institute? Is it very important?" Fyodor Mikheyich asked in a hoarse voice.

Grachikov sighed. "Once it's signed and sealed, there's no point in questioning it. Every project of ours is important."

The principal sighed too.

"What am I to do, Ivan Kapitonovich? Once they get government confirmation, that's it. We've only got two days till the deadline."

Grachikov was thinking.

Fyodor Mikheyich turned further towards him so that his knees rested against the desk; he leaned on the desk and propped up his head in his hands.

"I know. Why don't we dash off a telegram direct to the Council of Ministers? There's just enough time left ... talk about the relation of school to everyday life ... I'll sign it. I'm not afraid."

Grachikov looked at him very closely for a minute. Suddenly all trace of severity disappeared from his face and it broke into a sympathetic smile. He spoke in his most characteristic manner—in a charming, lilting voice, in long elaborate sentences.

"Tell me, Fyodor Mikheyich, my dear friend, how do you picture this government ordinance? Do you think that the whole Council of Ministers sits round a long table and discusses what to do with your building and nothing else, and just then someone brings in your telegram? A government ordinance means that on certain days one of the Deputy Premiers interviews this minister or that committee chairman. The Minister comes to the meeting with several papers and among other things says: 'There's this scientific research institute, you know the one, vitally important. We've decided to situate it in this town, and there happens to be a building ready there, by the way.' The Deputy Premier then asks: 'Who was it built for?' The Minister replies: 'For a technical school, but the school is housed in buildings that are perfectly tolerable. We sent a competent delegation there, and the comrades investigated the issue on the spot.' But, before giving his consent, the Deputy Premier asks one more question: 'Has the regional Party committee no objections? See? The *regional* Party committee. And they return your little telegram, saying: 'Check your facts.'" Grachikov smacked his lips. "When it's a question of an on-the-spot check, the regional Party committee has the last word."

Now he placed his hand on the receiver, but still he did not lift it.

"What I don't like about it is that the inspector from the regional Party committee was there and yet didn't raise any objections. If Victor Vavilich has already given his consent, then we're in a bad way, brother. He never changes his mind."

Grachikov, of course, was rather afraid of Victor Vavilich Knorozov—as was everyone in the province.

He lifted the receiver.

"Is that Konevsky? . . . Grachikov speaking. Listen, is Victor Vavilich in his office? When's he coming back? . . . I see . . . Well, if he does get back today, tell him I'd be very grateful if he'd see me . . . Yes, I'll even come from home this evening."

He put down the receiver and rolled it across his hand on its rest, from one side to the other, back and forth. He looked at the truncated pyramid of the telephone, then transferred his gaze to Fyodor Mikheyich, who was still holding his head in his hands.

"On the whole, you know," said Grachikov with sincerity, "I'm strongly in favour of technical schools. Yes, I really like them. In our country, everyone's trying to be an academician; unless someone has at least an engineering degree he's not considered educated. Yet what our country needs most of all is technicians. All technical schools are neglected—not just yours. And the kids you take!" He gestured in the air at a level slightly higher than the desk top, although Fyodor Mikheyich never took students as young as that. "Four years later"—he crooked his thumb—"You turn out what are supposed to be trained technicians. I was at your oral examination of the diploma projects in the spring, do you remember?"

"Yes," Fyodor Mikheyich nodded unhappily. As Ivan Kapitonovich sat behind his large, efficient-looking desk, with a green baize table alongside it, his manner was so amicable that one might have expected to see plates of pickles, biscuits, and jellies on a white tablecloth instead of a set of penholders, a calendar, a paperweight, telephones, a carafe, a tray and an ash tray. He was like a host, persuading his guest to try his delicacies and even to take some home with him.

"There was a lad of about nineteen, who was probably wearing a tie for the first time in his life, and his jacket didn't match his trousers—or is that fashionable nowadays? He hung diagrams up all over the blackboard, put down a sort of regulating or calibrating gauge, which he had made himself; the gauge was clicking and flashing while the lad walked up and down waving a baton over the diagrams and talking his head off. I really envied him. What words and ideas he had at his command—the inadequacy of existing gauges; the principle on which his gauge functioned; how it showed the amount of anode current; how it was calibrated; its economic effectiveness; its coefficient of structural efficiency! And he was just a kid! It made me feel really embarrassed. I thought, here I have been tramping this earth for half a century, and what's my specialty? That I once used to be able to work a machine tool in a factory? But they scrapped those machines long ago. The fact that I know Party history and Marxist dialectic? But everyone has to know them, there's nothing special about that. It just isn't good enough! Nowadays if you're not a specialist of some sort, you're not a real Party worker. And all the lads who work in my old factory are like him, too. How can I tell them how to raise their productivity? I had my eyes and ears wide open, taking in all I could. If I were younger, Mikheyich, I'd gladly sign on at your technical school for evening classes . . ." And noticing that the principal was still in a state of utter depression, he laughed. ". . . In the old building!"

But Fyodor Mikheyich did not smile. He again let his head sink into his shoulders and sat in darkest gloom.

The secretary reminded Grachikov that he had another appointment.

5

Although no one had told them anything, by the following morning all the students knew what had happened.

The morning was overcast and there was rain in the air.

Those who came to school hung round in little groups outside in the cold. They were not allowed in the lecture halls, as the student monitors were tidying up there; they were not allowed in the laboratories either, because of preparations; so, as before, they drifted together to form a crowd on the stairs.

The place was humming with noise. The girls were sighing and giggling. Everyone was talking about the building, the hostel and lodgings. Mishka Zimin, a big tough boy who had been the fastest at digging trenches, began yelling: "Have we been slogging away for nothing? How are you going to explain that away, Igor?"

Igor, a committee member, the same dark boy in the reddish-brown shirt who the day before had listed the teams for transferring the lab equipment, was standing on the top landing, looking embarrassed.

"Be patient, it'll sort itself out."

"Who'll sort it out?"

"We'll see to it . . . We could write to . . ."

"That's an idea," a girl interrupted enthusiastically. She had thin, scraped-back hair parted in the middle and the keen look of a dedicated pupil. "Let's send a letter of complaint to Moscow. That's bound to work."

She was a docile girl but was on the verge of throwing up her studies because she could not go on paying seventy roubles a month out of her grant just for a bed.

"Yes, we've had enough." An attractive girl with delicate black curls, wearing a loose, casual jacket, slapped the handrail. "All nine hundred of us can sign it."

"That's right!"

"Good idea!"

"Don't you think we'd better find out first if we're allowed to collect signatures like that?" Voices from the other side of the staircase dampened their enthusiasm.

Valka Rogozkin was the best athlete in the school; the fastest runner in the 100 and 400 metres and the best jumper; he also had the loudest voice. He was stretched out, almost lying on the sloping rail of the staircase; one of his legs was resting on the step and he had lifted the other over the rails, which were supporting his chest. His arms were clasped round the rails and he was resting his chin on them. From this precarious position, ignoring catcalls from the girls, he stared up at Igor. On the curve of the rail, as though in fearless disregard of the twenty-foot drop behind him, sat a quiet, dark, broad-shouldered boy called Valka Guguyev.

"Listen to me!" shouted Valka Rogozkin in a piercing voice. "That won't do any good. It would be a much better plan if every one of us just didn't turn up tomorrow."

"Yes, we'll go to the stadium instead!" someone shouted in approval.

"But who says you can do that?" Igor said cautiously.

"Why do we need permission?" Rogozkin blurted out. "Of course no one's going to give us permission.

We just won't turn up! That's all there is to it, kids!" Carried away by his idea, he began to shout even louder. "After a few days a completely different delegation will arrive—by aeroplane this time—and then they won't just give us back our new building, but another one as well."

The crowd was starting to get excited.

"But won't they stop our grants?"

"That would be going too far."

"They might expel us!"

"That's not the right way to set about it!" Igor shouted above the noise. "And that's not how we're going to do it. Forget the idea!"

Because of the noise, no one noticed Dusya coming up the stairs with a galvanised bucket. As she drew level with Rogozkin, she transferred the bucket to her other hand and took a swing at him with her free one. She would have thumped him on his backside with all her strength, only he saw her in time and jumped down so nimbly that Dusya barely touched him.

"Hey!" Rogozkin let out a yell. "Dusya!" Half joking, he wagged his finger at her threateningly. "That's not fair play! Another time I'll . . ."

"Well, don't you carry on like that then!" Dusya menaced him with her fist. "I'll knock the living daylights out of you! You think handrails are made for that, do you?"

Everyone laughed loudly. Everyone in the school loved Dusya because of her forthright manner.

She went on up the stairs, forcing her way through the students. Her face was wrinkled yet lively, with a firm chin. She was a person who probably deserved a better job than the one she had.

"That's crap, Dusya!" said Mishka Zimin, using the current students' catch phrase. "Come on, tell us, why did they give our building away?"

"You mean you don't know?" Dusya put on an act. " 'Cause there are far too many parquet floors in it. You'd go balmy polishing that lot!"

And she went on her way, clinking her bucket amid cheerful laughter.

"Go on, Valka, do your stuff!" the students on the

top landing shouted to Guguyev, having spotted a bunch of girls who had just come in from outside. "Lyuska's coming!"

Valka Guguyev jumped down from the bend of the rails, pushed aside the people standing in his way, and took up a position in front of the straight handrail jutting out along the top landing. Placing the palms of his hands on it, he gauged its strength, took a good grip, then with a sudden slight thrust of his legs he raised his supple body into the air and gently, confidently, did a handstand over the stair well.

It was his star turn.

The whole staircase went silent. Everyone strained his head to see, the boys watching with respect, the admiring girls shivering with fear.

Lyuska, for whose benefit this was being performed, had already climbed up a few steps when she turned around and, opening wide her blue eyes, looked directly upwards to where Valka was balancing upside down; if he had fallen, he would have crashed straight on her and on to the stone floor. But he did not fall; keeping his balance almost without moving, Valka was holding his position over the stair well by sheer strength and was in no hurry to abandon it. What was more, his unprotected back was facing the well, and his legs, stretched out full-length and held together, were deliberately bent back in an arc over the drop. His upside-down head was straining backwards so that he could look straight at Lyuska—tiny, slim, fragrant in her pale raincoat with the turned-up collar and no beret. She looked especially pretty like this, with her short fair hair damp from the rain.

But was he looking at her? Even in the dull light of the staircase, the face and neck of this daring young man were visibly reddening from the flow of blood.

Suddenly there came whispered cries of *"Cave! Cave!"*

Guguyev swung himself down onto the landing, regained his feet noiselessly, and leaned innocently against the same handrail.

For a turn like that he could easily have been deprived of his grant, as had happened once before when he had rung the bell for the end of the lesson ten minutes before time (so as not to be late for the cinema).

Not having had enough time to start talking naturally, the students obediently made way for the tall, lanky Director of Studies, Grigory Lavrentich, as he walked gloomily up the stairs.

He had heard their cries of *"Cave,"* knew that this was a warning signal, and realised that the silence which met him was unnatural, but he could not spot the culprit. Especially as Rogozkin, who was always a troublemaker, attacked him on the spot.

"Grigory Lavrentich!" Rogozkin shouted for everyone on the staircase to hear. "Why has our building been taken away from us? We built it ourselves!" Putting on his simpleton act, he cocked his head to one side, waiting for an answer. He had acquired this habit of clowning at school, especially during lessons.

Everybody was silent, waiting to hear what the Director of Studies would say.

This was what being a teacher really meant: quickly finding the right thing to say, alone in front of a crowd, and each time in a different situation.

Grigory Lavrentich looked at Rogozkin with his penetrating, critical gaze. Still holding his head to one side, Rogozkin did not flinch.

"Well," the director said slowly, "you may get through college ... Though ... I don't know how ..."

"Is that a dig at my athletics matches?" Rogozkin retorted quickly. (Each spring and autumn he dropped his studies to go in for regional or national championships, but he always managed to catch up; he was not stupid.) "That's rubbish. If you'd like to know, I'm already planning a diploma project." He twirled his finger round his temple in a comical manner.

"Are you? That's fine. So you'll get through school. Then where will you go to work?"

"Wherever I'm sent," Rogozkin said glibly with exaggerated keenness, straightening his head and standing to attention.

"Then perhaps you'll be sent to work in the research institute that's going into the new building. Or perhaps others will land up there. So your work will be justified. And that goes for all of us."

"Oh, I see," said Rogozkin delightedly. "That's magnificent. Thank you!"

The director had already moved away. But before he could get as far as the corridor, Rogozkin called out with the same facetiousness: "No, wait, Grigory Lavrentich! I've changed my mind. I don't want to go to the new building."

"Where do you want to go?" the director asked, looking at him disapprovingly.

"I want to go to virgin lands!" Rogozkin shouted.

"Fill in an application, then." The Director of Studies almost smiled, and passed along the corridor into the principal's office.

Fyodor Mikheyich was not there: he had not managed to get an interview the day before, so he had gone to the regional Party committee again today. But the few teachers now waiting in the principal's office for a call from him had already given up hope.

Occasional drops of rain were splashing against the windowpanes. The uneven, bumpy piece of ground which stretched out as far as the level crossing looked dark and wet.

The heads of departments were bent over sheets of timetables, passing round coloured pencils and erasers as they worked out their teaching schedules. Sitting at a small table by the window near the Party safe, the school's Party secretary, Yakov Ananievich, was going through his files. Lydia Georgievna was standing by the same window. She had changed as quickly as only women can change: yesterday so cheerful, lively, and young, she looked today like an ailing, middle-aged woman. She was no longer dressed in blue-green but in black.

A short, balding, very neat, clean-shaven man with clear pink cheeks, Yakov Ananievich was talking as he worked. He would turn over each sheet of paper in the file carefully, without creasing it, as if it were a live thing, and if it happened to be a carbon copy he handled it with loving care. He spoke very gently and quietly, but also persuasively. "No, comrades. We won't hold a general meeting over this affair, or department meetings, or course meetings or even class meetings. It would only mean drawing too much attention to the issue. There's no point. They'll find out for themselves, anyway."

"They already know," said the Director of Studies, "but they're demanding an explanation."

"Well then," Yakov Ananievich replied calmly, seeing nothing contradictory in this, "you can give them an answer when you're talking to them in private—that's unavoidable. What should you say? Say that the institute is of national importance. Its work is closely allied to ours, and since electronics is now the basis of technological progress, no one should put obstacles in its path. Rather the reverse—they should clear the way for it." Everyone was silent; Yakov Ananievich leafed carefully through two or three more sheets of paper, looking for the right one. "In fact, you can get away without explaining any of it. Just say: 'The institute is vital to the state and it's not up to us to question its suitability.'" Leafing through a few more papers, he found the one he wanted, then again raised his clear, calm eyes. "But call meetings? Have a special discussion of the issue? No, that would be a political error. In fact, we must do the opposite: if the students or the Komsomol committee insist on a meeting, we must dissuade them from holding it."

"I disagree!" Lydia Georgievna turned abruptly towards him, and all her short, cropped hair quivered.

Yakov Ananievich looked at her in his sensible way and asked as precisely as ever: "But what can you disagree with in a matter like this, Lydia Georgievna?"

"First, with . . ." She went into the attack, gesturing with her whole body, her arms and hands. "First, with . . . well, with your tone of voice. You haven't merely given up, you're almost . . . pleased about it. Yes—it's as if you're pleased they've taken the building away from us!"

Yakov Ananievich spread his hands, not his arms but just his hands.

"But if this is a state requirement, Lydia Georgievna, how can I be displeased with it?"

"But I chiefly disagree with you on principle." She was no longer standing still but had begun to pace up and down the small space in the office and was gesticulating wildly.

"None of you is in such close contact with the students as I am, because I'm with the Komsomol from morning till night. And I know how they'll react to what you're telling us to do. The kids will think, and think rightly, that we're afraid of the truth. And will they respect us for that? Whenever anything good happens to us we proclaim it aloud, plaster the walls with notices about it, broadcast it over the loudspeaker system—isn't that so? But when it's something bad or something difficult to tell them—then let them find out wherever they can and whisper what they like. No!" Her voice rang out, but unfortunately for her, it reached the verge of tears for the second time that day. "No! We can't behave like that, especially with young people. Lenin taught us not to be afraid to speak freely. 'Free speech is a healing sword!' "

Untimely tears choked her and she rushed out to sob aloud.

Yakov Ananievich watched her go, with a pained expression, and closing his eyes, he shook his head with a great show of grief.

Lydia Georgievna walked quickly along the semidark corridor clutching her handkerchief screwed up in a ball. Here and there, students were tidying up, moving last year's trophies won on the sports day, cartoons of slackers, and wall newspapers.

Where the corridor widened out by the storeroom, there were some boxes of radio valves, and two third-year boys called out after her: during the cleaning-out process they had taken down the model of the building and now they did not know what to do with it. It was the same three-dimensional model they had carried in the October and May Day parades, raised on four poles, at the head of the school procession. Resting on the pile of boxes, now so familiar in every detail, the building stood realistically in front of them: white, painted blue and green in all the right places, with those two characteristic low turrets rising from the line of pilasters; with its two entrances, one large and one small; with the huge windows of the assembly hall and exactly the right number of normal-sized windows on the four floors, each of which had already been assigned to someone in particular.

Without looking straight at her, shifting guiltily, one of the boys asked: "Shall we . . . break it up? What use is it now? There's hardly room for it in here, anyway . . ."

6

Ivan Kapitonovich Grachikov did not like reminiscing about the war, especially about his own experiences. His reason was that the war had brought him much distress and little good; also that, as he'd been an infantryman, every day and each phase of the war was connected in his memory with the suffering, sacrifice, and death of good men.

Nor did he like the fact that, for twenty years after the war, military terms were still bandied about where they were completely unnecessary. At the factory he had tried to break other people of the habit and had himself avoided such expressions as "advancing on the technological front" . . . "we threw ourselves into the breach" . . . "we forced their lines" . . . "brought up reserves . . ." He thought that these expressions, instilling the ideas of war into peace itself, sickened people. The Russian language could manage very well without them.

Today, however, he had changed his rule. He and the principal of the technical school were sitting in the waiting room of the First Secretary of the regional Party committee (at the same time as other people were sitting in his own waiting room, waiting to see him). Nervous, Grachikov telephoned his secretary and smoked a couple of cigarettes. Then he took a close look at Fyodor Mikheyich's head, sunk miserably between his shoulders, and it occurred to him that his hair had grown greyer overnight. To rouse Fyodor Mikheyich from his gloom, Grachikov began to tell him about a funny incident in which people they both knew had figured, during that short period when their division had been behind the battle line. This had happened in 1943, after Fyodor Mikheyich had been wounded.

However, his anecdote had no effect; Fyodor Mikheyich did not laugh. Grachikov himself preferred not to stir up memories of war; but in telling this story, he was involuntarily reminded of what had happened the next day, when his division had received an urgent order to cross the river Sozh and deploy.

The bridge there had been blown up. The sappers had repaired it by night and Grachikov had been posted as duty officer at the crossing, with orders to let no one through until the division had crossed over. The bridge was narrow, the edges were crumbling, the planks were uneven, and no bunching could be allowed because single-engined Stukas had twice swooped out from behind the forest and dive-bombed them, although admittedly their bombs had fallen into the water. So the crossing, which had started before daylight, dragged on until well into the afternoon. Other units who also wanted to cross came up and collected there, but they had to wait their turn in the sparse pine forest. Suddenly six of a new type of covered lorry (Grachikov's batman called them "secret" lorries) came out of the wood, one behind the other. They overtook the column of the division and made straight for the bridge to squeeze their way on to it. "Ha-a-lt!" Grachikov shouted ferociously at the first driver, and ran to bar his way, but the lorry carried straight on. Grachikov's hand made for his holster, but hardly had it reached it when an elderly officer with a cape thrown over his shoulders opened the door of the first cab and shouted with equal ferocity: "Come here, Major!" With a twist of his shoulder, he threw back his cape; he was a lieutenant-general.

Grachikov ran up, now rather afraid.

"What was your hand reaching for?" the general

shouted threateningly. "D'you want to be court-martialled? Then let my lorries through!" Until he was ordered to let them through, Grachikov had been prepared to explain everything calmly, without any shouting, and might even have let them through. But when right clashed head-on with wrong and the latter was backed up by greater force, Grachikov stuck to his guns and cared nothing for what might happen to him. He stood to attention, saluted, and announced: "Comrade Lieutenant-General, I won't let you through!" "You wha-a-at?" the general yelled, and stepped down onto the running board. "What's your name?" "Major Grachikov, Comrade Lieutenant-General. Permit me to ask yours." "Tomorrow you'll be in a penal battalion!" he yelled in fury. "Very good, sir, but today you can take your turn," Grachikov retaliated, took a pace in front of the lorry's radiotor, and stood there, feeling as if his face and neck were turning crimson, but certain that he would not give way. The general drew himself in with rage, thought for a moment, then banged the door shut and turned his six lorries around . . .

At last several men came out of Knorozov's office; they were from the district board of farm management and from the Agricultural Department of the regional Party committee. Knorozov's secretary, Konevsky (whom a novice might well have taken for the Party secretary himself, considering the airs he gave himself and the size of his desk), came out into the reception room and turned around.

"Comrade Knorozov will see you alone," he announced firmly.

Grachikov winked at Fyodor Mikheyich and went in.

A livestock expert had stayed on in Knorozov's office. Straining his head around as far as he could and twisting his whole body as if his bones were made of rubber, he was looking at a large sheet of paper lying in front of Knorozov, on which were beautiful coloured diagrams and figures.

Grachikov greeted them.

Knorozov, tall and bald-headed, did not turn towards him but just squinted in his direction.

"Think yourself lucky agriculture's none of your business. But since you've come, you might as well stay. Just wait quietly."

He often reproached Grachikov for not having any responsibility for agriculture, as if urban industry somehow did not earn its keep. Now, as Grachikov well knew, Knorozov was aiming not only to specialise in agriculture but to make a name for himself in it.

"Well, then," Knorozov said to the livestock expert, lowering five long, outspread fingers slowly and weightily in a semicircle onto the large sheet of paper, as if placing a huge seal on it. He was sitting up straight, without using the back of the armchair for support, and the contours of his figure, from both side and front, seemed drawn in harsh, straight lines. "Well, then—I've told you what you must do now. And what you must do is what I tell you."

"Of course, Victor Vavilich." The livestock expert bowed.

"Take it then." Knorozov released the sheet of paper.

The livestock expert cautiously lifted up the paper in both hands from Knorozov's table and rolled it into a tube. Then, lowering his head, his bald patch to the fore, he crossed the spacious office with its numerous chairs standing in readiness for large conferences.

Thinking that he would now be sent to bring in the principal of the technical school, Grachikov did not sit down but leaned against the leather back of the chair in front of him.

Even sitting down at a desk, Knorozov looked imposing. His long head made him look even taller. Although far from young, he was not aged by his lack of hair; it actually made him look younger. He never made a single unnecessary movement, nor did his expression ever change except rarely. For this reason his face always looked as if cast in a mould; it did not reflect any trivial, fleeting emotions. A smile would have upset its balance, spoilt its harmony.

"Victor Vavilich," said Grachikov, pronouncing each syllable in full. Whenever he spoke to anyone, his sing-song voice itself invited moderation and courtesy.

"I won't keep you long. I've come with the principal—about the building for the electronics technical college. A delegation arrived from Moscow and announced it was transferring the building to a scientific research institute. Did you know about this?"

Still without looking at Grachikov, but rather staring ahead of him into a distance that was visible to him alone, he moved his lips the necessary minimum and replied abruptly: "Yes."

With that, the conversation was effectively over.

"You did know?"

"I did."

Knorozov was proud of the fact that he never deviated from something once he had said it.

Knorozov was in this region what Stalin had once been in Moscow: he never changed his mind or retracted a decision. And although Stalin had died long ago, Knorozov lived on. He was one of the leading examples of the "voluntarist" style of leadership and considered this his own greatest merit. He could not imagine that leadership could be exercised in any other way.

Feeling that his temper was beginning to rise, Grachikov forced himself to speak even more affably and persuasively: "Victor Vavilich, why don't they put up a special building for them—one suited to their requirements? Otherwise, the internal alterations alone will . . ."

"It's urgent," Knorozov interrupted him. "The matter is in hand. The institute must open as soon as possible."

"But is that worth all the alterations, Victor Vavilich? And"—he spoke quickly to prevent Knorozov from cutting him off—"the main thing is the educational angle. The students at the school worked hard on it for a whole year, entirely without pay and very enthusiastically. They . . ."

Knorozov turned his head—only his head, not his shoulders—towards Grachikov, and his voice now had a metallic ring. "I don't understand it. You're secretary of the town Party committee. Do I have to tell *you* about fighting for the honour of the town? There is not and never has been a single scientific research institute in our town. And it wasn't so easy for our people to get one. We must jump at the chance—before the Ministry changes its mind. Because of this, we'll move at once into a different class of town—towns on the scale of Gorky and Sverdlovsk."

He frowned. Either he was already seeing his town transformed into Sverdlovsk or he was inwardly aiming at some new, even higher post.

But although his remarks fell like steel girders, they did not convince Grachikov in the slightest; he felt the onset of one of those decisive moments in his life when he could do nothing but stick to his guns and refuse to give way. Because right had come face to face with wrong.

"Victor Vavilich." No longer speaking calmly, he rapped it out more abruptly than he had intended. "We're not medieval barons trying to outdo each other by adding more quarterings to our coat of arms. The honour of our town lies in the fact that these students put up that building themselves, and did it for the love of it, and it's our duty to back them up. But if you take the building away, they'll never forget we've cheated them. If you cheat people once, then they realise that you may cheat them again."

"We have nothing to discuss." A girder, larger than the previous ones, came crashing down. "The decision has been taken."

An orange flash exploded in Grachikov's eyes. His neck and face turned red as the blood rushed to them.

"Which means more to us in the end—stones or people?" Grachikov shouted. "Why are we arguing over a heap of stones?"

Furious, Knorozov stood up to his full height. He was all steel, completely inflexible.

"Demagogy!" he roared over the head of this man who had dared to assert his opinion.

His will power and strength were such that it seemed as though he had only to stretch out his hand for Grachikov's head to be struck from his body.

But Grachikov no longer had the power to decide whether to speak out or to keep quiet.

"Communism will not be built with stones but with

people, Victor Vavilich!" he shouted, all restraint gone. "It's a harder and longer task, but if we were to finish the whole structure tomorrow and it was built of nothing but stones, we would never have Communism!"

Both of them were silent and unmoving.

Ivan Kapitonovich noticed that his fingers were hurting. He had dug them into the back of the chair. He let them relax.

"You're not mature enough for the post of secretary of the town Party committee," Knorozov muttered. "We overlooked that."

"Don't imagine that I ever will be either!" Grachikov replied, already feeling a certain relief because he had said the most important thing. "I'll find work for myself."

"What kind of work?" Knorozov listened attentively.

"Any kind of unskilled work. I don't suppose that'll make you like me any the more," Grachikov said at the top of his voice.

The truth was that he was sick to the teeth of working without ever being consulted, without ever being allowed to discuss matters, but simply being ordered about from above. That was not the way his factory had been run.

Knorozov expelled the air through his clenched teeth with a long, whistling sound.

He placed his hand on the receiver.

He lifted it.

He sat down.

"Sasha, connect me with Khabalygin."

They were connected.

Neither of the men in the office spoke a word.

"Khabalygin? . . . Tell me, what are you going to do about the fact that this building is not built to your requirements?"

(What's this about Khabalygin "going to do" something?)

"What d'you mean—not large enough? They're very large . . . Urgent . . . yes, I see . . . In other words, you've got enough on your hands with the one building . . .?"

("On *your* hands . . .?")

"No, I won't give you the one next to it. You can build a better one yourself."

He put down the receiver.

"Call in the principal."

Grachikov went to call him, already preoccupied with this new piece of information: was Khabalygin moving into the research institute?

He returned with the principal. Fyodor Mikheyich drew himself up and fixed his gaze on Knorozov. He liked him. He had always admired him. He was happy when he went to his meetings and could imbibe and charge himelf with Knorozov's all-embracing will power and energy. Afterwards, he would cheerfully feel like carrying out his instructions in time for the next meeting, whether it involved raising the pass rate of his students, digging up potatoes, or collecting scrap metal. What Fyodor Mikheyich liked about Knorozov was that when he said yes he meant yes, and when he said no he meant no. Dialectics were all very well, but like many others, Fyodor Mikheyich prefered unambiguous decisions.

Now he had not come to dispute the issue but to hear sentence passed on his building.

"Have you been treated unfairly?" Knorozov asked.

Fyodor Mikheyich gave a weak smile.

"Chin up!" said Knorozov, quietly but firmly. "You don't usually give up because of a difficulty."

"I'm not giving up," said Fyodor Mikheyich hoarsely, and cleared his throat.

"They've started building a new hostel alongside you, haven't they? Right, when it's finished, you'll have a new technical school. D'you see?"

"Yes, I see," Fyodor Mikheyich concurred. But this time, for some reason, he felt no upsurge of enthusiasm. Thoughts immediately began whirling around his head: winter was coming on; another whole school year would have to be spent in the old building; the new college would again be without an assembly hall and a gymnasium; and they would still have no hostel.

"The trouble is, Victor Vavilich," said Fyodor Mikheyich, thinking aloud, "we'll have to alter the plans. The rooms are tiny, they are only designed for four people. We'll have to convert them into lecture halls, laboratories . . ."

"Take it or leave it!"

Cutting him off with a gesture, Knorozov dismissed them. They should not bother him with such trivialities.

On their way to the cloakroom, Grachikov slapped the principal on the back.

"Well, Mikheyich, don't worry. You'll build it, all right."

"We'll have to alter the ceiling over the basement," said the principal as more and more problems occurred to him. "It has to be much stronger to stand up to the weight of the machine tools. And because the reinforcement will raise the level of the ground floor, we'll also have to dismantle the first floor, which we've already finished."

"Ye-es," said Grachikov. "But look at it this way: they've given you a plot of land in a good place; the site has already been excavated and the foundation laid. So the future's certain: by the spring you'll have finished and be moving. We'll help you, and so will the Council of National Economy. You could even say it's a good thing they took away that building."

They went out into the street, both of them wearing dark coats and caps. A cool but pleasant wind was blowing, carrying with it a hint of rain.

"By the way"—Grachikov frowned—"You don't happen to know how Khabalygin stands with the Ministry, do you?"

"Khabalygin? Oh, they think a lot of him. He told me a long time ago that he's *very* well connected there. You mean you think he might help?" Fyodor Mikheyich asked with momentary optimism. But he rejected the idea himself. "No. If he had been able to help, he would have objected there and then, when the delegation was going round. But he agreed with them . . ."

Standing with his feet firmly apart, Grachikov looked down the street. He asked another question: "What is he? A relay expert, isn't he?"

"Well, hardly an expert. He used to work on transformers. He's just an executive who's had a certain amount of practical experience."

"But why did he in particular go round with the delegation, do you know?"

"That's true." Fyodor Mikheyich had been so confused by the events of the previous day that only now did this point occur to him. "Yes, why *did* he?"

"Well, don't worry," Grachikov sighed, and shook hands with him vigorously.

He went home, thinking about Khabalygin. This type of scientific research institute had nothing in common with a little factory making relay equipment. The salary and status of the director would be far greater; perhaps he was aiming for a Lenin Prize! It was Grachikov's firm conviction that one should not wait until a Party member actually contravened the criminal code. Anyone who was using his job, his status, or his connections to acquire not just a detached house or a summer cottage but even the merest trifle should be immediately expelled from the Party. There was no need to show him up or give him a public reprimand; he should be got rid of because it was not merely a transgression, a mistake, or a failing—it implied a completely alien mentality, that of an inherent capitalist.

A driver and his teacher wife had been caught cultivating a flower garden at home and selling the flowers in the market. For this they had been pilloried in the local paper. But how was Khabalygin to be caught?

Fyodor Mikheyich walked on slowly, making the most of the refreshing breeze. He felt sluggish and queasy from insomnia, from the two Nembutal tablets he had taken, and from everything he had been thinking about in the past twenty-four hours. But bit by bit the fresh wind cleared his head.

So, he thought, we've got to start all over again. Collect all nine hundred of them and explain: we haven't got a building. We must put one up. If we all help, it'll be quicker.

At first they won't like the idea. Then, once again, they'll get really keen on it as the work itself starts to attract them.

They'll believe in it.

And they'll put up the building.

One more year in which to make do with the old building—I suppose we'll manage.

Without noticing it, he had arrived at the new building, gleaming with metal and glass.

The second one, alongside it, had hardly risen above ground level and was covered in sand and mud.

After Grachikov's question, several disconnected little facts about Khabalygin had been aroused in his guileless memory, and the pieces slowly started to fit together: why had he postponed the handover of the project in August? And why had he looked so cheerful when the delegation had come?

Strangely enough, just as he had begun to puzzle about Khabalygin as he walked along, who should be the first person that Fyodor Mikheyich saw in the large back yard of the building site but Vsevolod Borisovich Khabalygin? Wearing a green trilby and a smart brown overcoat, he was walking confidently around over the sodden mud, ignoring the fact that his shoes were getting smeared with it, and giving orders to several workmen, obviously his own.

Two workmen and a driver were dragging posts out of the back of a lorry—some freshly painted ones and othes that had turned grey and had already been used, though their rotting ends had been chopped off. Two other workmen were bending over and doing something while Khabalygin was instructing them with an authoritative wave of his short arms.

Fyodor Mikheyich went closer and saw that they were driving in stakes. But there was something underhand about the way they were doing it: the stakes were not in a straight line but in a sort of long curve, so as to secure more of the yard for the institute and leave less for the technical school.

"Vsevolod Borisovich! How dare you! What are you doing?" the principal called out, furious at being cheated. "Fifteen- and sixteen-year-old kids need some space to breathe in, to run about in! Where can I let them go and play?"

Khabalygin had just placed himself on a strategic spot

which completed the last stretch of his maliciously planned fence. With his feet apart on either side of the future boundary, he had gained a good foothold and had already raised his arm to give the signal when he heard Fyodor Mikheyich coming up behind him. Holding his palm edgewise in front of his face, Khabalygin turned his head a fraction (his neck and shoulders were so fat he never could turn his head very well), twitched his upper lip so that his cheeks quivered, and muttered: "What? What's that?"

Without waiting for an answer, he turned away, checked his markers along the line of his hand, used his four fingers together to signal to one of them to level himself up, and finally, with a swing of his short arm sliced the air.

It seemed as if he were cleaving not the air but the very ground itself. No, not merely cleaving—the swing of his arm was the gesture of someone opening up a great new roadway. He swung it like some ancient chieftain pointing the way ahead to his warriors, like the first navigator who has at last found the true azimuth pointing to the North Pole.

And only when he had done his duty did he turn towards Fyodor Mikheyich and explain to him: "It must be done like this, comrade."

"Why *must* it?" Fyodor Mikheyich lost his temper and his head started to shake. "You mean for the good of the cause? Just you wait!" He clenched his fists, but he had no more strength left to speak, so he turned away and strode quickly towards the street, muttering: "Just you wait, just you wait, you swine! . . ."

The workmen went on carrying the stakes.

The Easter Procession

Connoisseurs tell us that an artist should not paint everything exactly as it is. They say that colour photography does this and that by means of curved lines and combinations of triangles and squares we should convey the essence of a thing rather than the thing itself. But I do not see how colour photography could pick out what is significant among the faces in an Easter procession at the patriarchal church of Peredelkino half a century after the Revolution and compose them meaningfully into a single picture. Depicted in conventional terms (even without the aid of triangles), a present-day Easter procession can tell us a great deal.

Half an hour before the bells start ringing, the forecourt of the patriarchal Church of the Transfiguration looks as gay as a Saturday-night hop in the recreation hall of some remote industrial town. Girls in bright scarves and ski pants (true, some of them are wearing skirts) are walking around in noisy groups of threes and fours; they jostle to get into the church, but it is very crowded in the porch, as the old women have been in their places since early evening, so the girls start yapping at them from the doorway. Then they stroll around the churchyard, shrieking uninhibitedly and calling out to each other, staring at the green, pink, and white lights hanging in front of ikons on the church walls and beside the graves of bishops and archpriests. The boys, ranging from hulking great toughs to scrawny weaklings, all have the same arrogant look on their faces. (What, one wonders, have these teenagers got to feel superior about? The fact that they're good at ice hockey?) Almost all of them are wearing caps, and if some of them are bareheaded it has nothing to do with the fact that they are on consecrated ground. About one

102

in four has been drinking, one in ten is drunk, and half of them are smoking—in that repulsive way with the cigarette stuck to the lower lip. There is no incense yet; instead of it, swathes of grey-blue cigarette smoke rise towards the Easter sky under the electric light of the churchyard in dense, hovering clouds. They spit on the asphalt path, jostle each other in fun, and whistle loudly. Some are using obscene language, and a bunch are jigging to dance music from transistor radios. Some of them kiss their girlfriends, who are then pulled from one boy to another, staring aggressively around as though the knives may come out at any minute. Once they start flashing their knives at each other, they may easily turn them on the members of the congregation, because the attitude of these youths to churchgoers is not the usual attitude of the young to the old or of guests to a host; they regard them as a housewife regards flies.

However, the knives are not brought out, as three or four policemen are strolling up and down nearby, just to keep an eye on things. The boys are not swearing noisily but simply as part of their normal conversation, so the police fail to notice that they are breaking the law, and smile amiably at the rising generation. And the police are not going to snatch the cigarettes out of their mouths or pull the caps off their heads, because this is a public place and the right not to believe in God is safeguarded by the constitution.

Huddling close to the cemetery fence and the church walls, the believers dare not protest but just keep glancing around, hoping that no one will jab them with a knife or force them to hand over their watches, which they need to check the last minutes before Christ's resurrection. Here, outside the church, the grinning, swirling mob far outnumbers the Orthodox. They are even more intimidated and suppressed than in the days of Tartar rule; the Tartars at least did not come to crowd out the faithful at the Easter Morning service.

These youths are not breaking the law; although they are doing violence, it is bloodless. Their lips twisted into a gangsterish leer, their brazen talk, their loud laughter, their flirting and snide jokes, their smoking and spitting—it all amounts to an insult to the Passion of

103

Christ, which is being celebrated a few yards away from them. It is expressed in the arrogant, derisory look worn by these snotty hooligans as they come to watch how the old folk still practise the rites of their forefathers.

Among the believers I catch a glimpse of one or two Jewish faces. Perhaps they are converts, or perhaps they are just onlookers. Glancing around warily, they too are waiting for the Easter procession. We all curse the Jews, but it would be worthwhile having a look around us to see what kind of Russians we have bred at the same time. These are not the militant atheists of the thirties, who snatched the consecrated Easter cakes out of people's hands, dancing and caterwauling and pretending to be devils. This generation is just idly inquisitive: the ice-hockey season on television is over, the football season has not started yet, and what brings them to church is sheer boredom. They push the churchgoers aside like so many sacks of straw; they curse the church for its commercialism, yet for some reason they buy candles.

One thing is odd: they are all outsiders, yet they all know each other—and by their first names. How is it they are such good friends? Do they all come from the same factory? Or is it that these occasions unite them in a kind of freemasonry?

The bell tolls loudly above our heads, but there is something false about it; the chimes sound somehow tinny instead of deep and sonorous. The bell is ringing to announce the procession. Now things really get going, although it is not the believers who are on the move but the crowd of shrieking youngsters, as they mill around in the churchyard in twos and threes. They are hurrying, even though they have no idea what they are looking for, which way to go, or where the procession will come from. They light red Easter candles, then show off by using them to light their cigarettes. They crowd together as if waiting for a foxtrot to begin; all it needs is a beer stall for these tall, curly-headed lads (at least our race gets no shorter) to start blowing white froth onto the graves.

The head of the procession has already left the porch

and is turning in this direction, to the accompaniment of a gentle peal of bells. Two laymen are walking ahead asking the comrades to leave as much space as possible. Three paces behind them comes an elderly, balding churchwarden, carrying a heavy cut-glass lantern fixed to a pole. He looks up cautiously at the lamp as he tries to keep it steady, and glances from side to side with equal apprehension ... And this is the start of the picture which I would so like to paint, if only I could: the churchwarden's terror that the builders of the new society may close in, jump on him, and beat him up. The spectators can sense his fear.

Girls in trousers, holding candles, and boys with cigarettes stuck in their mouths, in caps and unbuttoned coats—some with immature, moronic expressions of totally unfounded self-confidence; others with simple, credulous faces: a lot of these must be in the picture—tightly packed, watching a spectacle which cannot be seen elsewhere for any money. Behind the lantern come two men carrying a religious banner, and they too, instead of walking apart, are huddling together from fear.

After them come ten women in pairs, holding thick lighted candles. They must also be in the picture, elderly women with faces set in an unworldly gaze, prepared for death if they are attacked. Two out of the ten are young girls of the same age as those crowding round with the boys, yet how pure and bright their faces are. The ten women, walking in close formation, are singing and looking as solemn as though the people around them were crossing themselves, praying and falling to their knees in repentance. They do not breathe the cigarette smoke; their ears are deaf to the vile language; the soles of their feet do not feel how the churchyard has been turned into a dance floor.

And so the real procession begins. A slight tremor runs through the crowd on both sides and the noise has died down a little.

The women are followed by seven men, priests and deacons in bright copes. As they are walking out of step and bunched together, they get in each other's way, and there is almost no room to swing their censers or to

105

raise the ends of their stoles in blessing. Yet this is the procession in which, had he not been dissuaded from taking part, the Patriarch of All Russia should have walked and conducted the service . . .

The tightly packed little party hurries by—and that is all there is of the procession. No one else. There are evidently no worshippers in the procession, for if there were they would by now have left the church. No worshippers, yet this bunch of rowdies swarms along behind as though they were bursting through the broken doors of a warehouse to loot, tear open packets of food, brushing against the doorposts, spinning around in a whirlpool, crowding together, shoving their way through—and for what? They do not even know themselves. To see the priests making fools of themselves? Or are they just pushing for the sake of pushing?

It is extraordinary—a religious procession without worshippers, without people crossing themselves, a religious procession of people with caps on, smoking cigarettes, with transistors in their breast pockets. The front row of the crowd as it squeezes its way into the church-yard must also be in the picture; then it will be complete.

An old woman turns aside to cross herself and says to another: "It's better this year, there's no rowdiness. There are so many police."

Ah, so that's it. This is one of the better years.

These millions we have bred and reared—what will become of them? Where have the enlightened efforts and the inspiring visions of great thinkers led us? What good can we expect of our future generations?

The truth is that one day they will turn and trample on us all. And as for those who urged them on to this, they will trample on them too.

Easter Day
10 April 1966

Zakhar-the-Pouch

You asked me to tell you something about my cycling holiday last summer. Well, if it's not too boring, listen to this one about Kulikovo Field.

We had been meaning to go there for a long time, but it was somehow a difficult place to reach. There are no brightly painted notices or signposts to show you the way, and you won't find it on a single map, even though this battle cost more Russian lives in the fourteenth century than Borodino did in the nineteenth. There has been only one such encounter for fifteen hundred years, not only in Russia but in all Europe. It was a battle not merely between principalities or nation-states, but between continents.

Perhaps we chose a rather roundabout way to get there: from Epiphania through Kazanovka and Monastirshchina. It was only because there had been no rain till then that we were able to ride instead of pushing our bikes; to cross the Don, which was not yet in full spate, and its tributary, the Nepriadva, we wheeled them over narrow, two-plank footbridges.

After a long trek, we stood on a hill and caught sight of what looked like a needle pointing into the sky from a distant flat-topped rise. We went downhill and lost sight of it. Then we started to climb again, and the grey needle reappeared, this time more distinct, and next to it we saw what looked like a church. There seemed to be something uniquely strange about its design, something never seen except in fairy tales: its domes looked transparent and fluid; they shimmered deceptively in the cascading sunlight of the hot August day—one minute they were there and the next they were gone.

We guessed rightly that we would be able to quench our thirst and fill our water bottles at the well in the valley, which proved to be invaluable later on. But the peasant who handed us the bucket, in reply to our question: "Where's Kulikovo Field?" just stared at us as if we were idiots.

"You don't say Kulikóvo, you say Kulíkovo. The village of Kulíkovka is right next to the battlefield, but Kulikóvka's over there, on the other side of the Don."

After our meeting with this man, we travelled along deserted country lanes, and until we reached the monument several kilometres away, we did not come across a single person. It must have been because no one happened to be around on that particular day, for we could see the wheel of a combine harvester flailing somewhere in the distance. People obviously frequented this place and would do so again, because all the land had been planted with crops as far as the eye could see, and the harvest was almost ready—buckwheat, clover, sugar beet, rye, and peas (we had shelled some of those young peas); yet we saw no one that day and we passed through what seemed like the blessed calm of a reservation. Nothing disturbed us from musing on the fate of those fair-haired warriors, nine out of every ten of whom lay seven feet beneath the present topsoil, and whose bones had now dissolved into the earth, in order that Holy Russia might rid herself of the heathen Mussulman.

The features of the land—this wide slope gradually ascending to Mamai Hill—could not have greatly changed over six centuries, except that the forest had disappeared. Spread out before us was the very place where they had crossed the Don in the evening and the night of September 7, 1380, then settled down to feed their horses (though the majority were foot soldiers), sharpen their swords, restore their morale, pray, and hope—almost a quarter of a million Russians, certainly more than two hundred thousand. The population of Russia then was barely a seventh of what it is now, so that an army of that size staggers the imagination.

And for nine out of every ten warriors, that was to be their last morning on earth.

On that occasion our men had not crossed the Don from choice, for what army would want to stand and fight with its retreat blocked by a river? The truth of history is bitter but it is better to admit it: Mamai had as allies not only Circassians, Genoese, and Lithuanians but also Prince Oleg of Ryazan. (One must understand Oleg's motives also: he had no other way of protecting his territory from the Tartars, as it lay right across their path. His land had been ravaged by fire three times in the preceding seven years.) That is why the Russians had crossed the Don—to protect their rear from their own people, the men of Ryazan: in any other circumstances, Orthodox Christians would not have attacked them.

The needle loomed up in front of us, though it was no longer a needle but an imposing tower, unlike anything I had ever seen. We could not reach it directly: the tracks had come to an end and we were confronted by standing crops. We wheeled our bicycles round the edges of the fields and, finally, starting nowhere in particular, there emerged from the ground an old, neglected, abandoned road, overgrown with weeds, which grew more distinct as it drew nearer to the monument and even had ditches on either side of it.

Suddenly the crops came to an end and the hillside became even more like a reservation, a piece of fallow land overgrown with tough rye-grass instead of the usual feather-grass. We paid homage to this ancient place in the best way possible—just by breathing the pure air. One look around, and behold!—there in the light of sunrise the Mongol chief Telebei is engaged in single combat with Prince Peresvet, the two leaning against each other like two sheaves of wheat; the Mongolian cavalry are shooting their arrows and brandishing their spears; with faces contorted with blood lust, they trample on the Russian infantry, breaking through the core of their formation and driving them back to where a milky cloud of mist has risen from the Nepriadva and the Don.

Our men were mown down like wheat, and we were trampled to death beneath their hoofs.

Here, at the very axis of the bloody carnage, provided that the person who guessed the spot did so correctly, are the monument and the church with the unearthly domes which had so amazed us from afar. There turned out to be a simple solution to the puzzle: the local inhabitants have ripped off the metal from all five domes for their own requirements, so the domes have become transparent; their delicate structure is still intact, except that it now consists of nothing but the framework, and from a distance it looks like a mirage.

The monument, too, is remarkable at close quarters. Unless you go right up to it and touch it, you will not understand how it was made. Although it was built in the last century, in fact well over a hundred years ago, the idea—of piecing the monument together from sections of cast iron—is entirely modern, except that nowadays it would not be cast in iron. It is made up of two square platforms, one on top of another, then a twelve-sided structure which gradually becomes round; the lower part is decorated in relief with iron shields, swords, helmets, and Slavonic inscriptions. Farther up, it rises in the shape of a fourfold cylinder cast so that it looks like four massive organ pipes welded together. Then comes a capping piece with an incised pattern, and above it all a gilded cross triumphing over a crescent. The whole tower—fully thirty metres high—is made up of figured slabs so tightly bolted together that not a single rivet or seam is visible, just as if the monument had been cast in a single piece—at least until time, or more likely the sons and grandsons of the men who put it up, had begun to knock holes in it.

After the long route to the monument through empty fields, we had assumed that the place would be deserted. As we walked along, we were wondering why it was in this state. This was, after all, a historic spot. What happened there was a turning point in the fate of Russia. For our invaders have not always come from the West . . . Yet this place is spurned, forgotten.

How glad we were to be mistaken! At once, not far from the monument, we caught sight of a grey-haired old man and two young boys. They had thrown down their rucksacks and were lying in the grass, writing something in a large book the size of a class register. When we approached, we found that he was a literature teacher who had met the boys somewhere nearby, and that the book was not a school exercise book, but none other than the Visitors' Comments Book. But there was no museum here; where, then, in all this wild field was the book kept?

Suddenly a massive shadow blotted out the sun. We turned. It was the Keeper of Kulikovo Field—the man whose duty it was to guard our glorious heritage.

We did not have time to focus the camera, and in any case it was impossible to take a snapshot into the sun. What is more, the Keeper would have refused to be photographed (he knew what he was worth and refused to let himself be photographed all day). How shall I set about describing him? Should I begin with the man himself? Or start with his sack? (He was carrying an ordinary peasant's sack, only half full and evidently not very heavy since he was holding it without effort.)

The Keeper was a hot-tempered muzhik who looked something of a ruffian. His arms and legs were hefty, and his shirt was dashingly unbuttoned. Red hair stuck out from under the cap planted sideways on his head, and although it was obviously a week since he had shaved, a fresh reddish scratch ran right across his cheek.

"Ah!" he greeted us in a disapproving voice as he loomed over us. "You've just arrived, have you? How did you get here?"

He seemed puzzled, as if the place were completely fenced in and we had found a hole to crawl through. We nodded towards the bicycles, which we had propped up in the bushes. Although he was holding the sack as though about to board a train, he looked as if he would demand to see our passports. His face was haggard, with a pointed chin and a determined expression.

"I'm warning you! Don't damage the grass with your bicycles!"

With this, he let us know immediately that here, on Kulikovo Field, you were not free to do as you liked.

The Keeper's unbuttoned coat was long-skirted and enveloped him like a parka; it was patched in a few places and was the colour you read about in folk tales—

somewhere between grey, brown, red, and purple. A star glinted in the lapel of his jacket; at first we thought it was a medal, but then we realised it was just the ordinary little badge, with Lenin's head in a circle, that everyone buys on Revolution Day. A long blue-and-white-striped linen shirt, obviously home-made, was hanging out from underneath his jacket and was gathered at the waist by an army belt with a five-pointed star on the buckle. His second-hand officer's breeches were tucked into the frayed tops of his canvas boots.

"Well?" he asked the teacher, in a much gentler tone of voice. "How's the writing going?"

"Fine, Zakhar Dmitrich," he replied, calling him by name. "We've nearly finished."

"Will *you*"—more sternly again—"be writing too?"

"Later on." We tried to escape from his insistent questions by cutting in: "Do you know when this monument was built?"

"Of course I do!" he snapped, offended, coughing and spluttering at the insult. "What do you think I'm here for?"

And carefully lowering his sack (which clinked with what sounded like bottles), the Keeper pulled a document out of his pocket and unfolded it; it was a page of an exercise book on which was written, in capital letters and in complete disregard of the ruled lines, a copy of the monument's dedication to Dmitry Donskoi and the year—1848.

"What is that?"

"Well, comrades," sighed Zakhar Dmitrich, revealing by his frankness that he was not quite the tyrant that he had at first pretended to be, "it's like this. I copied it myself from the plaque because everyone asks when it was built. I'll show you where the plaque was, if you like."

"What became of it?"

"Some rogue from our village pinched it—and we can't do anything about it."

"Do you know who it was?"

"Of course I know. I scared off some of his gang of louts, I dealt with them all right, but he and the rest got

112

away. I'd like to lay my hands on all those vandals, I'd show 'em."

"But why did he steal the plaque?"

"For his house."

"Can't you take it back?"

"Ha, ha!" Zakhar threw back his head in reply to our foolish question. "That's the problem! I don't have any authority. They won't give me a gun. I need a machine gun in a job like this."

Looking at the scratch across his cheek, we thought to ourselves it was just as well they didn't give him a gun.

Then the teacher finished what he was writing and handed back the Comments Book. We thought that Zakhar Dmitrich would put it under his arm or into his sack, but we were wrong. He opened the flap of his dirty jacket and revealed, sewn inside, a sort of pocket or bag made of sacking (in fact, it was more like a pouch than anything else), the exact size of the Comments Book, which fitted neatly into it. Also attached to the pouch was a slot for the blunt indelible pencil which he lent to visitors.

Convinced that we were now suitably intimidated Zakhar-the-Pouch picked up his sack (the clinking *was* glass) and went off with his long, loping stride into the bushes. Here the brusque forcefulness with which he had first met us vanished. Hunching himself miserably, he sat down, lit a cigarette, and smoked with such unalleviated grief, with such despair, that one might have thought all those who had perished on this battlefield had died only yesterday and had been his closest relatives, and that now he did not know how to go on living.

We decided to spend the whole day and night here: to see whether nighttime at Kulikovo really was as Blok described it in his poem. Without hurrying, we walked over to the monument, inspected the abandoned church, and wandered over the field, trying to imagine the dispositions of the battlefield on that eighth of September; then we clambered up onto the iron surface of the monument.

Plenty of people had been here before us. It would

be quite wrong to say that the monument had been forgotten. People had been busy carving the iron surface of the monument with chisels and scratching it with nails, while those with less energy had written more faintly on the church walls with charcoal: "Maria Polyneyeva and Kikolai Lazarev were here from 8/5/50 to 24/5 . . ." "Delegates of the regional conference were here . . ." "Workers from the Kimovskaya Postal Administration were here 23/6/52 . . ." And so on and so on.

Then three young working lads from Kovomoskovsk drove up on motorbikes. Jumping off lightly onto the iron surface, they started to examine the warm grey-black body of the monument and slapped it affectionately; they were surprised at how well made it was and explained to us how it had been done. In return, from the top platform we pointed out everything we knew about the battle.

But who can know nowadays exactly where and how it took place? According to the manuscripts, the Mongol-Tartar cavalry cut into our infantry regiments, decimated them, and drove them back towards the crossings over the Don, thus turning the Don from a protective moat against Oleg into a possible death trap. If the worst had happened, Dmitry would have been called "Donskoi" for the opposite reason. But he had taken everything into careful account and stood his ground, something of which not every grand duke was capable. He left a boyar dressed in his, Dmitry's, attire, fighting beneath his flag, while he himself fought as an ordinary foot soldier, and he was once seen taking on four Tartars at once. But the grand-ducal standard was chopped down and Dmitry, his armour severely battered, barely managed to crawl to the wood, when the Mongols broke through the Russian lines and drove them back. But then another Dmitry, Volinsky-Bobrok, the governor of Moscow, who had been lying in ambush with his army, attacked the ferocious Tartars from the rear. He drove them back, harrying them as they galloped away. Then he wheeled sharply and forced them into the river Nepriadva. From that moment the Russians took heart: they re-formed and turned on the Tartars, rose from the ground and drove all the khans, the enemy commanders, even Mamai himself, forty versts away across the river Ptan as far as Krasivaya Mech. (But here one legend contradicts another. An old man from the neighbouring village of Ivanovka had his own version: the mist, he said, had not lifted, and in the mist Mamai, thinking a broad oak tree beside him was a Russian warrior, took fright— "Ah, mighty is the Christian God!"—and so fled.)

Afterwards the Russians cleared the field of battle and buried the dead: it took them eight days.

"There's one they didn't pick up—they left him behind!" the cheerful fitter from Novomoskovsk said accusingly.

We turned around and could not help but burst out laughing. Yes!—one fallen warrior was lying there this very day, not far from the monument, face down on mother earth—his native land. His bold head had dropped to the ground and his valiant limbs were spread-eagled; he was without his shield or sword and, in place of his helmet, wore a threadbare cap, and near his hand lay a sack. (All the same, he was careful not to crush the edge of his jacket with the pouch in it, where he kept the Comments Book; he had pulled it out from underneath his stomach and it lay on the grass beside him.) Perhaps he was just lying there in a drunken stupor, but if he was sleeping or thinking, then the way he was sprawled across the ground was very touching. He went perfectly with the field. They should cast an iron figure like that and place it here.

However, for all his height, Zakhar was too skinny to be a warrior.

"He doesn't want to work on the kolkhoz, so he found himself a soft government job where he can get a suntan," one of the lads growled.

What we disliked most of all was the way Zakhar flew at all the new arrivals, especially those who looked as if they might cause him trouble. During the day a few more people arrived; when he heard their cars he would get up, shake himself, and pounce on them with threats, as if they, not he, were responsible for the monument. Before they had time to be annoyed,

115

Zakhar himself would give vent to violent indignation about the desolation of the place. It seemed incredible that he could harbour such passion.

"Don't you think it's a disgrace?" he said, waving his arms aggressively, to four people who got out of a Zaporozhetz car. "I'll bide my time, then I'll walk right through the regional department of culture." (With those long legs he could easily have done it.) "I'll take leave and I'll go to Moscow, right to Furtseva, the Minister of Culture herself. I'll tell her everything."

Then, as soon as he noticed that the visitors were intimidated and were not standing up to him, he picked up his sack with an air of importance, as an official picks up his briefcase, and went off to have a smoke and a nap.

Wandering here and there, we met Zakhar several times during the day. We noticed that when he walked he limped in one leg, and we asked him what had caused this.

He replied proudly: "It's a souvenir from the war!"

Again we did not believe him: he was just a practised liar.

We had drunk our water bottles dry, so we went up to Zakhar and asked him where we could get some water. Wa-ater? The whole trouble was, he explained, that there was no well here and they wouldn't allocate any money to dig one. The only source of drinking water in the whole field was the puddles. The well was in the village.

After that, he no longer bothered to get up to talk to us, as if we were old friends.

When we complained about the inscriptions having been hacked away or scratched over, Zakhar retorted: "Have a look and see if you can read any of the dates. If you find any new damage, then you can blame me. All this vandalism was done before my time; they don't dare try it when I'm around! Well, perhaps some scoundrel hid in the church and then scribbled on the walls—I've only got one pair of legs, you know!"

The church, dedicated to St. Sergei of Radonezh, who united the Russian forces and brought them to battle and soon afterwards effected the reconciliation between Dmitry Donskoi and Oleg of Ryazan, was a sturdy fortress-like building with tightly interlocking limbs: the truncated pyramid of the nave, a cloister surmounted by a watchtower, and two round castellated towers. There were a few windows like loopholes.

Inside it, everything had been stripped and there wasn't even a floor—you walked over sand. We asked Zakhar about it.

"Ha, ha, ha! It was all pinched!" He gloated over us. "It was during the war. Our people in Kulikovo tore up all the slabs from the floors and paved their yards, so they wouldn't have to walk in the muck. I made a list of who took the slabs . . . Then the war ended, but they still went on pinching the stuff. Even before that, our troops had used all the ikon screens to put round the edges of dugouts and for heating their stoves."

As the hours passed and he got used to us, Zakhar was no longer embarrassed to delve into his sack in front of us, and we gradually found out exactly what was inside it. It contained empty bottles (twelve kopecks) and jam jars (five kopecks) left behind by visitors—he picked them up in the bushes after their picnics—and also a full bottle of water, because he had no other access to drinking water during the day. He carried two loaves of rye bread, which he broke bits off of now and again and chewed for his frugal meals.

"People come here in crowds all day long. I don't have any time to go off to the village for a meal."

On some days he probably carried a precious half bottle of vodka in there or some canned fish; then he would clutch the sack tightly, afraid to leave it anywhere. That day, when the sun had already begun to set, a friend on a motorbike came to see him; they sat in the bushes for an hour and a half. Then the friend went away and Zakhar came back without his sack. He talked rather more loudly, waved his arms more vigorously, and, noticing that I was writing something, warned us: "I'm in charge here, let me tell you! In '57 they decided to put a building up here. See those posts over there, planted round the monument? They've been here since then. They were cast in Tula. They were supposed to join up the posts with chains, but the

117

chains never came. So they gave me this job and they pay me for it. Without me, the whole place would be in ruins!"

"How much do you get paid, Zakhar Dmitrich?"

After a sign like a blacksmith's bellows, he was speechless for a moment. He mumbled something, then said quietly: "Twenty-seven roubles."

"What? The minimum's thirty."

"Well, maybe it is ... And I don't get any days off, either. Morning to dusk I'm on the job without a break, and I even have to come back late at night too."

What an incorrigible old liar he is, we thought.

"Why do you have to be here at night?"

"Why d'you think?" he said in an offended voice. "How can I leave the place at night? Someone's got to watch it all the time. If a car comes, I have to make a note of its number."

"Why the number,"

"Well, they won't let me have a gun. They say I might shoot the visitors. The only authority I've got is to take their number. And supposing they do some damage?"

"What do you do with the number afterwards?"

"Nothing. I just keep it ... Now they've built a house for tourists, have you seen it? I have to guard that too."

We had, of course, seen the house. Single-story, with several rooms, it was near completion but was still kept locked. The windows had been put in, and several were already broken; the floors were laid, but the plastering was not yet finished.

"Will you let us stay the night there?" (Towards sunset, it had begun to get cold; it was going to be a bitter night.)

"In the tourist house? No, it's impossible."

"Then who's it for?"

"No, it can't be done. Anyway, I haven't got the keys. So you needn't bother to ask. You can sleep in my shed."

His low shed with its sloping roof was designed for a half a dozen sheep. Bending down, we peered inside. Broken, trampled straw was scattered around; on the floor there was a cooking pot with some leftovers in it, a few more empty bottles, and a desiccated piece of bread. However, there was room for our bikes, and we could lie down and still leave enough space for Zakhar to stretch out.

He made use of our stay to take some time off.

"I'm off to Kulikovo to have supper at home. Grab a bite of something hot. Leave the door on the hook."

"Knock when you want to come in," we said, laughingly.

"O.K."

Zakhar-the-Pouch turned back the other flap of his miraculous jacket, to reveal two loops sewn into it. Out of his inexhaustible sack he drew an axe with a shortened handle and placed it firmly in the loops.

"Well," he said gloomily, "that's all I have for protection. They won't allow me anything else."

He said this in a tone of the deepest doom, as if he were expecting a horde of infidels to gallop up one of these nights and overthrow the monument, and he would have to face them alone with his little hatchet. We even shuddered at his voice as we sat there in the half light. Perhaps he wasn't a buffoon at all? Perhaps he really believed that if he didn't stand guard every night the battlefield and the monument were doomed?

Weakened by drink and a day of noisy activity, stooping and barely managing to hobble, Zakhar went off to his village and we laughed at him once more.

As had been our wish, we were left alone on Kulikovo Field. Night set in, with a full moon. The tower of the monument and the fortress-like church were silhouetted against it like great black screens. The distant lights of Kulikovka and Ivanovka competed faintly with the light of the moon. Not one aeroplane flew overhead; no motorcar rumbled by, no train rattled past in the distance. By moonlight the pattern of the nearby fields was no longer visible. Earth, grass, and moonlit solitude were as they had been in 1380. The centuries stood still, and as we wandered over the field we could evoke the whole scene—the campfires and the troops of dark horses. From the river Nepriadva came the sound of swans, just as Blok had described.

We wanted to understand the battle of Kulikovo in its entirety, grasp its inevitability, ignore the infuriating ambiguities of the chronicles: nothing had been as simple or as straightforward as it seemed; history had repeated itself after a long time-lag, and when it did, the result was disastrous. After the victory, the warriors of Russia faded away. Tokhtamysh immediately replaced Mamai, and two years after Kulikovo, he crushed the power of Muscovy; Dmitry Donskoi fled to Kostroma, while Tokhtamysh again destroyed both Ryazan and Moscow, took the Kremlin by ruse, plundered it, set it afire, chopped off heads, and dragged his prisoners back in chains to the Golden Horde, the Tartar capital.

Centuries pass and the devious path of history is simplified for the distant spectator until it looks as straight as a road drawn by a cartographer.

The night turned bitterly cold, but we shut ourselves in the shed and slept soundly right through it. We had decided to leave early in the morning. It was hardly light when we pushed our bicycles out and, with chattering teeth, started to load up.

The grass was white with hoarfrost; wisps of fog stretched from the hollow in which Kulikovka village lay and across the fields, dotted with haycocks. Just as we emerged from the shed to mount our bicycles and leave, we heard a loud, ferocious bark coming from one of the haycocks, and a shaggy grey dog ran out and made straight for us. As it bounded out, the haycock collapsed behind it; wakened by the barking, a tall figure arose from beneath it, called for the dog, and began to shake off the straw. It was already light enough for us to recognise him as our Zakhar-the-Pouch, still wearing his curious short-sleeved overcoat.

He had spent the night in the haycock, in the bone-chilling cold. Why? Was it anxiety or was it devotion to the place that had made him do it?

Immediately our previous attitude of amused condescension vanished. Rising out of the haycock on that frosty morning, he was no longer the ridiculous Keeper but rather the Spirit of the Field, a kind of guardian angel who never left the place.

He came towards us, still shaking himself and rubbing his hands together, and with his cap pushed back on his head, he seemed like a dear old friend.

"Why didn't you knock, Zakhar Dmitrich?"

"I didn't want to disturb you." He shrugged his shoulders and yawned. He was covered all over in straw and fluff. As he unbuttoned his coat to shake himself, we caught sight of both the Comments Book and his sole legal weapon, the hatchet, in their respective places.

The grey dog by his side was baring its teeth.

We said goodbye warmly and were already pedalling off as he stood there with his long arm raised, calling out: "Don't worry! I'll see to it! I'll go right to Furtseva! To Furtseva herself!"

That was two years ago. Perhaps the place is tidier now and better cared for. I have been a bit slow about writing this, but I haven't forgotten the Field of Kulikovo, or its Keeper, its red-haired tutelary spirit.

And let it be said that we Russians would be very foolish to neglect that place.

The Right Hand

When I arrived in Tashkent that winter I was practically a corpse. I came there expecting to die.

But I was given another lease of life.

A month passed, then another and a third. Outside, the vivid Tashkent spring unfolded and advanced into summer; it was already very warm and lush greenery was everywhere when I started to venture out of doors on my shaky legs.

I still did not dare to admit to myself that I was getting better; in my wildest dreams I still measured my extra span of life not in years but in months. I would tread slowly along the gravel and asphalt paths in the park which was laid out between the blocks of the clinic. I would often have to sit down for a rest and sometimes, when overcome with nausea, I had to lie down with my head as low as possible.

I was like the sick people all around me, and yet I was different: I had fewer rights than they had and was forced to be more silent. People came to visit them, relatives wept for them, and their one concern, their one aim in life was to get well again. But if I recovered, it would be almost pointless: I was thirty-five years of age and yet in that spring I had no one I could call my own in the whole world. I did not even own a passport, and if I were to recover, I should have to leave this green, abundant land and go back to my desert where I had been exiled "in perpetuity." There I was under open surveillance, reported on every fortnight, and for a long time the local police headquarters had not even allowed me, a dying man, to go away for treatment.

I could not talk about all this to the free patients around me; had I done so, they would not have understood. On the other hand, I had ten years of long and careful reflection behind me and already knew the truth of the saying that the true savour of life is not to be gained by big things but from little ones—things like my ability to shuffle along hesitantly on my weakened legs; my cautious breathing, to avoid stabbing pains in the chest; and a single potato, undamaged by the frost, that I fished out of my soup.

So for me this spring was the most painful and the loveliest of my life.

I was surrounded by things I had either forgotten or had never seen, so everything interested me—even the ice-cream cart, the roadsweeper with his hose, the women selling bunches of long radishes, and especially the foal who had strayed through a gap in the wall onto the grass.

With every passing day I dared to wander farther away from the clinic, through the park, which must have been laid out at the end of the last century, when these good, sturdy buildings, with their ornamental brickwork at the corners, were also put up. From the magnificent sunrise, throughout the long southern day, and deep into the electric-yellow evening, the park was alive with movement. The healthy people would scurry around while the sick would make their unhurried promenade.

At the point where several avenues merged into the one leading to the main gates, there stood a large white alabaster Stalin, grinning sarcastically behind his stone whiskers. Other, smaller statues were spaced out evenly along the path leading to the gates.

Then there was a stationer's kiosk. It sold plastic pencils and tempting notebooks. But I decided it was better to do without them, not merely because I had to keep a strict watch on my spending but also because previous notebooks of mine had fallen into the wrong hands.

A fruit stall and a teahouse were situated right by the gates. We patients in our striped pyjamas were not allowed into the teahouse, but you could watch what was going on through the openwork fence. I had never in my life seen a real teahouse, with those individual pots of green or black tea for each person. The teahouse had a European section with small tables, and an Uzbek section with a large dais. The people at the tables ate and drank quickly, left a small payment in an empty bowl, and departed. But on the dais people sat or sprawled around for hours on end, some of them even for days. On sackcloth mats beneath a rush awning which had been put up at the beginning of the hot weather, they consumed pot after pot of tea while playing dice, as if the whole long day was completely free of cares.

The fruit stall did sell to the patients, but the few kopecks I had earned in exile shied away from the prices. I stared hard at the piles of dried apricots, raisins, and fresh cherries, then walked away.

Farther on there was a high wall; the patients were not allowed beyond the gates. Two or three times a day the strains of a band playing funeral marches would waft over this wall into the hospital grounds.

The city had a million inhabitants, but the cemetery was right next door to us. We could hear the slow funeral processions for about ten minutes, until they had passed the grounds. The sound of the drum produced an odd result: its rhythm had no effect on the crowd of mourners, whose jerky movements were always slightly faster than the beat; the healthy bystanders would hardly stop to look around before hurrying off again to wherever they had to go (and they all knew exactly where they had to go); but the patients would stop when they heard these marches, poke their heads out of the windows of the wards, and listen for a long time.

The clearer it grew that I was recovering from the disease, and the more certain I became that I would remain alive, the more wistfully I looked around: I was already sorry to be leaving all this.

In the medical students' sports ground, white figures were hitting white tennis balls to each other. All my life I had wanted to play tennis, but I had never had the chance. Beneath its steep bank, the muddy yellow water of the river Salar was gurgling furiously. Wide-branching oak trees grew in the park, shady maples and delicate Japanese acacias. The octagonal fountain was

124

throwing up fresh, slender streams of silver as high as they could reach. And what grass on the lawns!— succulent and mercifully disregarded, unlike the grass in the prison camps, which the authorities ordered to be weeded out like an enemy, while in my place of exile grass could not grow at all. Just to lie in it face downwards, peacefully breathing in its herbal fragrance and its sun-warmed exhalation, was a taste of paradise.

I was not the only one lying there in the grass. Dotted about were students from the Medical Institute, slogging away at their bulky textbooks. Some of them, however, were absorbed in reading short stories which were not part of the examination syllabus, while others, the athletic ones, emerged from the changing rooms swinging their sports hold-alls. In the evening girls, indistinct and therefore three times more attractive, would walk round the fountain in creased or well-ironed frocks, crunching the gravel of the paths under their feet.

My heart was bursting with pity for someone: it might have been for myself and my contemporaries, frozen to death near Demiansk, burnt alive in Auschwitz, harried to exhaustion in Djezkazgan, or dying in the wastes of Siberia, because these girls would never belong to us. Or it might have been for these girls, because of the things I could never tell them and which they would never find out.

The whole day long, women—women, women!— would flow along the gravel and asphalt paths, young doctors, nurses, laboratory assistants, clerks, housekeepers, dispensers, and relatives visiting patients. They would pass me by in their austere white coats and their bright southern dresses, often semi-transparent, the richer ones in bright blues and pinks slowly twirling fashionable bamboo-handled Chinese parasols over their heads. Each one, as she flashed past, momentarily made up a complete plot for a novel: her past, the (nonexistent) chance of my getting to know her.

I was a pitiful wreck. My emaciated face bore the stamp of what I had been through—the wrinkles caused by the enforced gloom of camp life, the ashen colour of death on my leathery skin, the more recent poisoning caused by a venomous disease and toxic medicines which had added a greenish tinge to my cheeks. My back was hunched from the defensive habit of submission and self-effacement. My clown-like striped jacket barely reached as far as my stomach, my striped trousers ended above my ankles, and the edges of my footcloths, brown from long wear, were hanging out of the canvas uppers of my blunt-toed prison-camp boots.

Not one of these women would have dared to walk beside me. But I could not see myself, and the world impinged upon my consciousness through eyes that were as sensitive as theirs.

One day, towards evening, I was standing by the main gates, looking around me at the usual stream of people rushing past; parasols bobbed along, silk dresses and tussore trousers with bright sashes, embroidered shirts and skullcaps flickered by. There was a buzz of voices. People were selling fruit; behind the fence, others were drinking tea and throwing dice. At the same time, leaning against the fence, a small, ungainly man who looked like a beggar was addressing the crowd from time to time in a voice gasping for breath: "Comrades ... Comrades ..."

The busy, gaily-coloured crowd was not listening to him. I went up to him. "What's the matter, brother?"

The man had an enormous belly, larger than a pregnant woman's, which hung down like a sack. It had burst through his dirty khaki tunic and trousers. His shoes, their soles worn away, were clumsy and dusty. His thick, unbuttoned overcoat with its soiled collar and frayed cuffs, unsuitable for this weather, weighed down his shoulders. On his head he wore an ancient, torn peaked cap, fit for a garden scarecrow. His eyes, swollen with dropsy, were glazed.

With great effort he raised one clenched hand, and I pulled a sweaty, crumpled piece of paper out of it. It was an application from citizen Bobrov, written in an angular hand with a pen that had scratched the paper, requesting admission to hospital; slanting across the application were two stamps, one in blue ink and one in red. The one in blue ink was from the Town Health

Committee giving reasoned grounds for its refusal to admit him. The one in red ink, however, ordered the clinic of the Medical Institute to accept the man as an in-patient. The blue ink bore yesterday's date; the red ink—today's.

"Look," I explained to him loudly, as if he were deaf. "You've got to go to Reception, in Ward One. So just go straight on past these . . . statues . . ."

But then I noticed that his strength had abandoned him at the very moment that he reached the goal of his journey; not only was he incapable of asking any more questions or dragging his feet over the smooth asphalt path; he was even too weak to carry his shabby bag, which weighed no more than three or four pounds. So I made up my mind and said: "All right, old fellow, I'll take you. Let's go. Give me your bag."

He understood. He handed me his bag with relief, leaned on my proffered arm, and moved forward by dragging his shoes along the asphalt path, hardly lifting his feet off the ground. I guided him by his elbow, holding on to his coat, which was reddish-brown from the dust. His swollen stomach seemed to pull the old man forward and downwards. He frequently heaved a deep sigh.

Thus we advanced, two dishevelled figures, along the same avenue where, in my thoughts, I had linked arms with the most beautiful girls in Tashkent. For a long time we slowly dragged ourselves past the alabaster statues.

At last we turned off. Beside our path stood a bench with a back rest. My companion asked to sit down for a while. I too could feel an attack of nausea coming on, as I had been standing too long. We sat down. From here we could see the fountain.

While we were still walking along, the old man had said a few things to me, and now that he had recovered his breath, he resumed his story. He had to get to the Urals, and the residence permit in his passport was for the Urals, which was the whole trouble. He had been taken ill somewhere near Takhia-Tashem (where, I remember, they had started building a canal). At Urgench they had kept him in hospital for a month, drained the water from his stomach and legs, made him worse, and then discharged him. He had interrupted his journey at Chardzhou and then at Ursatevskaya, but wherever he went for treatment he was turned away; instead, they had sent him on to the Urals, because that was his official place of residence. He had felt too weak to go there by train, and anyway he did not have enough money for the ticket. So two days ago he had managed to get to Tashkent in the hope of being admitted to hospital.

I did not ask what he was doing down south or what had brought him here. His illness was, according to his medical certificates, "advanced," but a glance at the man was enough to tell you that it was terminal. I had seen a lot of patients and I could tell that he no longer had the will to live. He had lost control of his lips, his speech was indistinct, and his eyes had a dull lifelessness about them.

Even his cap was a burden to him. With great difficulty he pulled it off his head, down onto his knees. He struggled to raise his arm again and wiped the sweat off his forehead with his dirty sleeve. The top of his head was bald, though it was ringed by some sparse, untidy hair, still pale red under its coating of dust. It was not old age that had reduced him to this state but disease.

Folds of superfluous skin hung from his neck, which had grown pitifully thin, like a chicken's, and his triangular Adam's apple protruded visibly. I wondered how he held his head up, and we had scarcely sat down when it lolled forward onto his chest, supported by his chin.

There he collapsed, with his cap on his knees and his eyes closed. He seemed to have forgotten that we had only sat down for a moment to recover our breath and that he had to go on to Reception.

Before our eyes, the almost noiseless jet of the fountain was casting its silver thread upwards. Beyond it, two girls passed, side by side. I watched them walk away. One was wearing an orange skirt, the other a maroon one. I found both of them extremely attractive.

My neighbour sighed audibly, rolled his head across his chest, and, raising his yellowish-grey lashes, squinted up at me. "Do you happen to have a cigarette, comrade?"

"You can forget that idea, old fellow," I barked at him. "You and I haven't got a hope unless we give up smoking. Take a look at yourself in a mirror. A cigarette! Really!" (I had only just succeeded in breaking myself of the habit a month before.)

Panting for breath, he again raised his eyes and looked at me from underneath his yellow lashes, rather like a dog. "All the same, comrade, give us three roubles."

I thought about whether to give them to him or not. After all, I was still a prisoner, while he was a free man. For all the years I had worked in prison camps I had been paid nothing. And when they did start to pay me they took all of it back in deductions: for the escort, for lighting the perimeter, for police dogs, for the officers, for the prison stew.

I took my oilskin purse out of the small breast pocket of my clown's jacket and inspected the notes in it. I sighed, then handed the old man a three-rouble note.

"Thanks," he said hoarsely. Struggling to hold his arm out, he took the note and put it in his pocket; at once his arm flopped down and slapped against his knee. His chin sagged forward until his head was again resting on his chest.

We fell silent. A woman passed by, then two more girl students. I found all three of them very attractive. It had been years since I had heard girls' voices or the tapping of their stiletto heels.

"You're lucky they gave you an admission form, otherwise you might have had to hang around here for a week or so. It often happens. Lots of people have to put up with it."

He pulled his chin away from his chest and turned towards me. In his eyes a spark of sense glinted, his voice quivered, and he spoke more distinctly: "They're putting me in here, son, because I'm a deserving case. I'm a veteran of the Revolution. Sergey Mironovich Kirov personally shook me by the hand during the fighting at Tsaritsyn. I should be getting a special pension."

A slight movement of his cheeks and lips—the shadow of a proud smile—registered on his unshaven face.

I examined his rags, then looked him over once more. "Why don't you get it, then?"

"That's life," he sighed. "Now they don't even acknowledge my existence. Some of the records were burnt, others were lost. And I can't get any witnesses. Sergey Mironovich was murdered . . . It's all my fault. I didn't keep my documents . . . I've just one thing here . . ."

He lifted his right hand and fumbled in his pocket with his round, swollen finger joints, but here his burst of activity expired, and he again dropped his arm and his head and sat stock-still.

The sun was already sinking behind the hospital buildings and we would have to hurry to Reception (it was still a hundred paces away). In my experience, getting admitted to hospital is always beset with difficulties.

I took the old man by the shoulder. "Wake up, old fellow. Look, see that door over there? See it? I'm going over there to start persuading them. Come on your own if you can, but if not, wait for me. I'll take your bag."

He nodded as if he understood.

Reception was part of a large, shabby hall, divided off by rough partitions; at one time there had been a communal bathroom, a dressing room, and a hairdresser's here. In the daytime it was always crowded with patients whiling away the long hours until they would be admitted, but now, to my surprise, there was not a soul there. I knocked at the plywood hatch, which was closed. A very young nurse with a snub nose opened it; her lips were painted not red but a thick violet.

"What do you want?" She was sitting at a table reading a spy comic, as far as I could see.

She had very lively eyes.

I gave her the application with the two stamps on it

and explained: "He can hardly walk. I've just brought him in."

"How dare you bring anyone in!" she cried sharply, without even looking at the piece of paper. "Don't you know the routine? We only admit patients at nine a.m.!"

She was the one who did not know the "routine." I stuck my head through the hatch and as much of my arm as I could manage, so that she could not slam it shut on me. Twisting my lower lip and pulling a face like a gorilla, I hissed in a menacing voice: "Listen, woman. And get this into your head—I'm not going to be bossed about by you!"

She took fright, moved her chair farther back into her little room, and said: "There's no admission, citizen. Only at nine a.m."

"Look . . . read this bit of paper!" I growled at her in my nastiest voice.

She read it.

"Well, so what? The normal routine applies. And there may not be any places tomorrow. There weren't any this morning."

She announced that there had been no places that morning with a sort of satisfaction, as if the remark would puncture me.

"But the man's just passing through, don't you see? He's got nowhere to go."

As I backed out of the hatch and stopped talking in my harsh prison-camp rasp, her face took on its former expression of cheerful callousness. "They're all passing through. Where can we put them? They have to wait. He'll have to find a room somewhere."

"But just come and have a look. You'll see the condition he's in."

"Whatever next? Do you expect me to go round collecting patients? I'm not an orderly, you know!"

And she proudly twitched her snub nose. Her reply was as snappy and as automatic as clockwork.

"Then what the hell are you doing sitting here?" I banged on the plywood wall with my fist, and a thin layer of whitewash scattered like pollen. "Lock the place up!"

"No one asked for your opinion, you lout!" She exploded with anger, jumped up, ran round, and appeared out of the narrow corridor. "Who do you think you are, anyway? Don't you teach me how to do my job! The ambulance'll bring him in."

Except for her crude violet lips and her matching nail varnish, she would not have been at all bad-looking. Her nose was her attractive feature, and she made great play with her eyebrows. Because it was so stuffy, she had undone the top buttons of her white coat and I could see her nice little pink scarf and Komsomol badge.

"What? If he hadn't come here by himself but had been picked up in the street by an ambulance, you would have admitted him? Is that your rule?"

She stared haughtily at my absurd figure and I stared back at her. I had completely forgotten that my footcloths were poking out of my boots. She snorted, looked at me coldly, and continued: "Yes, *patient*. That *is* the rule."

And she went back behind the partition.

I heard a rustling sound behind me. I looked around. My companion was already standing there. He had heard and understood everything. Clutching onto the wall and hauling himself towards the large bench put there for visitors, he was scarcely able to wave his right hand, which was clutching a tattered piece of paper.

"Here you are," he appealed to me in a faint voice. ". . . Here you are, show her this . . . let her . . . here . . ."

I managed to support him and lowered him onto the bench. With helpless fingers he tried to pull his only certificate out of his wallet but just could not manage it.

I took the top piece of paper from him, which was stuck down along its folds because it was falling apart, and opened it. On it were typed, in violet ink, lines with the letters dancing up and down over the creases:

WORKERS OF THE WORLD UNITE!
This certificate is presented to Comrade Bobrov N.K. for active service in 1921 in the distinguished

"World Revolution" Special Detachment of_____
Province for personally eliminating large numbers of
counterrevolutionary terrorists.

>   Signed: Commissar_____

A pale violet seal was attached to it.

Scratching my chest, I asked him quietly: "What's
this 'Special Detachment'? What did it do?"

"Aha," he replied, scarcely able to keep his eyes
open. "Show it to her."

I noticed his hand, his right hand—so small, with its
brown, swollen veins and its round, puffed joints, practically incapable of pulling a certificate out of his wallet. And I remembered the way horsemen used to strike
down men on foot with a single, sweeping backhand
stroke.

Strange . . . That right hand had once swung a sabre
in a full arc and chopped off heads, necks, and shoulders. And now it could not even hold a scrap of
paper . . .

I went up to the plywood hatch and again tried to
persuade her to listen. The registrar did not raise her
head but continued reading her comic. On the open
page I saw a handsome man in uniform leaping onto a
windowsill with a pistol.

I quietly placed the torn certificate on top of her
book and turned away. I kept rubbing my chest to
avoid being sick as I walked towards the door. I had to
lie down as quickly as possible.

"What have you put this paper here for? Take it
away!" the girl shot at me through the hatch as I
walked away.

The veteran shrank into the bench. His head and
even his shoulders seemed to sink into his torso. His
helpless fingers dangled, outspread. His unbuttoned
coat hung down, his bulbous, unbelievably swollen belly sagging into the fold of his thighs.

An Incident at
Krechetovka Station

"Hello, is that the dispatcher's office?"

"Uh-huh."

"Who is that? Dyachikhin?"

"Uh-huh."

"Cut out the uh-huh. I want Dyachikhin."

"Shunt the tankers from number 7 to number 3, go on. Dyachikhin speaking."

"This is Lieutenant Zotov, duty officer. Listen, what the hell are you up to? Why haven't you done anything about dispatching the Lipetsk train, number six seventy ... six seventy what, Valya?"

"Eight."

"Six seventy-eight."

"Got nothing to pull it with."

"What do you mean—nothing?"

"There's no engine, that's what. That you, Varnakov? Varnakov, over there on number 6 there are four coal trucks. Can you see? Put them with the tankers."

"Look here, what do you mean no engine when I can see six of them standing in a row outside?"

"They're condemned ones."

"Condemned?"

"Condemned engines. From the dump. They're being evacuated."

"All right, but you've got two shunting engines working."

"Comrade lieutenant, they've got *three* shunters—I've seen them."

"The escort sergeant is standing here beside me, and he's just told me you have three. Give us one."

"I can't do that."

"What do you mean—can't? Do you realise how

important this train is? It mustn't be delayed for a second. And you . . ."

"Put them up the hump."

". . . and you've been holding it up for nearly twelve hours."

"Never."

"Are you running a kindergarten or a dispatcher's office? Why is it I hear babies crying?"

"I can't help it, they've all pushed in. Comrades, how many times do I have to tell you? Please clear the room. I can't get any of you on the train. I've got army supplies waiting . . ."

"There's blood plasma on this train! For a military hospital! Don't you understand?"

"Sure I understand. Hello, Varnakov? Now uncouple, go to the water column, and get the other ten."

"Look here, if you don't get that train off in the next half hour, I'll report you to my superiors. This is serious. You'll answer for it."

"Vasil Vasilich, give me the receiver, let me speak to him."

"I'm putting the military dispatcher on the line."

"Nikolay Petrovich? Podshebyakina speaking. Listen, what's going on at the depot? One engine has already been refuelled."

"All right, comrade sergeant, go and wait in the escort van and if they still haven't got you an engine in forty minutes—let's say by half past six—come and report to me."

"Very good, sir. Permission to carry on, sir?"

"Fall out, sergeant."

The escort sergeant turned smartly about, bringing his hand sharply down from the salute as he left the room.

Lieutenant Zotov straightened the glasses which gave a hard look to his gentle features, glanced at Podshebyakina the dispatcher, a young girl in railway uniform with a mass of blond curls, talking into the mouthpiece of an old-fashioned telephone, and left her small office to go into his own equally small one, which had no other door.

The station commandant's office was a corner room

on the ground floor, and above it, exactly over that corner, the drainpipe was broken. As the thick stream of water poured noisily down the wall, gusts of wind blew and sprayed it alternately past the left-hand window onto the platform and past the right-hand window into a narrow little passageway. After the bright frosty October days when the whole station had been covered with hoarfrost every morning, it had lately turned wet and since the previous day it had rained so hard and so steadily that one couldn't help wondering just how the sky could hold so much water.

Still, the rain had at least tidied things up a bit: gone was that untidy rabble of civilians permanently swarming all over the platforms and the tracks, spoiling the look of the station and hampering the work. They had all taken shelter, so there was no one crawling under the trucks on all fours or clambering up the steps at the coach ends, there were no more local people jostling around with buckets of boiled potatoes, no more vendors wandering between the trains with their arms and shoulders draped with underwear, dresses, and sweaters as though the place was a second-hand clothes' market ... (Lieutenant Zotov found this trade very embarrassing; it somehow ought not to be allowed but couldn't be stopped, because the authorities had not released any goods for the evacuees to buy.)

The only ones not driven away by the rain were the people on duty. Out of the window a guard could be seen standing on an open truck with shrouded cargo. The rain streamed down him as he stood there without even trying to shake it off. A shunting engine was pulling tankers on track 3, and a pointsman wearing a tarpaulin cape with a hood was waving it on with the handle of his flag. There, too, was the short dark figure of the wagon inspector passing down the train on track 2 and diving under each carriage. Otherwise, there was only the slanting, cutting rain. Driven by a cold, persistent wind, it beat against the roofs and sides of goods wagons and the fronts of locomotives; it lashed the rusty iron ribs, scorched and twisted, of a score of skeleton carriages (their bodies had been burned in an air raid somewhere or other, but the chassis were still intact and were now being taken to the rear). The rain poured on the troop of four field guns standing uncovered on flatcars. Merging with the approaching dusk, the rain drew a grey shroud over the first green disk of the signal arm and over the occasional showers of crimson sparks that flew out of the chimneys of the heated carriages. The asphalt of platform 1 was entirely covered by a sheet of glassy, bubbling water which did not have time to drain away; the rails still glistened wetly in gathering darkness; and quivering puddles, unable to soak away, lay on the dark brown ballast of the railway track.

None of this made a sound save for the dull rumble of the ground and the faint notes of the pointsman's bugle. (Engine whistles had been forbidden since the first day of the war.)

Only rain could be heard booming in the shattered drainpipe.

Outside the other window, in the pathway alongside the warehouse fence, stood a young oak. Buffeted and drenched, it had still held on to a last few brown leaves, but today even these had been blown off.

There was no time to stand and gape. He had to roll down the paper blackout blinds at the windows, put the light on, and get down to work. There was a lot to be done before the next shift came on at 9 p.m.

Zotov did not let down the blinds, but he took off his uniform cap with the green band which he always wore when on duty, even indoors. He took off his glasses and slowly rubbed his eyes with his fingers, exhausted with the strain of copying all those encoded train numbers from one pencilled list to another. But it was not tiredness that crept over him on that prematurely dark afternoon. It was a gnawing sense of despair.

The despair was not even about his wife, left behind with her unborn child far away in Byelorussia under German occupation; it was not about his lost past, because as yet Zotov had no past; nor was it about his lost possessions, because he had none and did not want ever to have any.

It was the totally bewildering way the war was going that made Zotov so miserable that he felt he wanted to howl out loud. From the official news bulletins it was impossible to discover where the front line was; it was not even clear who held Kaluga or who held Kharkov. But it was common knowledge among the railwaymen that no more trains were being sent through the junction to Tula and that the farthest you could get beyond Yelets was Verkhovie. Every now and then, German bombers would break through as far as the Ryazan-Voronezh railway and drop a few bombs, some of them on Krechetovka. And ten days ago a couple of crazy German motorcyclists had turned up from nowhere and raced into Krechetovka, firing their machine-pistols as they went. One was killed on the spot, the other got away, but the shooting had started a panic in the station and the head of a special unit in charge of demolition in the event of evacuation had managed to blow up the water column with the explosives already placed there. So they had called in a repair train, which had been working there for three days.

However, Krechetovka did not matter—the point was, why was the war going like this? Where was the revolution all over Europe, why weren't our troops advancing virtually unscathed against every possible coalition of aggressors? Instead, there was this mess. And how much longer would it last? "How much longer?" This was the only thought in Zotov's head—by day, whatever he was doing, or at night in bed. And when he was not on duty but spent the night in his billet, he still woke up at six in the morning to the chimes on the radio, desperate with the hope that today at last he would hear the resounding news of victory. But all that came out of the black cone of the loudspeaker were the same dreary bulletins about the Vyazma and Volokolamsk fronts. Anguish gripped his heart at the thought that Moscow might be surrendered. Zotov never spoke his thoughts aloud—to do so would be dangerous—and he was afraid even to say them to himself. Trying not to think about it, he thought about it all the time.

And yet this question, however depressing, was not the only one. To surrender Moscow was not the end of the world—Moscow fell to Napoleon, too. There was another burning question: what might happen afterwards? Suppose they reached the Urals?

Vasya Zotov considered it a crime that such cowardly thoughts should even run through his head. It was blasphemy, it was an insult to the omniscient, omnipotent Father and Teacher who was always there, who foresaw everything, who would do all that had to be done and would never let it happen.

But railwaymen used to come in from Moscow who had been there in the middle of October and told monstrous, impossible tales of factory directors on the run, of shops and banks being looted, and again Lieutenant Zotov's heart was clutched by unspoken torment.

Not long ago, on his way here, Zotov had spent two days in a reserve officers' camp. They had put on an evening's amateur entertainment during which a thin, pale-faced lieutenant with lanky hair read some poetry. It was his own, uncensored and sincere. At first Vasya didn't realise he had remembered any of it, but later some verses had floated up from his memory. And now, when walking around Krechetovka, or travelling by train to the regional headquarters or by cart to the village soviet where he was assigned to give basic military training to teenagers and old men, Zotov kept repeating these words as though they were his own:

> *"Our villages burn, our towns, our home . . .*
> *And the thought that lashes us into a stance:*
> *O when, O when will the moment come*
> *That we halt the German advance?"*

And then it went something like this:

> *"If Lenin's great cause should now be lost,*
> *What is there left for us to live for?"*

Since the very beginning of the war Zotov had felt no desire to be spared. His insignificant life meant something only if he could help the Revolution. But however much he begged to be sent to the front line, he was left mouldering as a rail-transport officer.

To be spared for his own sake seemed senseless. To remain alive for the sake of his wife or his unborn child—not even that seemed essential. But if the Germans were to get as far as Lake Baikal and Zotov, by some miracle, was still alive, he knew that he would flee on foot through Kyakhta to China, or India, or across the ocean—but only in order to join a re-formed army there and to return under arms to Russia and to Europe.

And so he stood there in the dusk, listening to the rain and blustering wind outside, and as he hunched his shoulders he repeated that lieutenant's poem.

The darker it became in the room, the brighter glowed the hot, cherry-red door of the stove, and a little shaft of diffused light came through the glass pane of the door leading into the next room, where the military dispatcher on duty had already turned her light on.

Although not subordinate to the duty R.T.O., she could not manage without him because she was not supposed to know either the contents or the destinations of military trains, only the wagon numbers. Old Frosya, whose job it was to record these numbers, came in now, noisily shaking the mud off her boots.

"God, what a downpour," she complained. "Still, it does seem to be letting up a bit."

"But you'll have to list the wagons on number 765 again, Frosya," said Valya Podshebyakina.

"All right, I'll do them again. Just let me fix my lamp."

The door was not thick and it was not firmly shut; Zotov could hear their conversation.

"It's a good thing I managed to get some coal," Frosya was saying. "I've nothing to worry about now, the kids'll last out on potatoes. But Dashka Melentyeva hasn't lifted all hers yet. She'll never do it now, in all this mud."

"Looks like frost. It's cold enough."

"It'll be an early winter. What with this war, and an early winter as well ... And how many potatoes have you lifted?"

Zotov sighed and started pulling down the blackout

blind, carefully pressing it against the window frame so that no light could escape through a crack.

Here was something he could not understand, and it made him feel hurt and even lonely. All these working people around him used to listen to the news bulletins as glumly as he did, and walked away from the loudspeakers with the same feeling of unspoken hurt. But Zotov saw a difference: those around him seemed to have something more to live for than the news from the front; they had their potatoes to lift, their cows to milk, their wood to saw, their windows to seal. They talked about these things most of the time and were much more preoccupied with them than with the news from the front.

Stupid woman—got her coal and now she's "got nothing to worry about"—not even Guderian's tanks?

The wind was shaking the little tree by the warehouse, and a pane in the window tinkled faintly. Zotov let down the last blind and switched on the light. And immediately the warm, well-swept, though bare room became cosy, somehow secure, and his thoughts about things became more cheerful.

Right under the light, in the middle of the room, stood the duty officer's desk. Behind it, next to the stove, was a safe, and by the window stood an ancient oak station settee designed to seat three. (Thick wooden letters carved in its back proclaimed the name of the railway line.) One could lie down for a nap on this couch at night, but the pressure of work seldom allowed it. There were also a couple of rough chairs. Between the windows hung a coloured portrait of Kaganovich in a railwayman's uniform. A map of the rail network had once hung there too, but the captain who was the station commandant had ordered it to be taken down, because outsiders came into the room and if there were an enemy among them he would need only a quick look to get his bearings and see where the lines led to.

"I've been trading," old Frosya was boasting next door. "A pair of silk stockings for half a dozen potato cakes. There may not be any more stockings until the end of the war. You tell your mom to wake up; tell her to make some potato cakes and take them down to the

141

trains. They'll grab the lot. Grun'ka Mostryukova got the funniest thing from them the other day—a woman's nightie, it was supposed to be, but with slits cut in it— guess where! . . . well, really! The women all came round to her house and watched her try it on, nearly died laughing, they did! . . . You can get soap from them too—and cheap. Soap is scarce now, you can't buy it. You tell your mom to wake up."

"Oh, I don't know, Frosya . . ."

"Don't you need stockings, then?"

"Of course I need stockings, badly, but it's a shame, somehow from evacuees . . ."

"The 'vacuees is just who you should take things from. They've got material, suits, soap, just like they were going to market. There's some there, you should see their greedy mugs, want a boiled chicken—nothing else will do. People've seen some of them with hundred-rouble notes, bundles of them, suitcases full. Anyone'd think they were taking a bank with them. Only it's not their money we want, they can keep that."

"What about the evacuees billeted on you, then?"

"My lot are different—haven't got a stitch to their name. No clothes, no shoes. They just got away from Kiev in what they stood in; it's a miracle they ever got here. Polinka got a job at the post office, the pay's miserable—and what can you do with it, anyway? I showed their grandma the cellar, opened it. 'Look,' I says, 'there you are, there's potatoes, there's pickled cabbage, help yourself, and I don't want anything for the room, either.' I always feel sorry for the poor, Valya dear, but the rich—no mercy for them."

Two telephones stood on Zotov's desk—one belonging to the office, an old wind-up one in a yellow wooden box, like the military dispatcher's; the other his own, a field telephone with a buzzer connected to the captain's room and the guardroom at the station ration store. The ration-store detachment was the only military force of the Krechetovka command. Although their main duty was to guard the food supplies, they cleaned and kept the fires in, and even now a bucketful of large shiny pieces of coal stood in front of the stove to be piled on.

The office telephone rang. Zotov, who had thrown

off the momentary depression he had felt in the twi-light, strode over and picked up the receiver, using his free hand to pull on his cap, and began to shout answers into the telephone. He always shouted when making long-distance calls, sometimes because the line was bad, but more often from force of habit.

Someone was ringing from Bogoyavlenskaya wanting to know exactly which traffic lists he had received and which he had not. These traffic lists were sent in code by telegraph from the next R.T.O.'s post down the line and showed the destinations of the trains. Only an hour ago Zotov had taken a few of these lists to the girl telegraphist and received some from her. It was his job quickly to sort out the incoming ones, to see which trains were to be grouped together and which stations they were to be sent on to. Then he had to instruct the railway military dispatcher which trucks to couple to-gether, and finally he had to make out and send off fresh traffic lists, keeping copies for himself, which he pinned together. Zotov put down the receiver, fell heavily into his chair, leaned shortsightedly over the desk, and was at once engrossed in his traffic lists.

But the noise from next door disturbed him slightly. A man had come in, stamping his boots, and flung down a sack full of iron on the floor. Frosya asked whether the rain was stopping. The man muttered something and then must have sat down.

Water was no longer cascading quite so noisily from the broken drainpipe, but the wind had freshened and was beating at the windows.

"What did you say, dad?" shouted Valya Podshe-byakina.

"I said it's freezing up," replied the old man, in a voice that was still vigorous.

"You can hear all right, can't you, Gavrila Niki-tich?" Old Frosya shouted too.

"I can hear all right," said the old man. "Only I get this clicking in my ear."

"Then how do you check the wheels, grandpa? You have to tap them, don't you?"

"I can tell by looking."

"You don't know him, Valya. He's from
143

Krechetovka, his name's Kordubailo. All the inspectors at every station around here learned their job from him. He retired ten years before the war. And now here he is back at work."

And old Frosya was off again. Zotov was just starting to get irritated by her chatter and was about to go and shut her up when the talk in the next room turned to yesterday's incident with a trainload of "returnees"— troops who had been surrounded, had capitulated to the Germans, and after being retaken by Soviet forces were being shipped off to detention camps. Zotov had heard about the incident from the other assistant R.T.O., who had been duty officer on the previous day and had had to take the appropriate action, since Krechetovka did not have its own military police detachment. Yesterday morning two trains had arrived at Krechetovka simultaneously. One, from Shchigry via Otrozhka, had been a thirty-car train of "returnees," and for all thirty trucks full of these desperate men there were only five NKVD security guards, who could naturally do nothing with them.

The second train had come from Rtishchevo, carrying flour. Some of the flour was in sealed trucks and some in sacks in open wagons. The returnees had sized up the situation, had stormed the open wagons, climbed up, slit open the sacks with their knives, filled their canteens with flour, used their tunics as sacks and filled them too. Two sentries of the escort guarding the flour train had been standing on the track, one at each end. The sentry at the front of the train, no more than a boy, had shouted at them several times to get off, but they had paid no attention to him and no one had come to his assistance from the guard's van. So he had lifted up his rifle, fired, and with that single shot had hit one of the returnees in the head and killed him right there on top of the flour sacks.

Zotov listened carefully to the conversation—they had got it all wrong, they didn't understand it at all. Unable to contain himself, he went in to explain. He stood at the open door and looked at them through his plain, round spectacles.

To the right, the slender Valya was sitting at her

144

deskful of papers and graphs with their coloured squares.

Under the window, which was covered with the standard blue blackout paper, ran a plain bench, on which Frosya was sitting. She was one of those tough, weather-beaten, middle-aged Russian women who are used to having things their own way both at home and at work. A wet, grey-green tarpaulin cape that she wore on duty hung stiffly on the wall; she was sitting in wet boots and a shabby civilian overcoat, mending the wick from a square hand lantern.

Stuck to the outer door was a little pink poster, of the kind seen everywhere around Krechetovka: "Beware of typhus!" The paper was a sickly pink, like typhoid rash, or like the scorched iron bones of the bombed trucks.

Old man Kordubailo sat on the floor leaning against a wall, near the stove but close enough to the door not to dirty the floor. His old leather bag with his heavy tools and his mittens, covered in diesel oil, were thrown on the floor so as not to block the way. The old man had obviously flopped down just as he was; he had not bothered to take off his coat or even shake off the rain, and his cape and boots had dripped puddles onto the floor. He had drawn up his legs and between them on the floor was an unlit lantern like Frosya's. Under his raincoat the old man was wearing a scruffy black duffel-coat, belted in with a dirty brown belt. He had thrown back the hood, and planted firmly on his still thick, tousled hair was a railwayman's cap of great antiquity. The cap covered his eyes, and the light caught only his huge bluish nose and his thick lips, with which the old man was puffing soggily at a home-made cigarette. His dishevelled grey beard was still streaked with black.

"What else could he have done?" Valya argued, tapping her little pencil. "He was on duty, he was the guard!"

"Well, yes"—the old man nodded agreement, dropping large bits of red ash on the floor and the lid of his lantern. "Yes, that's right. Still, everybody wants to eat."

145

"What are you on about?" The girl frowned. "What do you mean 'everybody'?"

"I mean you and me, for instance." And Kordubailo sighed.

"You don't know what you're talking about, grandad! They're not hungry, you know. They get their rations. You don't think they travel without rations, do you?"

"Well, I suppose not," agreed the old man, and again a hot shower fell from his cigarette, this time onto his knee and the hem of his duffel-coat.

"Look out, Gavrila Nikitich, you'll set yourself on fire," warned Frosya.

Without shaking them off, the old man calmly watched the shreds of burning tobacco fizzle out on the dark quilted material of his trousers, still wet with rain, and when they had burnt out he slightly raised his tousled grey head. "Have you girls ever tried eating raw flour mixed with water?"

"Why should I eat it raw?" Frosya was shocked. "I'd mix it up, knead it, and bake it."

The old man smacked his thick, pale lips and said after a pause—he always talked like this; his swords came out lamely and awkwardly as though on crutches: "Then you've never seen hunger, my dears."

Lieutenant Zotov stepped over the threshold and broke into the conversation. "Listen, old man, you know what taking the oath means, don't you?" Zotov had a marked northern accent.

The old man gave the lieutenant a bleary-eyed look. He was not a very big man, but his boots were big and heavy, soaking wet, and smeared in places with mud.

" 'Course," he muttered. "I took it five times."

"Well, who did you swear the oath to? Tsar Nicky?"

The old man shook his head. "Before that."

"What? Alexander III?"

The old man smacked his lips regretfully and went on smoking.

"There you are. Nowadays they take the oath to the people. Isn't there a difference?"

The old man dropped more ash on his knee.

"And whose flour is it? It belongs to the people,

146

doesn't it?" Valya said angrily, tossing back her tumbling curls. "That flour wasn't going to the Germans, was it?"

"That's right." The old man quite agreed. "But those boys weren't Germans either, they're our people too."

He finished smoking, bent the stub of his cigarette, and put it out on the lantern lid.

"You stupid old man," Zotov was roused. "Don't you know about law and order? Suppose we all just help ourselves—I take a bit, you take a bit—do you think we'll ever win the war?"

"And why did they slice the sacks open?" Valya said indignantly. "That's no way to act. Is that what we expect from our boys?"

"The sacks must have been sewn up," said Kordubailo, wiping his nose with his hand.

"But why waste it? Why let it spill out onto the track?" Frosya too was indignant. "All that flour bursting out and pouring away, comrade lieutenant! Think how many children could have been fed on it!"

"That's right," said the old man. "But in this rain all the flour in those open trucks would get wet anyway."

"It's no use talking to him," said Zotov, furious with himself for getting mixed up in a pointless conversation about something that was obvious anyway. "Don't make so much noise in here. You're keeping me from working."

Having finished cleaning her wick, Frosya lit it and replaced it inside the lantern. She got up to reach for her creased, stiff cape.

"Sharpen a pencil for me, will you, Valya dear? I'm going to get the numbers of number 765."

Zotov returned to his room.

The outcome of yesterday's incident might have been much worse. Seeing one of their comrades killed, the returnees had dropped the flour sacks and thrown themselves on the young sentry with an angry roar. They grabbed his rifle—which he apparently gave up without resistance—began to beat him up, and would have simply torn him to pieces if his relief had not turned up just in time. He pretended to arrest him and led him away.

Whenever returnees are being transported, every station commandant does his best to push them through as fast as possible. Last night Zotov had checked in another trainload of returnees—number 245413, from Paveletsk to Archedinsk—and quickly checked it out again. The train stood at Krechetovka for about twenty minutes; the returnees were asleep and did not get out. When there are a lot of them together, returnees are a frightening lot of toughs. Though not an army unit and not armed, they cannot forget that only yesterday they were part of the army, the same soldiers who in July were fighting at Bobruisk, in August at Kiev, in September at Orel.

Zotov felt he could not face them; probably this was how the young guard had felt when he gave up his rifle without firing another shot. Zotov was ashamed that he had been posted to the rear. He envied them and would have been prepared to share their somewhat tarnished reputation if only he could say that he had been through the same fighting, shellfire, and river crossings that they had.

All Vasya Zotov's friends and contemporaries were at the front. And he was—here ... So he must work all the more resolutely. Not only must he work hard to do his shift duty perfectly, but there was so much else to be done besides. He must do all he could and do it as well as he could, especially now that the twenty-fourth anniversary of the Revolution was so near at hand. It was his favourite holiday of the year, always a happy occasion in spite of the onset of winter, but this time—how agonising.

Besides his routine duties, another problem which had arisen during his shift had been dogging Zotov for a whole week. There had been an air raid. The Germans had given a bad mauling to an army supply train which had also been carrying provisions. If they had completely destroyed it, that would have been the end of that. But luckily a lot had been saved, and now Zotov was expected to make a full inventory in quadruplicate: goods completely damaged (lists to be obtained from the addresses and fresh supplies indented for); goods 40% to 80% damaged (disposal to be assessed separately); goods 10% to 40% damaged (to be delivered with appropriate explanations, or partly replaced); and, finally, goods that were undamaged. To complicate matters, although the stuff from the bombed train had now all been moved into warehouses, this had not been done straightaway, and since there were civilians of all kinds loitering around the station, there was reason to suspect pilfering. Besides, in order to assess the percentage of damage, experts from Michurinsk and Voronezh had to be called in and the crates in the warehouse had to be endlessly shifted around, and there was a shortage of men to do it.

Any fool can bomb a train, but just try sorting out the mess!

Zotov was a stickler for precision in everything. He had already checked over most of the lists; he could put in a bit of work on them today and was hoping to have it all finished in a week. But even this job was routine, and Zotov had found another task for himself. Here he was, a man with a university education and a systematic mind, doing the job of a responsible army officer and gaining useful experience. He saw clearly both the failings in the mobilisation plans that had been in effect at the outbreak of war and the faults in the army supply system. He also saw many improvements big and small that could be made in the command structure. Was it not his clear duty to make such observations, note them down, work on them, and submit them as a report to the People's Commissariat of Defence? Even if his labours were too late to be used in this war, how important they might be for the next!

This was the task for which he had to find the time and the strength. (Naturally, if he were to mention this idea to the captain or to area headquarters, they would only laugh. Fools.)

So, hurry up and deal with those traffic lists! Zotov rubbed one chubby palm against the other, picked up his indelible pencil in his stubby fat fingers, and, with one eye on the code book, entered the numbers of trains, trucks, and carriages—some in whole numbers, some in fractions—in his clear round hand on various sheets of paper. This was work in which no mistakes were allowed—just like aiming a gun. He wrinkled his brow with concentration and pushed out his lower lip.

At this point Podshebyakina came and knocked on the little glass window in his door. "May I come in, Vasil Vasilich?" Without much pause, she came in, carrying another list.

Strictly speaking, she was not supposed to come in at all but was meant to get an answer to her question while standing in the doorway or in her own room. But Zotov's and Valya's shifts had coincided more than once in the past and he was too naturally polite to keep her out. He therefore merely shut the code book and casually covered the columns of figures he was writing with a clean sheet of paper.

"I'm in a muddle, Vasil Vasilich. Look . . ." There was no other chair nearby and Valya leaned against the edge of the table and showed Zotov her register with its wavering lines and uneven figures. "Look, in train number 446 there's a carriage number 57831. Where's it going to?"

"Let's have a look." He pulled out a drawer, wondered which of the three folders to take, opened one (in such a way that Valya could not peer over his shoulder), and immediately found what he wanted. "Number 57831 is going to Pachelma."

"Uh-huh," said Valya. She wrote down "Pach" and remained draped over his table, sucking her pencil and staring at her register.

"Your 'ch' isn't written clearly," Zotov pointed out. "It looks like 've' and that carriage will end up at Paveletsk."

"Really?" said Valya coolly. "I wish you'd stop picking on me, Vasil Vasilich."

She looked at him from under a lock of her hair. But she corrected the "ch."

"Then there's another thing . . ." she said slowly, and again put the pencil in her mouth. Her thick, almost flaxen hair cascaded down from her brow, covering her eyes, but she never pushed it back. It looked so clean and soft and Zotov thought how nice it would be to run his hands through it. "Oh, yes, flatcar number 105110."

150

"Short flat?"

"No, long one."

"Can't be."

"Why?"

"It's one digit short."

"So what shall I do now?" She threw back her curls. Her lashes were as flaxen as her hair.

"You'll have to look for it, that's what. You must be more careful, Valya. Is it the same train?"

Glancing down at the folder, Zotov began to check the numbers. But Valya looked at the lieutenant, at his funny protruding ears, his lumpy nose, and his pale blue eyes flecked with grey which she could see clearly through his glasses. He was a hard boss, this man, but not unkind. And what she particularly liked was that he always behaved himself, never took liberties.

"Aha!" Zotov was furious. "You really deserve a hiding! Not '05' but '005,' idiot."

"Oh—*two* noughts," Valya exclaimed and added a nought.

"You've been through high school. Aren't you ashamed of yourself?"

"Don't, Vasil Vasilich, what's high school got to do with it? And where's the truck going, anyway?"

"To Kirsanov."

"Uh-huh." Valya wrote it down.

But she did not go. Still leaning over the table beside him, she looked thoughtful as she fingered the splinter in the tabletop, bending it back and letting it snap down.

The man's eyes involuntarily passed over her small girlish breasts, usually hidden under her clumsy uniform tunic but now clearly discernible as she leaned over the table.

"The shift will be over soon," said Valya with a pout of her fresh, pale pink lips.

"There's still work to be done before it's over." Zotov frowned and stopped looking at the girl.

"I suppose you'll be going back to that old landlady of yours."

"Where else?"

"Don't you ever go out and see anyone?"

"At a time like this?"

"What's so nice about your landlady's place? You haven't even got a proper bed. You have to sleep on top of a trunk."

"How do you know that?"

"Oh, people talk."

"This is no time for soft living, Valya, least of all for me—I feel so ashamed, not being at the front."

"But why? You're doing a useful job here, aren't you? There's nothing shameful about that. You'll get your turn in the trenches yet, I shouldn't wonder. You might even get killed ... And in the meantime we're only human, we must live."

Zotov took off his cap and rubbed his smarting forehead. (His cap was too small for him, but there had been no others at the store.)

Valya was busy drawing a long, claw-shaped doodle on the corner of her register.

"Why did you leave the Avdeyevs? Wasn't it better there?"

Zotov looked down and blushed furiously. "I just left, that's all." Surely the Avdeyevs hadn't told the whole town?

Valya went on doodling, making her claw sharper and sharper.

Neither spoke.

Valya looked at his round head out of the corner of her eye. Without his spectacles, he would look just like a little boy. Wisps of his thin fair hair stood up here and there like question marks.

"And you never go to the cinema. You must have some interesting books. Maybe you could lend me something to read."

"How do you know about my books?"

"I just guessed."

"I haven't got any books with me. I left them at home."

"I bet you just don't want to lend them."

"I tell you I haven't got any. Where could I put them? A soldier's only allowed his kit bag, that's all."

"Then we can lend you some."

"Have you got many?"

"A shelf full."

"What have you got?"

"Oh, things like . . . *The Blast Furnace, The Silver Prince* . . . and some others."

"Have you read them all?"

"Some of them." She suddenly lifted her head, opened her eyes wide, and said in one breath: "Vasil Vasilich, please come and live with us! You can have Vovka's room. It's next to the stove, so it's warm. Mother will cook for you. Why do you want to stay with that landlady?"

They looked at each other, each busy with his own thoughts.

Valya saw the lieutenant hesitate and thought he might agree. And why shouldn't he, the silly fool? Soldiers always say they're not married, but he says he is. All the soldiers billeted in the town live with nice families, are warm, and are well looked after. Now that her father and brother had been called up, Valya thought there ought to be a man about the house. Then they would come home from duty together, late at night, through the muddy, blacked-out streets (they would have to go arm in arm), and they would sit down cheerfully to dinner, make jokes, tell each other things . . .

With something approaching fear, Vasya Zotov glanced at this girl openly inviting him to her home. She was barely three years younger than he, and she addressed him by his name and patronymic not because of the difference in their ages but out of respect for his rank. He realised it wouldn't stop at the well-heated room and tasty dinners cooked out of his rations. He grew excited. Her blond curls were so close and he longed to touch them and stroke them.

But that was out of the question. He loosened his collar with its red badges of rank on green tabs, although the collar was not tight, and he straightened his glasses.

"No, Valya, I'm not moving anywhere. Anyway, let's get back to work. We've wasted enough time gossiping . . ."

He put on his green cap, which made his guileless, snub-nosed face look very stern.

The girl frowned at him and drawled: "Aw'lll right then, Vasil Vasilich." She sighed. Wearily and as though with an effort, she straightened herself up from the table and left the room, with the register hanging limply from her hand.

He blinked his eyes foolishly. Perhaps if she came back again and spoke to him firmly, he would give in. But she didn't come back.

Vasya could not explain to anyone around why he chose to live in a dirty, badly heated house with an old woman and her three grandsons and sleep on an uncomfortable chest that was too short for him. In the harsh days of '41 amid the mass of newly mobilized men, he found himself more than once being laughed at when he told them that he loved his wife, that he was going to be faithful to her throughout the war and had complete trust in her. They were good fellows, true friends, but they all laughed with a wild, cheerful bravado, clapped him on the shoulder, and told him not to be a fool. Since then he had never said anything like that out loud but he felt a terrible sadness, especially when he woke in the dead of night and wondered what it must be like for her, miles away, under German occupation and pregnant.

But it was not for his wife's sake that he refused Valya just now, but for Paulina ... And then again, maybe not even for Paulina, but for ...

Paulina was a girl from Kiev with short dark hair and a pale face who lived with Frosya and worked at the post office. If he had the time, Vasya used to go to the post office to read the latest newspapers (they came in bundles, several days late). In this way he could read all the papers at once and not just one or two. Of course, a post office is not a reading room and no one was obliged to let him read there, but Paulina understood him and would bring out all the papers for him and put them on the end of the counter, where he would stand and read them in the cold. For Paulina, as for Zotov, the war was not the mere inhuman turning of some relentless wheel; it represented all her personal

154

life and all her future, and it was in order to divine that future that, like Zotov, she would leaf nervously through the papers, looking for any crumbs of information that might explain the course of the war. They often read standing alongside, eagerly showing each other important items. For them, newspapers took the place of the letters they never received. Paulina pored over all the battle reports in the communiqués, wondering whether her husband was there, and on Zotov's advice she would even wrinkle her smooth forehead and read through articles on infantry and tank tactics in *Red Star*. As for Ehrenburg's articles, Zotov would excitedly read them aloud to her. He even asked Paulina to give him the unclaimed newspapers so that he could cut out some of these articlees and keep them.

He had become attached to Paulina, her child, and her mother in a way that in normal times would never happen. He used to bring her little boy sugar from his rations. But not once as they turned the pages together did he dare even to touch her white hand—not because of her husband, or his wife, but because of the sacred bond of grief that united them.

Of all the people in Krechetovka—indeed, anywhere this side of the front line—Paulina had become dearer to him than anyone else. She had become his conscience and the guardian of his fidelity, so how could he become Valya's lodger? What would Paulina think of him?

But, even apart from Paulina, how could he in all conscience console himself with a woman when everything he loved was under threat of destruction?

And then, too, he felt embarrassed to admit to Valya and his fellow officers that he did read in the evenings, that he had a book—a single book which he had picked up in some library in the hectic moves of that year and which he carried around in his kit bag.

It was the first volume of *Das Kapital*, a fat little book with blue covers, printed on the rough brownish paper of the thirties.

All the five years that he had been a student, he had dreamt of reading this cherished book. He had borrowed it time and again from the university library, kept it for a term and sometimes even for a whole year, intending to summarize it, but he had never managed to find the time, which was always taken up with endless meetings, voluntary work, and examinations. Without finishing one page of the summary, he would return the book when he went away for the summer vacation. Even when they were doing political economy, the very time to read *Das Kapital,* the lecturer had advised them against it—"It's too much for you"—and had urged them to concentrate on Lapidus's textbook and their lecture notes. And he was quite right; they only just managed to get through all the work.

But now in the autumn of '41, when all around glowed the fires of destruction, Vasya Zotov was at last able, in this God-forsaken spot, to find time for *Das Kapital.* This is what he did in the time left to him after his work, his evening classes, and the jobs he did for the district Party committee. In the Avdeyevs' house, he would sit down in the parlour at a small rickety table surrounded by philodendrons and aloes and lit by an oil lamp (the local generator could not provide enough current for all the houses), and he would read, smoothing out the coarse paper with his hand. He read each passage three times: the first time to get the gist of it, the second in more detail, and the third summarising and trying to get it all into his head. The gloomier the news from the front, the more earnestly did he bury himself in his fat blue volume. Vasya believed that once he had mastered even this first volume and committed it in its noble entirety to his memory, he would become invincible, invulnerable, irrefutable in any ideological combat.

But such evenings were rare and he only made a few pages of notes, because Antonina Ivanovna kept interfering.

She was the other lodger. She had come from Liski and immediately on arrival had become the manageress of the canteen. She was efficient and so obviously tough that no one felt like starting trouble in her canteen. There, as Zotov later found out, for a rouble an earthenware soup bowl of hot grey water with a few bits of macaroni floating in it was thrust through the hatch and people who did not care to lap the soup straight from the bowl gave another rouble's deposit for a battered wooden spoon. As for Antonina Ivanovna, having ordered the Avdeyevs to get the samovar ready in the evenings, she would put bread and best-quality butter on her landlady's table. She was in fact only about twenty-five, but she was a solid-looking woman with a smooth, white skin. She always had a welcoming word for the lieutenant, who would answer absent-mindedly, and for a long time he confused her with one of the landlady's relatives who used to come and visit. Hunched over his book, he never noticed and never heard her when like himself she returned late from work and passed back and forth through his room from the landlady's quarters to her bedroom. Suddenly she would come up to him and ask: "What is it that you're always reading, comrade lieutenant?" He would cover the book with his notebook and answer evasively. Another time she would ask: "Don't you think it's risky that I don't lock my door at night?" Zotov would answer: "What's the risk? I'm here and I'm armed." Some days later, engrossed in his book, he sensed that she had stopped going backwards and forwards and was apparently still in the room. He looked round and was transfixed: right there in his room she had made up a bed on the divan and was lying in it with her hair spread over the pillow and her white shoulders showing provocatively above the quilt. He gaped at her, not knowing what to do next. "I'm not disturbing you, am I?" she said mockingly. Vasya stood up, utterly at a loss. He even took a big step towards her—but the sight of that well-fed body, sated on purloined food, repelled him.

He was so choked with hate that he could not even speak. He turned, banged *Das Kapital* shut, just managed to put it in his kit bag, and rushed to the nail where his coat and cap hung. He snatched his belt with its heavy revolver, and holding it in his hand without strapping it on, he made for the door.

He came out into impenetrable darkness. Neither the blacked-out windows nor the clouded sky let out a shred of light, and a wet, cold autumn wind tore and

157

lashed at him. Stumbling into puddles, potholes, and mud, Vasya started out towards the station, not realising that he was still carrying his gun belt. He was burning with such a feeling of impotent humiliation that he nearly burst into tears tramping through the dark and the mud.

From that moment, life became impossible for him at the Avdeyevs'. To give her her due, Antonina Ivanovna no longer spoke to him but started bringing home an ugly great stallion of a man, a civilian but in military boots and tunic as the times demanded. Zotov tried to work, but she left the door ajar on purpose so that for a long time he could hear their laughter and her squeals and groans.

It was then that he moved to the half-deaf old woman's who had nothing but a chest covered with a horse blanket.

But it seemed that gossip had spread through Krechetovka. Surely it would never reach Paulina's ears? What disgrace . . . These thoughts distracted him from his work. He picked up his indelible pencil again and forced himself once more to scrutinise the traffic lists and once more write down in his clear round handwriting the numbers of trains and trucks, and draw up fresh lists, each with one carbon copy. He would have finished the work had there not been a complication about a big goods train from Kamyshin which was to be split up. Only the commanding officer himself could make the decision. Zotov gave one buzz on the field telephone, picked up the receiver, and listened. Then he gave a longer buzz. And a third long buzz. The captain did not answer. That meant he was not in his office. Maybe he was resting in his billet after supper. He was bound to come before the end of the shift to hear the reports.

In the next room Podshebyankina occasionally rang the station dispatcher. Frosya came and went again. Then he heard the heavy tread of boots. Someone knocked at the door, opened it slightly, and asked in a clear voice: "May we come in?"

Without waiting for an answer, they came in. The first one—a lithe figure, tall as a guardsman, his face flushed from the cold—stepped into the middle of the room, clicked his heels, and reported: "Escort commander of train number 95505, Sergeant Gaydukov. Thirty-eight passenger carriages, all present and correct and ready to move off, sir!"

He had on a new fur cap, a smart long greatcoat cut like an officer's with a vent, a broad leather belt with a star-shaped buckle, and highly polished cowhide boots.

The second man, thickset, with a tanned leathery face, peered round the sergeant's back, shuffled a bit, and remained near the door. He reluctantly raised his hand to his fur cap with its dangling earflaps, and said quietly, in an unmilitary manner: "Escort commander of train number 71628, Corporal Dygin. Four sixteen-ton carriages."

His soldier's greatcoat, belted with a narrow canvas belt, hung askew as though its hem had been chewed up in some machine. He wore canvas boots, creased like concertinas.

Sergeant Dygin had thick eyebrows and heavy jowls like the actor Chkalov—not the young and dashing Chkalov, who had just died, but a battered and careworn edition of the man.

"Ah—good, good!" said Zotov, and got up. Neither his rank nor his job obliged him to rise to meet any sergeant who happened to come in. But he was genuinely glad to see everyone and was anxious to do his best by everyone. As assitant R.T.O., Zotov had no one under his command, and these people who came for five minutes or forty-eight hours were the only ones to whom he could show the proper care and efficiency due from an officer.

"I know, your traffic lists are already here." He found them on the table and looked them through. "Here they are—95505 . . . 71628 . . ." he said, raising his benevolent eyes to the sergeants.

Their coats and caps were only slightly spotted with rain.

"Why are your clothes dry? Has the rain stopped?"

"More or less." The handsome Gaydukov tossed his head with a smile. He stood stiffly, though not quite at attention. "It's blowing harder from the north."

He was about nineteen and had that premature first flush of manhood, like sunburn, that innocent young faces get from being at the front. (It was this front-line tan on their faces that had brought Zotov to his feet.)

The assistant R.T.O. had little to say to them. There was in any case no question of talking about the contents of their trains, because their trucks might be sealed, the crates nailed down, and they themselves probably had no idea what they were carrying. But they wanted plenty from the R.T.O. of this transit station. They stared at him—the one looking cheerful, the other hangdog.

Gaydukov needed to find out at once if this R.T.O. in his cushy rear-echelon billet was an officious bastard who would insist on inspecting the train and its load.

Not that Gaydukov was in the least worried about his load; he not only guarded it, he loved it. It consisted of several hundred magnificent horses and an adequate supply of baled hay and oats that an intelligent supply officer had dispatched with them on the same train, there being little hope of finding any fodder en route.

Gaydukov had grown up in the country, had been fond of horses since childhood, and treated them as friends; although it was not his job to do so, he voluntarily helped the duty grooms to water them, feed them, and look after them. Every time he opened the door and climbed up the dangling wire ladder into the truck with his lantern in his hand, all sixteen horses in the truck—bays, chestnuts, and greys—would turn their long, alert, intelligent heads towards him, some laying their heads over the backs of their neighbours, and would look at him with their large, sad, unblinking eyes, attentively flicking their ears. They seemed to be asking him not just for hay but to tell them about this rumbling, lurching box, why they were in it and where they were being taken to. And Gaydukov would inspect them, shouldering his way between their warm rumps, ruffling their manes and, if he were alone, stroking their muzzles, talking to them. Going to the front was worse for them than for men; the front line was as much good to a horse as a fifth leg.

Gaydukov's fear was that the R.T.O. (obviously a

decent type, who wouldn't give any trouble) might look into the men's carriage. Although the troops in Gaydukov's escort consisted mostly of recruits, he had already seen service in a forward area and in July had been wounded on the Dnieper. He had spent two months in hospital, had worked there in the stores, and now he was off to the front again. So he not only knew the rules; he also knew the proper way to break them. His twenty young lads just happened to be escorting the horses on this trip: once they had been handed over, the men would be drafted into a division. In a few days their new uniforms would be dirtied by the wet mud of the trenches—and they would be lucky if there were even any trenches: there might be no more than hummocks as cover for their young heads when the German mortar bombs started exploding over them. It was the mortars that had bothered Gaydukov most in the summer. This was why he wanted them to spend these last days in the warm, among friends, and in as cheerful an atmosphere as possible. In their roomy carriage, two iron stoves glowed day and night, burning up huge lumps of coal scrounged from other trainloads. Their train was being sent through quickly, without any holdups, but somehow they managed to water the horses once a day and to indent for their rations every three days.

If a train was moving fast, there were always people wanting to get on it. And although the regulations strictly forbade admitting civilians to military quarters, neither Gaydukov himself nor his deputy, who had picked up Gaydukov's easy ways, could bear to see people freezing in the autumn cold and running crazily alongside the trains. Not that they took on everyone, but they did not turn many away. There was one crafty wagon-inspector whom they had let on in exchange for a litre of moonshine vodka, and a red-haired old man carrying baskets who got on for a hunk of lard. Some were let on for nothing. Then there were the ones the boys could never refuse: their hearts melted towards them and they would stretch out their hands and lift up into the carriage any women or girls who, like them, were travelling, travelling somewhere, for some purpose. Once in the warmth and hubbub of the uproarious carriage, the red-haired old man had muttered about the First World War, how he had nearly won the St. George's Medal, and the only shy one of the girls had sat by the stove like a little ruffled owl. In the heat, the other girls had long since thrown off their overcoats and their quilted jackets and even their blouses. One girl, wearing only her red shift and flushed all over, was washing shirts for the lads. One of the boys was helping her wring them out, and when he got too fresh, she would take a swipe at him with a wet, twisted shirt. Two girls were cooking for the soldiers, adding their home-produced lard to the dry army rations, while another girl sat and mended anything that was torn. Once away from the station, they would have supper, sit by the fire, and sing to the noisy lurching of the carriage as it sped along. Later, without bothering too much about who was on or off duty (they would anyway all be equally exhausted from watering the horses), they would crawl into the hard bunks, made of unplaned wood, to sleep huddled together. And some of today's young women, who like yesterday's had not long ago seen their husbands off to the war (and some of the girls too; few could resist it), would lie down and make love to the boys in the shadows away from the lamp. Why not be good to a soldier going to the front line? These days might be his last . . .

All that Gaydukov wanted now from the R.T.O. was for him to let the train through as quickly as possible, and perhaps to try and worm out of him some information about their route. He wanted to know where to let the girls off; and it was of interest to him to know which sector of the front they were bound for. The train might even pass near someone's home.

"I see," said the Lieutenant slowly, looking at the travel documents. "You haven't come all the way together. Where did they join you up?"

"A few stations back."

Zotov pursed his lips as he squinted at the paper. "But why have you been sent here?" he asked the older man, who looked like the actor Chkalov. "Were you in Penza?"

162

"Yes," answered Dygin hoarsely.

"Then why the hell do they send you through Ryazhsk? It's idiotic!"

"Are we going on together?" asked Gaydukov. (On the way to the office he had found out Dygin's destination and wanted some idea of his own.)

"You'll be together as far as Gryazi."

"And after that?"

"Military secret," said Zotov in his rather attractive northern accent as he turned his head and peered through his spectacles at the tall sergeant.

"Come on," urged Gaydukov, leaning towards the lieutenant. "We're going through Kastornaya, aren't we?"

"You'll see." Zotov meant to give his answer in a stern voice, but his lips broke into a faint smile and Gaydukov knew that it was Kastornaya.

"Are we leaving this evening?"

"Yes. Mustn't delay you."

"I can't go," Dygin announced weightily. His voice was hoarse and aggressive.

"You mean, you personally? Are you ill?"

"None of my escort can go."

"What do you mean? I don't understand. Why not?"

"Because we're not dogs!" Dygin burst out, his eyeballs rolling furiously under their lids.

"What's this talk?" Zotov frowned and straightened himself up. "You'd better be careful, sergeant."

Then he noticed that the green triangular sergeant's badge was screwed into only one of the lapels of Dygin's greatcoat. The other was empty. There was a triangular depression and a little hole in the middle. The unbuttoned ear flaps of his Budyonny helmet hung down to his chest like great dock leaves.

Scowling, Dygin croaked: "Because we haven't eaten for eleven days."

"What??" The lieutenant jerked back. His glasses fell off one ear; he caught them and put them on again. "How can that be?"

"Just like that. It happens . . . Very simple."

"Haven't you got your ration-indent forms?"

"Can't eat paper."

"How have you kept alive, then?"

"We're alive."

How have you kept alive? That pointless, childish question by this bespectacled little officer was the last straw and Dygin despaired of getting any help at Krechetovka Station. How have you kept alive! Hunger and fury involuntarily tightened his jaws as he glared Volga-fashion at this well-scrubbed little pipsqueak of an officer in his clean, warm room. Seven days ago they had scrounged two sackfuls of beetroot from a pile at some station and for a whole week they had boiled nothing but that beetroot in their cooking pots, stewed it and eaten it. Now they were sick of beetroot and their guts would refuse to take it. The night before last, when they had stopped at Alexandro-Novsky, Dygin had looked at his starving reservists—they were all older than him, and he was no chicken—made up his mind, and got up. The wind was under the carriages and whistling through the cracks. He must get something—anything—to quiet their stomachs. He had gone out into the darkness and returned an hour and a half later to fling three loaves onto his bunk. The soldier sitting next to him was stunned: "There's even a white loaf!" "Well, so what?" Dygin had said, glancing at it indifferently. "I haven't even noticed." He saw no point in telling all this to the R.T.O. now. How have you kept alive, indeed! These four men had been travelling for ten days through their native land and it might as well have been a desert. They were escorting a consignment of 20,000 entrenching tools still covered in protective grease. They were taking them—Dygin had known this from the start—from Gorky to Tiflis. But every other train, it seemed, was more urgent than their damned load and its frozen grease. They had been on the move for over two weeks and they were still less than halfway. Every miserable little dispatcher, if he could be bothered to, would have their four trucks uncoupled and left standing in some siding. They had drawn three days rations in Gorky, then three more days' worth at Saransk, and since then they had never managed to reach a ration store when it was open. All this would have been bearable, and they would even

164

have starved for another five days, if only they had been certain of eventually drawing their rations for the full fortnight. But their bellies were rumbling and their spirits were groaning because it was the rule at every ration store: no rations ever issued in arrears. Whatever they had missed was gone forever.

"But why haven't your rations been issued to you?" the lieutenant insisted.

"Will you issue them?" Dygin released his jaw.

As so often before, he had jumped down from the carriage and found out from a passing soldier that there was a ration point at this station. But it was already dark and rules were rules, so it was pointless to try.

Sergeant Gaydukov forgot his cheerful stance facing the lieutenant, turned towards Dygin, and slapped him on the shoulder with his big hand.

"Hey, why didn't you tell me, friend? We'll give you something right away."

Dygin did not flinch at the slap and did not even turn but went on staring dumbly at the officer. He was sickened at himself for being so hopeless at looking after his old men; for the whole eleven days they had not asked for any food from either civilians or soldiers, knowing there was nothing to spare at a time like this. No one had asked for a lift in their wretched coach, which was forever being uncoupled. Their tobacco had run out, and because their coach was full of cracks, they had boarded up three of the four windows, so that it was dark inside even in daytime. All hope gone, for days on end at the long stops they had sat around in silence poking fuel into their dim little stove, stewing beetroot, and occasionally prodding it with a knife.

Gaydukov sprang briskly to attention. "Permission to fall out, sir?"

"Fall out, sergeant." He ran off.

Zotov would see to it that these poor bastards got some first aid in the shape of some flour and tobacco. That whining old woman had so far given nothing in return for her train ride—so let her give something to the lads; there'd be more than enough to spare. And they would tap that inspector's suitcase; he would take the hint.

"Ye-es, it's after six," the lieutenant was thinking aloud. "Our ration store's shut."

"They're always shut ... Only open from ten to five. As soon as I got in the queue at Penza, I heard a noise: it was our train pulling out. We went through Morshansk at night. And Ryazhsk too."

"Wait a moment!" The lieutenant got busy. "I'm not going to leave things like this. We'll soon see!" He picked up the receiver of the field telephone and gave one long ring.

No reply.

He rang three times.

No reply.

"Hell!" Three more rings. "That you, Guskov?"

"Yes, sir."

"Why isn't the duty telephonist there?"

"He's gone. I've got some sour milk. Shall I bring you some, sir?"

"Don't be an idiot. I don't want any." (He did not say this for Dygin's benefit. He was constantly having to tell Guskov not to bring him things, on principle. This was to keep matters on a strictly proper footing; otherwise, he would never get Guskov to obey orders. In fact, Zotov had reported Guskov to the captain more than once for insubordination.)

"Listen, Guskov. An escort of four men has just arrived and they haven't had any rations for eleven days."

Guskov whistled down the telephone. "What's the matter with the silly bastards?"

"It just happened. We must help. Look, somehow or other we've got to get hold of Chichishev and Samorukov right away so they can issue them the rations they're entitled to."

"Where'll we find them? It won't be easy."

"Where? In their billets, of course."

"Streets are filthy, mud up to your knees, and it's dark as ..."

"Chichishev lives quite near."

"But Samorukov's the other side of the tracks. Anyway, he wouldn't come, sir."

"Chichishev will come."

Chichishev was an accountant who had been called up into the army from the reserve. Although he had been given the rank of sergeant major, no one looked on him as a soldier, simply as a typical elderly accountant whose whole personality had been moulded by his job. He could not even talk without his abacus. He would ask "What's the time? Five o'clock?" and at once he would flick five beads across his abacus in order to understand. Or he might ruminate: "If a man's alone ... [snap! one bead] ... life's hard. So [snap! a second bead] he gets married." As long as the queue of people yelling and shoving their ration cards at him was separated from him by a barred window with only a little opening left for the thrusting hands, then Chichishev was very firm, he shouted at the soldiers, pushed their hands away, and closed the opening to stop the draught. But if he had to face a crowd in the open or if a squad pushed its way into his little cubbyhole, he would immediately lower his round head into his little shoulders, call them "mates," and stamp their cards. He was equally fussy and obsequious to his superiors and never dared refuse anyone who wore an officer's badge. The ration store was not under the R.T.O.'s command, but Zotov reckoned that Chichishev would not refuse.

"Samorukov won't come," Guskov insisted.

In rank, Samorukov was a sergeant major too, but he despised lieutenants. A healthy, overfed beast, he was simply the quartermaster in charge of the ration store, although he behaved like an officer. With great dignity he would turn up at the store a quarter of an hour late, check the seals, unfasten the padlocks, raise and bolt the hatch in position—and all with a look of condescension on his disagreeable, fat-cheeked face. And no matter how many soldiers and convalescents crowded round the hatch cursing and jostling to get closer in their haste to catch trains or report for duty, Samorukov would calmly roll up his sleeves to the elbow, baring his fat, butcher's forearms. Then he would check Chichishev's stamps on the crumpled, tattered ration indents with niggling exactitude and calmly weigh out the rations (often enough giving short weight,

167

too), quite unconcerned whether or not the troops might be in a hurry to catch a train. He had purposely chosen a billet far away from the station so that he would not be disturbed in his off-duty time and had made a point of finding a landlady who had a kitchen garden and a cow.

The thought of Samorukov made Zotov choke. He found the breed as hateful as the Fascists and regarded it as no less of a threat. He could not understand why Stalin did not issue a decree to shoot all the Samorukovs out of hand, right outside the ration store, in front of a crowd of people.

"No, Samorukov won't come," Zotov thought to himself in agreement. Angered by Samorukov, yet possessed by a cowardly fear of the man, Zotov would not have dared to disturb him if these inexperienced men had not eaten for three days, or even five—but eleven days!

"This is what you must do, Guskov. Don't send a soldier, go to him yourself. And don't say that four men are hungry; say that the captain wants to see him urgently. The message is from me. Got it. And make him come to me. I'll see to the rest."

Guskov was silent.

"Well, why don't you say something? Got the order? Say 'Yes, sir,' and be off."

"But have you asked the captain?"

"What business is it of yours? I am responsible here. The captain has gone out. He's not here now."

"The captain wouldn't give an order like that," Guskov argued. "There's no regulation that says you should unseal the store in the middle of the night and seal it up again for the sake of two loaves of bread and three salt herrings."

That was quite true.

"Why the hurry, anyway?" reasoned Guskov. "Let them wait until ten in the morning. What's one night? Lie on your belly and your back keeps you warm."

"But their train is leaving now. It's a fast train, would be a pity to uncouple them, they're late as it is. Somebody's waiting for their consignment, somebody needs it."

"Well, if the train is leaving, Samorukov won't get here in time anyway. There and back through the mud—even with a lantern—it's an hour and a half at least. Two hours."

Again, Guskov was right.

Jaws clenched, the ear flaps of his cavalry helmet hanging down, his face dark and weather-beaten, Dygin glared at the telephone, trying to understand what was being said at the other end. He nodded and looked resigned. "That's it, then—missed another day."

Zotov sighed, covered the mouthpiece so that Guskov wouldn't hear.

"Well, what can we do, friend? Nothing doing today. Maybe you could go to Gryazi on this train? It's a good train. You'll be there by morning."

He nearly convinced him, but Dygin had sensed the lieutenant's weak spot.

"I won't go. You can arrest me. I won't go."

Someone knocked at the glass pane of the door. There stood a stout man wearing a black-and-grey-check tweed cap. He bowed politely, apparently asking permission to enter, but he was inaudible through the door.

"Come in, come in," shouted Zotov, and said into the phone: "Okay, Guskov, ring off. I'll think of something."

The man behind the door did not understand at first, then opened the door a little and asked once more: "May I come in?"

Zotov was struck by his voice. It was rich and deep, aristocratic yet controlled, as though not to draw attention to its quality. He was dressed in a long, heavy, reddish-brown civilian jacket with shortened sleeves, but on his feet he was wearing army boots with puttees. In one hand he was holding a small greasy army kit bag; with the other he raised his rather smart cap and bowed to both men as he entered.

"Good evening."

"Good evening."

"Could you tell me, please," asked the stranger very politely, yet holding himself with dignity, as though he were not dressed in this peculiar fashion but very elegantly. "Who is the R.T.O. here?"

"I am the assistant R.T.O."

"Then it's probably you I should see."

He looked for a place to put his check cap, which looked as though it had coal dust sprinkled on it, found nowhere, stuck it under his other arm, and with his free hand began to unbutton his coat with a look of concentration. The coat had no collar, or rather the collar had been torn off, and a warm woollen scarf was wrapped round his bare neck. Having undone his coat, the stranger revealed beneath it a greatly faded, dirty, summer army uniform. Then he began to unbutton his tunic pocket.

"Now wait a minute," Zotov brushed him away. "Now let's see." He frowned at the sullen, motionless Dygin. "I'll do the only thing that I'm fully entitled to. I'll uncouple you now. You'll get your rations at ten in the morning."

"Thanks," said Dygin, looking at him with bloodshot eyes.

"Never mind the thanks. It's against regulations. You had a good train. I don't know which one we can couple you to now."

"We've been on the go for two weeks. A day more or less won't make much difference." Dygin cheered up. "I know what our consignment is."

"No, no." Zotov shook his finger at him. "It's not for you and me to decide these things." He glanced sideways at the stranger, went right up to Dygin, and said almost inaudibly, though his accent was still noticeable: "Since you know what your consignment is, just think about it. How many people could dig themselves trenches with your spades? Two divisions! Digging in means saving your life. Twenty thousand spades is twenty thousand soldiers' lives. Isn't that so?"

Zotov again gave a sidelong glance. Realising that he was in the way, the stranger turned towards the wall and with his free hand covered—or rather warmed—first one ear, then the other.

"Are you cold?" Zotov asked with a loud laugh.

The stranger turned round, smiling. "Yes, you know,
170

it's become terribly cold. There's a furious wind. And wet, too."

The wind was indeed whistling, lashing against the corner of the building. It made the ill-fitting pane in the right-hand window tinkle behind the blind. And the water in the drainpipe was gurgling again.

This odd character with his unshaven chin had a charming smile, one that went straight to the heart. His head was not shaved army-style but he had thin, short-ish, greying hair. He looked neither like a soldier nor like a civilian.

"Here," he said, holding the paper he had taken from his pocket, "here is my . . ."

"Just a moment." Zotov took the paper without looking. "Sit down, please. Here's a chair." But, taking another look at his absurd getup, he went back to the table, gathered up the forms and the code book, locked them up in the safe, beckoned to Dygin, and took him to the military dispatcher's office.

Podshebyakina was arguing on the telephone, and old Frosya was crouching by the stove, trying to get dry. Zotov went up to Podshebyakina and took her by the hand, the one that was holding the receiver.

"Valyusha . . ."

The girl turned quickly and looked at him coyly, thinking how affectionately he had taken her hand. But she still had to finish her conversation: "Number 1002 going straight through. We have nothing for it. Put it on the Tambov line, Petrovich."

"Valya dear, tell Frosya to go right away and take down the numbers of these four carriages, or just tell the men to uncouple them. The sergeant here will go with her, and let the dispatcher's office shunt them into a siding until the morning."

Still crouching, Frosya turned her large, craggy face towards the lieutenant and stuck out her lower lip.

"All right, Vasil Vasilich," smiled Valya. Although she had finished her conversation, she went on holding the receiver because he was still touching her hand. "Right away."

"And those four carriages are to be sent off as soon as there is an engine. Do your best."

"Good, Vasil Vasilich." Valya was all smiles.

"Well, that's it," the lieutenant said to Dygin.

Frosya heaved a sigh like a blacksmith's bellows, grunted, and straightened up.

Dygin silently raised his hand to his temple and held it there.

He looked lop-eared in his unfastened helmet, and there was nothing military about him at all.

"Just been drafted? Been working in a factory?"

"Yes." Dygin looked straight at the lieutenant with gratitude.

"Screw your triangle back in." Zotov pointed to his missing sergeant's badge.

"It's gone. Broken."

"Either fasten your helmet or roll up the flaps."

"Roll up the flaps, indeed," snapped Frosya. "Look at the filthy weather. Come on, son."

"Okay. Good luck. Tomorrow there'll be another lieutenant on duty here. You must get him to send you off as soon as possible."

Zotov went back to his room and closed the door. Four months ago he himself had no idea how to tighten his belt, and having to lift a hand to salute seemed particularly ludicrous and absurd.

As Zotov came in, his visitor did not rise from his chair, but made a movement demonstrating his readiness to get up if necessary. His kit bag was now lying on the floor and the check cap on top of it.

"Sit down, sit down." Zotov sat down at his desk. "Well, what is it?"

The stranger unfolded the piece of paper. "I've missed my train." He smiled apologetically.

Zotov read the piece of paper. It was a travel warrant from the R.T.O. at Ryazhsk; glancing at the stranger, he put the routine check questions.

"Surname?"

"Tveritinov."

"First names?"

"Igor Dementyevich."

"Are you really over fifty?"

"No. Forty-nine."

"What was the number of your train?"

"No idea."

"What, didn't they tell you the number?"

"No."

"Then why is the number here? Who gave it? You?'

(It was train number 245413, the Archedinsk train that Zotov had checked through the night before.)

"No. I told them in Ryazhsk where it was from and what time, and the R.T.O. must have guessed."

"Where did you get left behind?"

"At Skopino."

"How did that happen?"

"Well, to tell you the truth"—the same apologetic smile appeared on Tveritinov's large lips—I went to trade something for a bit of food. And the train went. Nowadays they go without whistles, bells, or loudspeakers—very quietly."

"When was that?"

"The day before yesterday."

"Can't you catch up with it?"

"No, evidently not. How could I go? It's too wet for an open truck. And on a truck platform—you know, the kind with a little ladder—there's a terrible draught and sometimes the guards drive you off. I'm not allowed onto boxcars either they've no authority or there's no room. I did see a passenger train once, a real miracle, but there were two conductors on each step and they were pushing people away so they couldn't even catch hold of the handrail. As for goods trains, once they've moved, you can't get on, and while they are standing without an engine, there's no guessing where they're going to. They don't have an enamel plate saying: Moscow—Mineralnye Vody. You can't ask anyone; they think you're a spy. And then my clothes are so odd. Anyway, it's dangerous to ask questions these days."

"Naturally, in wartime."

"It was the same before the war."

"I didn't notice."

"It was." Tveritinov's eyes narrowed for a moment. "After '37."

"Why 1937?" asked Zotov with surprise. "What happened in 1937? The Spanish Civil War?"

"No, no." Tveritinov smiled apologetically again and looked away. "No."

His soft grey muffler hung down unknotted to below his belt along his open coat.

"Why aren't you in uniform? Where's your army coat?"

"I never got an army coat. They didn't give me one."

"Where did you get that ... getup?"

"Some kind people gave me ..."

"Mmm, I see." Zotov thought for a moment. "But I must say, you still managed to get here pretty quickly. Yesterday morning you were talking to the Ryazhsk R.T.O. and tonight you're here. How did you come?"

Tveritinov gazed at Zotov with his big, gentle, trusting eyes. Zotov found his way of speaking unusually attractive: the way he stopped if he thought the other wanted to interrupt; the way he emphasised a point with a slight gesture of his fingers instead of waving his arms.

"I had an enormous stroke of luck. I got out of a half-truck at some station ... These last two days I've begun to understand railway terminology. I thought a 'half-wagon' must at least be something like a truck, maybe half a roof. I climbed up there on a ladder, but it was just a huge iron box, a trap, nowhere to sit, nothing to lean on. It had had coal in it before, and when we moved, the dust kept swirling up and never settled. That's where things got really nasty. And on top of it all, it began to rain."

"So why were you so lucky?" Zotov burst out laughing. "I don't understand. Look what's happened to your clothes."

When he laughed, two large, deep lines stretched from the corners of his mouth up to his lumpy nose.

"The luck came when I got out of the half-truck, shook myself, had a wash, and suddenly saw an engine being coupled onto a train going south. I ran along the train—not a single heated carriage, and all the doors were sealed. And then I noticed a man got out to relieve himself and went back into an unlocked wagon.

I went in after him. And there, imagine, was a truck full of quilted blankets."

"And wasn't it sealed?"

"No. And what's more, they'd obviously been tied into bundles of five or ten at first and now many of the bundles were untied and they were ideally comfortable. Several people were sleeping there already."

"Well, I'm damned!"

"I wrapped myself up in three or four of them and slept like a log for days on end. I had no idea whether we were moving or standing still. Especially since I had had no rations for three days. So I slept and slept, forgot all about the war and everything else. I dreamt about my family ..." His crumpled, unshaven face lit up.

"Hold on!" Zotov suddenly came to and jumped up from his chair. "That train you're talking about ... When did it arrive here?"

"Let's see. Minutes ago. I came straight to your office."

Zotov rushed to the door, flung it open, and ran out.

"Valya, Valya. That through train for Balashov, one thousand and something, or whatever it was you said ..."

"A thousand and two."

"Is it still here?"

"Gone."

"Are you sure?"

"Sure."

"Damn." He clutched his head. "Here we are, sitting like damned bureaucrats, shuffling our papers, not noticing anything and not even earning our pay. Try getting through to Michurinsk-Uralsky."

He ran back and asked Tveritinov: "Do you remember the number of your truck?"

"No," smiled Tveritinov.

"Was it a two- or four-axle truck?"

"I don't understand such things."

"What do you mean, you don't understand? Was it little or big? How many tons?"

"As they used to say in the Civil War: forty men and eight horses."

175

"Sixteen tons, then. And no escort?"

"Seems not."

"Vasil Vasilich!" shouted Valya. "The military dispatcher's on the line. Do you want the R.T.O.?"

"I don't know, maybe not. Perhaps it's not a military consignment."

"Then will you allow me to explain it to them?"

"Yes, please do, Valechka. God knows, maybe these quilts are just being evauacated. Tell them to go carefully through the train, find the truck, see who it belongs to, seal it—in other words, get it sorted out."

"Very well. Vasil Vasilich."

"Well, see to it, Valechka. You're really very good at your job."

Valya smiled at him. Curls tumbled over her face.

"Hello. Michurinsk-Uralsky . . ."

Zotov closed the door and paced nervously across the room, beating one fist against the other.

"The work—it's never-ending," he said in his strong northern accent. "And they won't give me an assistant. All those quilts could be pinched and no one would give a damn. Maybe there's a shortage already."

He walked up and down for a while longer, then sat down and took off his glasses to wipe them with a rag. His face straightaway lost its alert, businesslike expression, became childlike, and, except for his green cap, defenceless.

Tveritinov waited patiently. He looked miserably at the blackout blinds, the coloured portrait of Kaganovich in the uniform of a railway marshal, the stove, the bucket, the shovel. The heat of the room made his coat, thick with coal dust, weigh heavily on him. He threw it off his shoulders and took off his scarf.

The lieutenant put on his glasses and looked at the travel warrant. The warrant was not, strictly spreaking, a real document, because it had been drawn up from the applicant's own words, who might have been telling the truth or not. Instructions were to treat returnees with extreme caution, especially if they were travelling on their own. Tveritinov could not prove that he really had been left behind in Skopino. Maybe it was Paveletsk? Perhaps he had had the time to go to Moscow and back on some mission?

However, it was in his favour that he had managed to get here in such a short time.

But then, what guarantee was there that he really had been on that train?

"So you had a nice warm journey?"

"Of course. I would gladly have travelled the rest of the way like that."

"So why did you get out?"

"To report to you. I was told to do that in Ryazhsk."

Tveritinov had a large head and big features. His forehead was broad and high, his eyebrows big and bushy, his nose prominent. His chin and cheeks were overgrown with dirty, grizzled stubble.

"How did you know that this was Krechetovka?"

"There was a Georgian sleeping next to me; he told me."

"A soldier? What rank?"

"I don't know. He just poked his head from out of the quilts."

Tveritinov's answers were becoming halfhearted, as though he was losing something with each word he spoke.

"I see." Zotov put down the travel warrant. "What other documents have you got?"

"None, really." Tveritinov smiled sadly. "How could I have documents?"

"I see. None at all?"

"When we were surrounded, we took care to destroy whatever we had."

"But now, when you arrived back in Soviet territory, they must have given you something?"

"Not a thing. They made up lists, divided us into parties of forty, and sent us on."

That was how it must have been. Until a man gets left behind, he is a member of his group and therefore needs no documents. But Zotov still wanted some material evidence to justify his involuntary liking for this well-mannered man with dignified bearing.

"Come on, something, anything. Haven't you any bit of paper left in your pocket?"

"Well, just some snaps ... of the family."

"Let me see them." It was not an order but a request.

Tveritinov's brows lifted slightly. He smiled once more with that bewildered, hesitant smile and took a flat bundle of thick orange paper out of the same pocket of his tunic (the other pocket did not fasten, having no button). He opened it out on his knees, got out two three-by-five snapshots, looked at the one and the other, then half rose to hand them to the officer, but as it was not very far from the chair to the table, Zotov leaned over to take them. Zotov began to study them as Tveritinov, still holding the open bundle on his knees, straightened his back and tried also to look at them from a distance.

One of the snaps was of a girl of about fourteen wearing a striped grey open-necked dress with a sash. It must have been early spring because the leaves were still tiny and one could see through the branches of the trees. The sun was shining and she was standing in a little garden. She had a long, slender neck. Her face was finely drawn and even though it was a still photograph it seemed to tremble. The picture gave the impression of something immature, of something that had been left unsaid; far from being cheerful, it was heartrending.

The little girl greatly appealed to Zotov. His expression relaxed. "What's her name?" he asked quietly.

Tveritinov was sitting with his eyes shut. "Lyalya," he said, even more quietly. Then he opened his eyes and corrected himself: "Irina."

"When was it taken?"

"This year."

"Where was it?"

"Near Moscow."

Six months! Six months had passed since the moment when someone had said: "Smile, Lyalyenka!" and clicked the shutter. Since then tens of thousands of gun barrels had thundered and millions of fountains of black earth had erupted and millions of people had

178

been whirled as if by a monstrous roundabout; people
had walked from Lithuania, people had come by train
from Irkutsk. And now at this station, with a cold wind
whipping up the snow and rain, with trains standing
idle and people milling aimlessly by day and by night,
sleeping hugger-mugger on the black floors, how could
one believe that that little garden, that child, that dress
still existed?

In the second photo, a woman and a boy were sitting
on a sofa, looking at a big book with full-page illustra-
tions. The mother was slenderly built, evidently tall,
and the boy was about seven. He had a round face and
was not looking at the book but gazing with an intelligent expression at his mother, who was explaining
something to him. His eyes were big like his father's.

There was a special quality about the whole family.
Zotov himself had never met any families like that, but
little fragments in his memory—from the Tretyakov
Museum, from the theatre, or from books—had gradually built up in him the idea that such families existed.
Looking at these photos, Zotov sensed an atmosphere
of cultured security.

As he handed them back, Zotov said: "You must be
hot. Why don't you take off your things?"

"Yes," said Tveritinov, took off his coat, and looked
around, wondering where to put it.

"Over there, on the seat." Zotov pointed and even
made as if to help him.

Now the patches, the raggedness, the odd buttons on
Tveritinov's summer uniform could be seen. He had
put on his puttees so clumsily that the coils were slack
and hung down in loops. His whole appearance was in
mocking contrast to his distinguished, greying head.

Zotov could no longer restrain the sympathy he felt
for this man, who took everything so calmly; he had
been right in liking him from the first.

"Who are you?" he asked respectfully.

As he sadly wrapped up the photographs in the
orange paper, Tveritinov replied, with a smile: "An
actor."

"Really?" Zotov was amazed. "I should have guessed
straightaway. You look just like an actor." (Although

179

at this moment he could hardly have looked less like one.)

"I bet you're an Honoured Artist."

"No."

"Where did you work?"

"At the Dramatic Theatre in Moscow."

"I've only been in Moscow once. On an excursion. We went to the Moscow Arts Theatre. But I've often been to the theatre in Ivanovo. Have you ever seen the new theatre there?"

"No."

"Outside it's nothing much, a grey box, you know, reinforced concrete style, but inside it's marvelous. I used to love going to the theatre. It's not just an entertainment, it's an education, isn't it?"

(Of course, those papers about the bombed train were still screaming to be sorted out, but that was at least two full days' work. Whereas the chance to meet and spend an hour with a real actor was not to be missed.)

"What parts have you played?"

"Any number." Tveritinov smiled sadly. "So many years, you can't count."

"Oh, come on . . . For example?"

"Well . . . Colonel Vershinin . . . Doctor Rank . . ."

"Hm. Hm." (The names meant nothing to Zotov.) "Have you played in anything by Gorky?"

"Of course, naturally."

"I like Gorky's plays best of all. And everything by Gorky. He's the wisest, most human, the greatest writer we've got, don't you think?"

Tveritinov puckered his brows in the effort to find an answer, failed, and said nothing.

"I've an idea I do know your name. Aren't you an Honoured Artist?" Zotov was slightly flushed with pleasure at the conversation.

"If I were Honoured"—Tveritinov shrugged his shoulders—"I wouldn't be here now."

"Why? Oh, yes, you wouldn't have been mobilised."

"But we weren't mobilised. We volunteered for the militia."

180

"But surely Honoured Artists joined up voluntarily too."

"Yes, everyone, from the chief producer downwards. But then some person drew a line after a certain number, and those above the line stayed at home and those below went."

"Did you get any military training?"

"A few days. Bayonet practice. With sticks. And how to throw grenades. Wooden ones."

Tveritinov's eyes fixed on a point on the floor and became glassy.

"Then what—did they arm you?"

"They chucked us a few rifles when we were already on the move. The 1891 model. We marched as far as Vyazma. But near Vyazma we were caught in an ambush."

"Were many killed?"

"I think the majority were taken prisoner. A small group of us joined the returnees and they got us out. I have no idea now where the front is. You haven't got a map, have you?"

"There's no map, the news bulletins are vague, but I can tell you anyway: Sebastopol and a bit round it is ours; Taganrog is ours; we're holding on to the Donets Basin. But they've got Orel and Kursk."

"That's bad ... What's happening around Moscow?"

"It's particularly confused round Moscow. They've nearly reached the suburbs. Leningrad is completely cut off." Zotov's eyes and forehead wrinkled with despair. "And I can't get to the front."

"You'll get there, all right."

"If I do, it'll be only if we're in for a long war."

"Were you a student?"

"Yes. Actually, we were taking our final exams in the first days of the war ... If you could call them exams. We were supposed to do them in December. Then they told us: Just bring whatever drawings and calculations you've done, and that will do." Zotov began to talk with interest and animation, swallowing his words in his haste to say it all. "The whole five years I was there, it was like that. Just as we began the course,

181

the Franco trouble started. Then Austria fell, then
Czechoslovakia. Then the world war started, then the
Finnish war. Hitler invaded France, Greece, Yugosla-
via! How could we concentrate on textile machinery in
an atmosphere like that? But that's not the point.
Straight after graduation, the boys were sent on a driving and vehicle-maintenance course at the military
academy. But I was left behind because of my eyes, I'm
very shortsighted.

"I besieged the local military district headquarters
every single day. I already had some experience in that
sort of thing from 1937. The only thing I achieved was
to be given a travel warrant to go to the officers'
training school of the Supply Corps. I used that pass to
travel via Moscow, where I wormed my way into the
People's Commissariat of Defence. Finally I managed
to see some old colonel. He was in a great hurry; in
fact, he was already fastening his briefcase. 'Look,' I
said. 'Look, I'm an engineer, I don't want to be a
supply officer.' 'Show me your diploma.' But I didn't
have my diploma with me ... 'All right, here's one
question for you. If you can answer this, you must be
an engineer: what is a crank?' So I rattled off: 'A device
placed on the axis of rotation and linked to a con-
necting rod by a bearing in order to ...' He crossed out
'Supply Corps' from my documents and wrote 'To the
transport officers' school.' And he ran off, carrying his
briefcase. I was on top of the world. But when I got to
the transport school they weren't taking anyone; there
were only courses for R.T.O.'s. So the crank didn't
help, after all!"

Vasya knew quite well that this was no time for
chatting and reminiscing, but the chance to open his
heart to a sympathetic, intelligent person was so rare.

"But I expect you'd like to smoke, wouldn't you?"
Vasya came to himself. "Do have a cigarette, if you
want to." He glanced down at the man's travel warrant
... "Igor Dementyevich. Here's the tobacco, here's the
paper. I get a ration but I don't smoke."

He took a newly opened packet of cigarette tobacco
out of a drawer and offered it to Igor Dementyevich.

"I do," admitted Igor Dementyevich, and his face lit

182

up with anticipation. He got up and bent over the packet but did not start to roll a cigarette immediately; at first he just breathed in the aroma of the tobacco, uttering what sounded almost like a groan. Then, as he read the name of the tobacco, he shook his head unbelievingly: "Armenian."

He rolled a fat cigarette and licked it down with his tongue, at which Vasya lit a match for him.

"And in that truckload of quilts, was anyone smoking?" Zotov inquired.

"Not that I noticed Igor Dementyevich leaned back pleasurably. "I expect nobody had any tobacco."

Smoking with half-closed eyes, he asked: "What were you saying about 1937?"

"Well, you remember what it was like at the time," said Vasya heatedly. "The Spanish war was on. The Fascists took University City. The International Brigade! Guadalajara, Jarama, Teruel! How could anyone keep calm? We demanded to be taught Spanish, but no, they went on teaching us German. I got hold of a textbook, a dictionary, neglected my studies, my exams, and learned Spanish. The whole situation made me feel that we were part of it, that our revolutionary conscience would not allow us to stand aside. But the newspapers said nothing of the kind. How on earth could I get there? Obviously, it was just childish nonsense to run away to Odessa and get on a boat. Anyway, there were the frontier guards. So I went to the head of the fourth department of the Military Commissariat, then to the third department, the second, the first: Send me to Spain! They laughed: Have you gone mad? There are none of our people there, and what do you think you will do there? ... You know, I can see how much you like smoking; take the whole packet. I only keep it for visitors, anyway. I've got some more at home. No, no, please, put it in your kit bag and fasten it up; then I'll believe you. Tobacco these days is as good as a free pass, you may need it on your journey ... Then suddenly one day I read in *Red Star*—I used to read every single newspaper—a quotation from a French journalist: 'Germany and the U.S.S.R. regard Spain as a military training tround.' I can be very persistent, so I got a copy of that issue from the library and waited three days for an editorial denial. There wasn't one. Then I went to the local Military Commandant himself, and I said: 'Here, read this. There hasn't been a denial, so it's a fact: we are fighting there. Please send me to Spain as a private soldier.' The commandant banged the table: 'Don't you try and catch me out with tricks like that! Who put you up to this? If we need you, we'll call you. About turn.'"

Vasya laughed wholeheartedly as he recalled it all. His face wrinkled with laughter lines. He felt very much at ease with this actor and wanted to tell him more, about the arrival of the Spanish sailors and how he had replied to them in Spanish. He wanted to ask him what it had been like when they were surrounded by the Germans, and generally to discuss the course of the war with this intelligent, sophisticated man.

But Podshebyakina opened the door. "Vasil Vasilich, the dispatcher wants to know if you have anything for number 794. If not, we'll let it through."

Zotov looked at the timetable.

"Which one is that? To Povorino?"

"Yes."

"Is it here already?"

"It's due in about ten minutes."

"It doesn't seem to be carrying much in the way of military supplies. What else has it got?"

"It's got industrial supplies and a few heated passenger carriages."

"Well, that's a stroke of luck. That's wonderful. Igor Dementyevich, I'll put you on that train. It's a very good train for you, you won't have to change. No, Valechka, all my loads are taken care of, you can let it through. But tell them to stop it close to the station, on track 1 or track 2."

"All right, Vasil Vasilich."

"Have you rung through about the quilts?"

"Just as you told me." And she went out.

"It's a shame, though, that I can't give you any food. I haven't even a piece of dry bread in my drawer." Zotov pulled out the drawer as though not quite convinced that there was nothing there. But he got no more than the standard ration and he had already eaten the bread he had brought with him when he came on duty that morning.

"Suppose you haven't eaten anything since you got left behind?"

"For heaven's sake, don't worry, Vasil Vasilich." Tveritinov spread his fingers fanwise across his grubby tunic with its odd buttons. "I'm grateful enough to you as it is." His expression and voice were no longer sad. "You have warmed me, literally and figuratively. You are a kind man. Times are so hard now that one really appreciates it. Now, could you please explain to me where I am going and what I should do next?"

"First," explained Zotov with pleasure, "you will go to Gryazi. Pity I haven't got a map. Have you any idea where it is?"

"N-not really. I think I've heard the name."

"Everybody knows that station. If you arrive in Gryazi in the daytime, take this bit of paper of yours—I'll make a note on it that you've been to see me. Take it to the R.T.O., he'll give you an indent for the ration stores, and you'll get a couple of days' rations."

"I'm most grateful."

"But if you should arrive there at night, don't get off, stay put in that train. You'd have been in a fix in your truckload of quilts if you hadn't woken up in time. God knows where you would have ended up. From Gryazi your train will go to Povorino, but don't get out at Povorino either; just jump out for your rations, and don't get left behind. It'll take you to Archeda. That's where your train number 245413 is going to."

And Zotov handed Tveritinov his warrant. Putting the paper away in the same pocket of his tunic, the one that buttoned properly, Tveritinov asked: "Archeda? Now that's a place I've never heard of. Where's that?"

"It's very near Stalingrad."

"Near Stalingrad." Tveritinov nodded, but wrinkled his brow. Making a mental effort, he asked vaguely: "Sorry . . . Stalingrad? What was it called before?"

Something in Zotov snapped and he suddenly froze. Was it possible? A Soviet citizen and he didn't know

Stalingrad? That was quite, quite impossible! Impossible, impossible! Unthinkable.

However, he managed to retain control of himself. He pulled himself together, straightened his glasses, and said, almost calmly: "It used to be called Tsaritsyn."

(So he wasn't a returnee. He was a plant, an agent. With those manners, most likely a White émigré.)

"Oh, of course, of course. Tsaritsyn. The defence of Tsaritsyn."

(He might even be an officer in disguise. That's why he was asking for a map. He was overdoing it a bit with those clothes.)

That dirty word "officer" had long since been abolished from Russian, replaced by the word "leader," but even when not spoken aloud, it pierced Zotov like a bayonet.

(Like a simpleton, he had let himself be taken in. Right, keep calm, keep on the alert. What was he to do now?)

Zotov gave a long ring on his field telephone.

He held the receiver to his ear, hoping the captain would pick up his receiver straightaway.

But the captain did not.

"Vasil Vasilich, I feel rather bad about taking all your tobacco."

"No trouble. You're welcome to it."

(God, what a fool I was! Quite forgot myself. Completely let my guard down, couldn't do enough for him.)

"Well, in that case, may I have another smoke here? Or should I step outside?"

(Go outside?! How blatant. He realises he's made a slip, so now he wants to clear off.)

"No, no. Smoke here. I like tobacco smoke."

(Must think of something. How can I do it?)

He gave three rings. Somebody answered: "Guard-room here."

"Zotov speaking."

"Yes, comrade lieutenant."

"Where's Guskov?"

"He's . . . gone out, comrade lieutenant."

"Where's he gone? Why has he gone out? You make sure that he's back in five minutes."

(Gone to his woman, the swine.)

"Yes, sir."

(Must think of something.)

Zotov took a sheet of paper and, shielding it from Tveritino, wrote on it in large letters: "Valya, come in and say that number 794 is an hour late."

He folded the paper, went to the door, stretched out his hand, and said: "Comrade Podshebyakina, take this. It's about that train."

"Which one, Vasil Vasilich?"

"The numbers are written there."

Surprised, Podshebyakina stood up and took the paper. Zotov returned to his room without waiting.

Tveritinov was putting on his coat. "We won't miss the train, will we?" he said with a friendly smile.

"No, they'll let us know."

Zotov walked up and down the room without looking at Tveritinov. He pulled down the folds of his tunic at the back under his belt, shifted his revolver from the back to his right side, and straightened the green cap on his head. There was absolutely nothing to be done and nothing to say.

And Zotov could not lie.

If only Tveritinov would say something, but he was keeping a polite silence.

Outside the window the stream of water from the broken drainpipe gave an occasional gurgle as it was blown back and forth by the wind.

The lieutenant stopped by the desk, gripped the corner of it, and stared at his fingers.

(To prevent Tveritinov noticing any change, he ought to look at him with the same expression as before, but he could not bring himself to do it.)

"Well in a few days' time it'll be the holiday," he said, on guard for the reply.

(Go on, ask—ask me—*what* holiday? Then there'll be no more doubt about it.)

But the visitor merely said: "Ye-es . . ."

The lieutenant threw him a glance. The man nodded slowly and went on smoking.

"I wonder if there'll be a parade on Red Square?"

(Who cared about the parade? He wasn't really thinking about it at all but was simply talking to fill in time.)

There was a knock at the door.

"May I come in, Vasil Vasilich?" Valya stuck her head in. Tveritinov saw her and reached for his kit bag.

"Number 794 has been held up at the junction. It'll be an hour late."

"Oh, what a nuisance." (The sickening falsity in his own voice disgusted him.) "All right, Comrade Podshebyakina."

Valya disappeared.

From right outside the window on track 1 could be heard the muffled panting of a locomotive and the clank of buffers as a train drew to a halt; they could feel the ground shaking.

"What's to be done?" Zotov was thinking aloud. "I have to go to the ration stores."

"I can wait outside. I'll go wherever you like," Tveritinov said eagerly, smiling as he stood up, holding his kit bag.

Zotov took his coat off the nail. "Why should you go outside and freeze? You can't get into the waiting room, it's packed solid, they're lying on the floor. Would you like to come with me to the ration stores?"

It sounded somehow unconvincing and, feeling himself blush, he added: "Maybe, you know ... I could manage ... to scrounge you something to eat there."

If only Tveritinov had not been so overjoyed. But his face lit up and he said: "That would be the height of kindness on your part. I wouldn't dare to ask you."

Zotov turned away, looked at his desk, checked the door of the safe, and put out the light. "Well, let's go."

As he locked the door, he said to Valya: "If anyone calls, I'll be back in a minute."

Tveritinov went out in front of him in his absurd getup and his loose, untidy puttees.

They went down a cold dark little corridor with a blue lamp and out onto the platform.

From an invisible sky wet, heavy, whitish flakes that

were neither rain nor snow slanted down through the blackness of the night.

There on track 1 stood the train. It was quite black, but a little blacker than the sky, so that its carriages and roofs could just be made out. To the left, where the engine stood, the ashpit shone with an incandescent glow; hot bright ash dripped onto the track and was blown swiftly to one side. Farther away and higher up, a solitary round green light hung in the air. To the right, towards the end of the train, streams of fiery sparks showered onto the carriages. Dark figures, mostly of women, were hurrying along the platform towards these life-giving sparks. The heavy breathing of many people dragging huge, monstrous burdens merged into a single sound. Children, silent or crying, were dragged along. Two breathless men pushed Zotov aside as they lugged a heavy trunk. Someone else was dragging something even heavier behind him, lurching and grinding along the platform. (Why was it now, of all times, when travelling had become such a desperate struggle, that everyone had to take his babies and his grandmother with him? Why did they have to carry all those impossibly heavy bags, baskets as big as beds and trunks the size of wardrobes?)

Were it not for the ash under the engine, the signal, the sparks from the chimneys on the heated carriages, and the dim light of a lantern glimmering somewhere out on the distant tracks, one might never know that this was a railway station—a meeting point of countless trains, and not the depths of a forest or a dark stretch of open countryside that was once again submitting to winter in the slow-moving cycle of the years.

But the ear could hear the clanging of couplings, the sound of the pointsman's horn, the puffing of two engines, the clatter and hum of people roused to desperate activity.

"This way." Zotov took him into a little passage leading away from the platform. He was holding a lantern with a blue glass and several times shone it on the ground to show Tveritinov the way.

"Ouch, I nearly lost my cap then," complained Tveritinov.

The lieutenant walked in silence.

"Don't know if it's snow or not, but it gets down your collar," said his companion, keeping up the conversation. His coat did not even have a collar.

"Watch out for the mud," the lieutenant warned him.

They stepped right into sticky, slimy mud. There was nowhere dry to tread.

"Halt! Who goes there?" a sentry shouted deafeningly from somewhere nearby.

Tveritinov jumped.

"Lieutenant Zotov."

They went straight on, up to their ankles in mud, dragging their feet with difficulty where the mud was thickest. Rounding the corner of the ration-store building, they went up the steps to the porch. They stamped energetically and brushed the rain from their shoulders. His torch still shining as they went indoors, the lieutenant led Tveritinov into a messroom where there was an empty table and two benches (this was where the soldiers on duty at the ration stores ate and trained). For a long time they had been trying to find a length of wire to bring in an electric light, but this room with its unwhitewashed wooden walls was still lit weakly and fitfully by a lamp standing on the table. The corners were shrouded in darkness.

The door of the guardroom opened. A soldier stood in the doorway, a dark figure against the electric light that shone in from behind.

"Where's Guskov?" Zotov asked sternly.

"Halt! Who goes there?" barked a voice from outside.

There was a sound of boots stamping on the porch. Then Guskov came in, and behind him the soldier who had run to get him.

"Here I am, comrade lieutenant." Guskov made a vague gesture approximating a salute. In the half light, Zotov could guess that Guskov's face, always rather insolent, was twitching with irritation because he had been interrupted for some triviality by the lieutenant—to whom he was not even directly subordinate.

190

Zotov suddenly shouted angrily: "Sergeant Guskov! How many sentries are you supposed to have posted?"

Guskov was not frightened but surprised; Zotov never shouted. He answered quietly: "There are supposed to be two, but you know that . . ."

"I know nothing. You know what the guard regulations are; obey them immediately!"

Guskov's lip twitched again. "Private Bobnev, take your rifle and go on duty."

Clumping heavily, the soldier who had brought Guskov walked round his superiors and disappeared into the next room.

"You, sergeant, come with me to the commander's office."

By now Guskov had an inkling that something was up.

The soldier came back carrying a rifle with bayonet fixed, marched smartly past them, and took up his sentry post by the outer door.

(At this point Zotov was overcome with timidity. He could not find the right words to say.)

"You . . . I . . ." said Zotov quietly, barely able to raise his eyes to Tveritinov. "I must go and see to something . . ." His accent was particularly noticeable. "You sit down here for a minute. I won't be long. Wait for me."

Tveritinov's head in his broad cap and the shadows it cast on the wall and the ceiling looked strangely sinister. The coils of his scarf seemed to be throttling him like a boa constrictor.

"You're leaving me here? But, Vasil Vasilich, I'll miss the train if I stay here. At least let me wait on the platform."

"No, no. You stay here." Zotov hurried to the door.

Now Tveritinov understood. "You're arresting me?!" he shouted. "But what for, comrade lieutenant? Let me catch my train!"

And with the same gesture that he had previously used to express gratitude, he pressed his five fingers to his chest, fanwise. He took two quick steps after the lieutenant, but the sentry, grasping the situation, barred the way with his bayonet.

Zotov could not help looking back once more—for the last time in his life—to catch a glimpse of that face in the dim light of the lantern, the despairing face of King Lear in the burial chamber.

"What are you doing, what are you doing?" shouted Tveritinov in a voice that rang like a bell. "You're making a mistake that can never be put right!"

As he flung up his arms in their too-short sleeves, one hand holding the kit bag, he seemed to grow to the size of his dark, flapping shadow and the ceiling seemed to be pressing down on his head.

"Don't worry, don't worry," Zotov soothed him, feeling for the doorstep with his foot. "We've just got to clear up one little question."

And he went out. Guskov followed him.

As they passed the office of the military dispatcher, the lieutenant said: "Hold that train a bit longer."

Back in his room, he sat at the table and wrote:

To: *Security Section, Transport Branch, NKVD*

I am sending you herewith the prisoner Tveritinov, Igor Dementyevich, allegedly left behind at Skopino from train 245413. In conversation with me . . .

"Get ready," he said to Guskov. "You will take another soldier, escort this man to the junction, and hand him over to the Security Section."

Several days passed, the holiday came and went.

But Zotov could not shake off the memory of the man with the delightful smile and the snapshot of his daughter in her little striped dress.

Surely he had done everything he should have done.

Yes, but . . .

He wanted to find out whether the man really was a spy or if he had long since been released. Zotov telephoned the Security Section at the junction.

"Excuse me, but on November 1 I sent you a prisoner called Tveritinov. Could you tell me what's happened to him?"

"Being investigated," was the firm answer. "And

look here, Zotov. In that report of yours about the goods that were 80 percent damaged by fire, there are several points which are not clear. It's a very important matter. Someone might get into trouble."

All that winter Zotov worked at the same station as assistant R.T.O. More than once he was tempted to ring up and inquire but was afraid that it might seem suspicious.

Once the Security Officer came over from headquarters on a matter of duty. As if by the way, Zotov casually asked him: "Do you happen to remember a man called Tveritinov? I arrested him in the autumn."

"Why do you ask?" The Security Officer frowned significantly.

"Just wondered . . . what happened to him in the end?"

"Your Tverikin's been sorted out all right. We don't make mistakes."

After that, Zotov was never able to forget the man for the rest of his life . . .

PROSE POEMS

Freedom to Breathe

A shower fell in the night and now dark clouds drift across the sky, occasionally sprinkling a fine film of rain.

I stand under an apple tree in blossom and I breathe. Not only the apple tree but the grass round it glistens with moisture; words cannot describe the sweet fragrance that pervades the air. I inhale as deeply as I can, and the aroma invades my whole being; I breathe with my eyes open, I breathe with my eyes closed—I cannot say which gives me the greater pleasure.

This, I believe, is the single most precious freedom that prison takes away from us: the freedom to breathe freely, as I now can. No food on earth, no wine, not even a woman's kiss is sweeter to me than this air steeped in the fragrance of flowers, of moisture and freshness.

No matter that this is only a tiny garden, hemmed in by five-story houses like cages in a zoo. I cease to hear the motorcycles backfiring, radios whining, the burble of loudspeakers. As long as there is fresh air to breathe under an apple tree after a shower, we may survive a little longer.

Lake Segden

No one writes about this lake and it is spoken of only in whispers. As though to an enchanted castle, all roads to it are barred and over each one hangs a forbidding sign—a plain, blunt straight line.

Man or beast, faced by that sign, must turn back. Some earthly power has put that sign there; past it none may ride, none may walk, crawl, or even fly.

Guards with swords and pistols lurk beside the path in the nearby pine grove.

You may circle and circle the silent wood searching for a way through to the lake, but you will find none and there will be no one to ask, for no one goes into this wood. They have all been frightened away. Your only chance to venture through will be one afternoon in the rain along a cattle track, in the wake of the dull clink of a cowbell. And from your first glimpse of it, vast and shimmering between the tree trunks, you know before you reach its banks that you will be in thrall to this place for the rest of your life.

Segden Lake is as round as though traced out with a pair of compasses. If you were to shout from one side (but you must not shout, or you will be heard), only a fading echo would reach the other bank. It is a long way across. Woods immure the lakeside entirely, a dense forest of row upon unbroken row of trees. As you come out of the wood to the water's edge, you can see the whole of the forbidden shore: here a strip of yellow sand, there a grey stubble of reeds, there a lush swathe of grass. The water is smooth, calm, and unruffled, and apart from some patches of weed by the shore, the white lake bed gleams through the translucent water.

A secret lake in a secret forest. The water looks up and the sky gazes down upon it. If there is a world

198

beyond the forest, it is unknown, invisible; if it exists, it has no place here.

Here is somewhere to settle forever, a place where a man could live in harmony with the elements and be inspired.

But it cannot be. An evil prince, a squint-eyed villain, has claimed the lake for his own: there is his house, there is his bathing place. His evil brood goes fishing here, shoots duck from his boat. First a wisp of blue smoke above the lake, then a moment later the shot.

Away beyond the woods, the people sweat and heave, whilst all the roads leading here are closed lest they intrude. Fish and game are bred for the villain's pleasure. Here there are traces where someone lit a fire but it was put out and he was driven away.

Beloved, deserted lake.

My native land . . .

The Duckling

A little yellow duckling, flopping comically on its white belly in the wet grass and scarcely able to stand on its thin, feeble legs, runs in front of me and quacks: "Where's my mommy? Where's my family?"

He has no mommy, because he has been fostered by a hen: duck eggs were put in her nest, she sat on them and hatched them with her own. To shelter them from the bad weather, their home—an upturned basket without a bottom—has been moved into a shed and covered with sacking. They are all in there, but this one is lost. Come on then, little thing, let me take you in my hand.

What keeps it alive? It weighs nothing; its little black eyes are like beads, its feet are like sparrows' feet, the slightest squeeze and it would be no more. Yet it is warm with life. Its little beak is pale pink and slightly splayed, like a manicured fingernail. Its feet are already webbed, there is yellow among its feathers, and its downy wings are starting to protrude. Its personality already sets it apart from its foster brothers.

And we men will soon be flying to Venus; if we all pooled our efforts, we could plough up the whole world in twenty minutes.

Yet, with all our atomic might, we shall never—never!—be able to make this feeble speck of a yellow duckling in a test tube; even if we were given the feathers and bones, we could never put such a creature together.

The Ashes of a Poet

Where now there is a village called L'govo, the ancient town of Ol'gov once stood on this cliff above the river Oka. When the Russians of those days chose a site, next in importance after good, drinkable, running water was its beauty.

Saved by a miracle from murder at his brothers' hands, Ingvar Igorevich founded the Monastery of the Assumption here as a thank offering.

From this place, on a clear day you can see far across the water meadows to where, thirty-five versts away, on another such eminence stands the tall belfry of the Monastery of St. John the Divine.

Both were spared by the superstitious Khan Bahty.

From all others, Yakov Petrovich Polonsky chose this place as his own and gave instructions that he was to be buried here. Man, it seems, has always been prone to the belief that his spirit will hover over his grave and gaze down on the peaceful countryside around it.

But the domed churches have gone; the half of the stone walls that is left has been made up in height by a plank fence with barbed wire, and the whole of this ancient place is dominated by those sickeningly familiar monsters: watchtowers. There is a guardhouse in the monastery gateway, and a poster that says "Peace among Nations," with a Russian workman holding a little black girl in his arms.

We pretend ignorance. Among the huts where the guards live, an off-duty warder, dressed in a singlet, explains to us:

"There was a monastery here, in the second world. They say the first world was Rome, and Moscow is the third. It used to be a children's colony once, too, but the kids didn't know what the place was, so they messed up the walls and smashed the ikons. Then a collective farm bought the two churches for forty thousand roubles—for the bricks, to build a big cowshed with six rows of stalls. Worked on it myself. We were paid fifty kopecks for a whole one, twenty kopecks for a half brick. But they never came out clean—always had lumps of mortar stuck to them. They found a vault under the church with a bishop in it. He was just a skeleton, but his robe was still all right. A couple of us tried to pull the robe in two, but the stuff was that good it wouldn't tear . . ."

"Tell me—according to the map, there's a poet called Polonsky buried here. Where is his grave?"

"You can't see Polonsky. He's inside the perimeter."

So Polonsky was out of bounds. What else was there to see? A crumbling ruin? Wait, though—the warder was turning to his wife: "Didn't they dig Polonsky up?"

"Mm. Took him to Ryazan." The woman nodded from the porch as she cracked sunflower seeds with her teeth.

The warder thought this was a great joke: "Seems he'd done his time—so they let him out . . ."

The Elm Log

We were sawing firewood when we picked up an elm log and gave a cry of amazement. It was a full year since we had chopped down the trunk, dragged it along behind a tractor, and sawn it up into logs, which we had then thrown onto barges and wagons, rolled into stacks, and piled up on the ground—and yet this elm log had still not given up! A fresh green shoot had sprouted from it with a promise of a thick leafy branch, or even a whole new elm tree.

We placed the log on the sawing horse, as though on an executioner's block, but we could not bring ourselves to bite into it with our saw. How could we? That log cherished life as dearly as we did; indeed, its urge to live was even stronger than ours.

Reflections

On the surface of a swift-flowing stream the reflections of things near or far are always indistinct; even if the water is clear and has no foam, reflections in the constant stream of ripples, the restless kaleidoscope of water, are still uncertain, vague, incomprehensible.

Only when the water has flowed down river after river and reaches a broad, calm estuary or comes to rest in some backwater or a small, still lake—only then can we see in its mirrorlike smoothness every leaf of a tree on the bank, every wisp of a cloud, and the deep blue expanse of the sky.

It is the same with our lives. If so far we have been unable to see clearly or to reflect the eternal lineaments of truth, is it not because we too are still moving towards some end—because we are still alive?

The City on the Neva

Angels holding candelabra kneel around the Byzantine dome of St. Isaac's.

Three faceted gold spires echo one another across the Neva and the Moika. Everywhere lions, griffons, and sphinxes stand guard over treasure houses, or sleep. History, drawn by her six horses, gallops atop Rossi's ingenious crooked arch. Porticoes by the hundred, thousands of pillars, prancing horses, straining bulls . . .

What a blessing that no new building is allowed here. No wedding-cake skyscraper may elbow its way onto the Nevsky Prospekt, no five-story shoebox can ruin the Griboyedov Canal. There is no architect living, no matter how servile and incompetent, who can use his influence to build on any site nearer than the Black River or the Okhta.

It is alien to us, yet it is our greatest glory! What a pleasure it is today to stroll down those avenues. Yet all this beauty was built by Russians—men who ground their teeth and cursed as they rotted in those dismal swamps. The bones of our forefathers were compressed, petrified, fused into palaces coloured ochre, *sang de boeuf,* chocolate brown, green.

And what of our disastrous, chaotic lives? What of our explosions of protest, the groans of men shot by firing squads, the tears of our women: will all this too—terrible thought—be utterly forgotten? Can it, too, give rise to such perfect, everlasting beauty?

The Puppy

In our back yard a boy keeps his little dog Sharik chained up, a ball of fluff shackled since he was a puppy.

One day I took him some chicken bones that were still warm and smelt delicious. The boy had just let the poor dog off his lead to have a run round the yard. The snow there was deep and feathery; Sharik was bounding about like a hare, first on his hind legs, then on his front ones, from one corner of the yard to the other, back and forth, burying his muzzle in the snow.

He ran towards me, his coat all shaggy, jumped up at me, sniffed the bones—then off he went again, belly-deep in the snow.

I don't need your bones, he said. Just give me my freedom . . .

The Old Bucket

Yes, Kartun Forest is a depressing place for an ex-soldier to explore. There is a place in it where the traces of eighteen years ago are still preserved. Partly collapsed, it hardly looks like a line of trenches or the firing position of a troop of field guns but was most likely an infantry platoon strong-point where an anonymous band of hefty Russian soldiers, in their tattered greatcoats, had dug themselves in. Over the years the roof beams of the dugout have been removed, of course, but the trenches are still quite plain to see.

Although I never fought here, I was in action in another wood like it nearby. I walked from dugout to dugout trying to reconstruct the position. Suddenly, coming out of one dugout, I stumbled on an old bucket which had already seen better days when it had been left lying there eighteen years ago.

Even then, in that first wartime winter, it had been broken. Maybe some quick-witted soldier had picked it up in a burnt-out village, had battered the lower half of the sides into a cone and used it to connect his tin stove to a flue. Here, in this same dugout, for the ninety or perhaps hundred and fifty days that the front line was stabilised in this sector, smoke had poured through this broken bucket. It had glowed hellishly hot, men had warmed their hands over it, you could light a cigarette on it and toast bread in front of it. As much smoke had passed through that bucket as all the unspoken thoughts and unwritten letters of the men there—men, alas, probably long since dead.

Then one bright morning the tactical position changed, the dugout was abandoned, and as the officer urged them on—"Come on, get moving!"—an orderly doused the stove, packed it into the back of the truck until everything was stowed away, except that there was no room for the broken bucket.

"Chuck the filthy thing away!" shouted the sergeant major. "You'll find another one in the new place."

They had a long way to go, and in any case the warmer spring weather was not far off; the orderly stood there with the broken bucket, and with a sigh he dropped it by the entrance to the dugout.

Everybody laughed.

Since then the logs have been pulled off the roof, the bunks and the table removed from the inside, but that faithful bucket has stayed there beside its dugout.

As I stood over it, tears started to my eyes. How splendid they were, those friends of wartime days. The spirit that kept us going, our hopes, even that selfless friendship of ours—it has all vanished like smoke and there will never again be a use for that rusty, forgotten . . .

In Yesenin Country

Four monotonous villages strung out one after another along the road. Dust. No gardens, and no woods nearby. Rickety fences. Here and there some garishly painted shutters. A pig scratching itself against the pump in the middle of the road. As the shadow of a bicycle flashes past them, a flock of geese in single file turn their heads in unison and give it a cheerfully aggressive honk. Chickens scratch busily in the roadway and the yards, searching for food.

Even the village general store of Konstantinovo looks like a rickety henhouse. Salted herrings. Several brands of vodka. Sticky boiled sweets of a kind people stopped eating fifteen years ago. Round loaves of black bread, twice as heavy as the ones you buy in town, looking as if they are meant to be sliced with an axe rather than a knife.

Inside the Yesenins' cottage, wretched little partitions that do not reach the ceiling divide it up into what are more like cupboards or loose boxes than rooms. Outside is a little fenced-in yard; here there used to be a bathhouse, where Sergey would shut himself in the dark and compose his first poems. Beyond the fence is the usual little paddock.

I walk around this village, which is exactly like so many others, where the villagers' main concerns are still the crops, how to make money, how to keep up with the neighbours, and I am moved: the divine fire once scorched this piece of countryside and I can feel it burning my cheeks to this day. Walking along the steep banks of the Oka, I stare into the distance with wonderment—was it really that far-off strip of Khvorostov wood which inspired the evocative line:

The forest clamorous with a food-grouse's lament . . .

And is this the same peaceful Oka, meandering through water meadows, of which he wrote:

Hayricks of sun stacked in the waters' depth . . .

What a thunderbolt of talent the Creator must have hurled into that cottage, into the heart of that quick-tempered country boy, for the shock of it to have opened his eyes to so much beauty—by the stove, in the pigsty, on the threshing floor, in the fields; beauty which for a thousand years others had simply trampled on and ignored.

The Kolkhoz Rucksack

When you're in a suburban bus and one of them gives you a painful blow in the chest or on the back with its hard edge—don't swear, but take a good look at that plaited straw basket on its wide, frayed canvas strap. Its owner is carrying milk, cottage cheese, and tomatoes into town for herself and two of her neighbours, and she will bring back fifty loaves of bread, enough for two families.

It is tough, roomy, and cheap, that peasant woman's rucksack; it cannot be compared with its brightly coloured sporting brethren, for all their little pockets and shiny buckles. It holds such a weight that even the practised shoulder of a peasant cannot bear the pull of its strap through a quilted jacket.

So this is what the peasant women do: they sling the basket up onto the middle of their back and wear the strap around their head like a harness. Then the weight is evenly spread between their shoulders and their chest.

I'm not suggesting, my fellow pen-pushers, that you try wearing one of these baskets yourself. But if you find yourself getting bumped—go by taxi.

The Bonfire and the Ants

I threw a rotten log onto the fire without noticing that it was alive with ants.

The log began to crackle, the ants came tumbling out and scurried around in desperation. They ran along the top and writhed as they were scorched by the flames. I gripped the log and rolled it to one side. Many of the ants then managed to escape onto the sand or the pine needles.

But, strangely enough, they did not run away from the fire.

They had no sooner overcome their terror than they turned, circled, and some kind of force drew them back to their forsaken homeland. There were many who climbed back onto the burning log, ran about on it, and perished there.

A Storm in the Mountains

It caught us one pitch-black night at the foot of the pass. We crawled out of our tents and ran for shelter as it came towards us over the ridge.

Everything was black—no peaks, no valleys, no horizon to be seen, only the searing flashes of lightning separating darkness from light, and the gigantic peaks of Belaya-Kaya and Djuguturlyuchat looming up out of the night. The huge black pine trees around us seemed as high as the mountains themselves. For a split second we felt ourselves on terra firma; then once more everything would be plunged into darkness and chaos.

The lightning moved on, brilliant light alternating with pitch blackness, flashing white, then pink, then violet, the mountains and pines always springing back in the same place, their hugeness filling us with awe; yet when they disappeared we could not believe that they had ever existed.

The voice of the thunder filled the gorge, drowning the ceaseless roar of the rivers. Like the arrows of Sabaoth, the lightning flashes rained down on the peaks, then split up into serpentine streams as though bursting into spray against the rock face, or striking and then shattering like a living thing.

As for us, we forgot to be afraid of the lightning, the thunder, and the downpour, just as a droplet in the ocean has no fear of a hurricane. Insignificant yet grateful, we became part of this world—a primal world in creation before our eyes.

A Journey along the Oka

Traveling along country roads in central Russia, you begin to understand why the Russian countryside has such a soothing effect.

It is because of its churches. They rise over ridge and hillside, descending towards wide rivers like red and white princesses, towering above the thatch and wooden huts of everyday life with their slender, carved and fretted belfries. From far away they greet each other; from distant, unseen villages they rise towards the same sky.

Wherever you may wander, over field or pasture, many miles from any homestead, you are never alone: above the wall of trees, above the hayricks, even above the very curve of the earth itself, the dome of a belfry is always beckoning to you, from Borki Lovetskie, Lyubichi, or Gavrilovskoe.

But as soon as you enter a village you realise that the churches which welcomed you from afar are no longer living. Their crosses have long since been bent or broken off; the dome with its peeling paint reveals its rusty ribcage; weeds grow on the roofs and in the cracks of the walls; the cemetery is hardly ever cared for, its crosses knocked over and its graves ransacked; the ikons behind the altar have faded from a decade of rain and are scrawled with obscene graffiti.

In the porch there are barrels of salt and a tractor is swinging round towards them, or a lorry is backing up to the vestry door to collect some sacks. In one church, machine tools are humming away; another stands silent, simply locked up. Others have been turned into clubs where propaganda meetings are held ("We will Achieve High Yields of Milk!") or films shown: *Poem about the Sea, The Great Adventure.*

214

People have always been selfish and often evil. But the Angelus used to toll and its echo would float over village, field, and wood. It reminded man that he must abandon his trivial earthly cares and give up one hour of his thoughts to life eternal. The tolling of the eventide bell, which now survives for us only in a popular song, raised man above the level of a beast.

Our ancestors put their best into these stones and these belfries—all their knowledge and all their faith.

Come on, Vitka, buck up and stop feeling sorry for yourself! The film starts at six, and the dance is at eight . . .

At the Start of the Day

At surise thirty young people ran out into the clearing; they fanned out, their faces turned towards the sun, and began to bend down, to drop to their knees, to bow, to lie flat on their faces, to stretch out their arms, to lift up their hands, and then to drop back on their knees again. All this lasted for a quarter of an hour.

From a distance you might have thought they were praying.

In this age, no one is surprised if people cherish their bodies patiently and attentively every day of their lives.

But they would be jeered at if they paid the same regard to their souls.

No, these people are not praying. They are doing their morning exercises.

We Will Never Die

Above all else, we have grown to fear death and those who die.

If there is a death in a family, we try to avoid writing or calling, because we do not know what to say about death.

It is even considered shameful to mention a cemetery seriously. You would never say at work: "Sorry, I can't come on Sunday, I've got to visit my relatives at the cemetery." What is the point of bothering about people who are not going to invite you to a meal?

What an idea—moving a dead man from one town to another! No one would lend a car for that. And nowadays, if you're a nonentity, you don't get a hearse and a funeral march—just a quick trip on a lorry.

Once people used to go to our cemeteries on Sundays and walk between the graves, singing beautiful hymns and spreading sweet-smelling incense. It set your heart at rest; it allayed the painful fears of inevitable death. It was almost as though the dead were smiling from under their grey mounds: "It's all right ... Don't be afraid."

But nowadays, if a cemetery is kept up, there's a sign there: "Owners of graves! Keep this place tidy on penalty of a fine!" But more often they just roll them flat with bulldozers, to build sports grounds and parks.

Then there are those who died for their native land—it could still happen to you or me. There was a time when the church set aside a day of remembrance for those who fell on the battlefield. England does this on Poppy Day. All nations dedicate one day to remembering those who died for us all.

More men died for us Russians than for any other people, yet we have no such day. If you stop and think about the dead, who is to build the new world? In three wars we have lost so many husbands, sons. and lovers; yet to think of them repels us. They're dead, buried under painted wooden posts—why should they interfere with our lives? For *we* will never die!